用對的方法充實自己，
讓人生變得更美好！

凱信企管

用對的方法充實自己，
讓人生變得更美好！

全方位英語大師

英文寫作

技巧 30

文法與寫作直覺搭配
立馬下筆寫出高分作文

User's guide
使用說明

每一個技巧，都是寫作亮點！

掌握英文寫作 30 技巧，就是掌握結構、風格、可讀性等寫作原則，直擊內容、組織、句構、拼字等寫作評分要項，讓寫作不再是難題，寫作高分不再是難事。

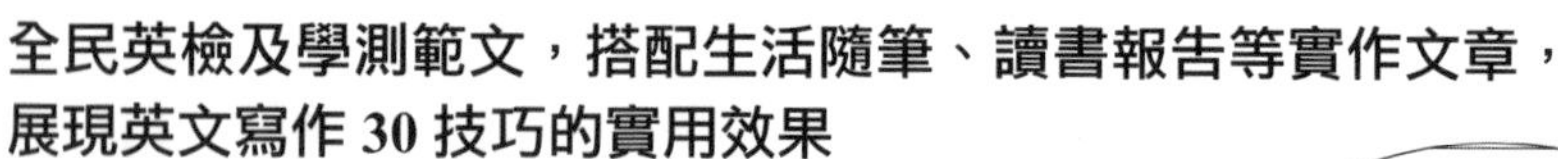

全民英檢及學測範文，搭配生活隨筆、讀書報告等實作文章，展現英文寫作 30 技巧的實用效果

寫作與閱讀、解題息息相關，都是遵照寫作原則產出的文字。知曉英文寫作 30 技巧足以增進閱讀理解、掌握解題脈絡，這是英語學習的進化。書中羅列國中會考與學測題組試題，驗證寫作技巧的強大效益，增進英文寫作的學習動機，達到全方位英語文學習的目標及效果。就著學習方法而言，熟讀課本語料、熟捻寫作技巧，有內容、有方法，一篇佳作便能自然完成。

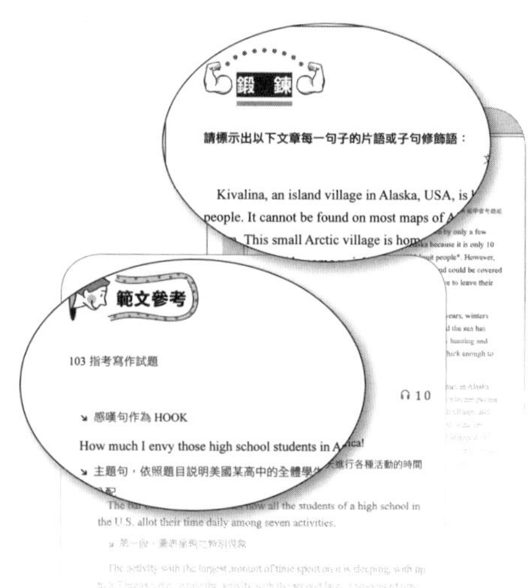

寫作導向文法講座，造就精湛筆頭功夫

文法使句子正確，句構完整而多變，符合寫作評分要項。然而，運用於寫作與測驗的文法講究不同，寫作文法首重主從分明、形意搭配，目標是準確而清晰地呈現文理與義理。「寫作導向的文法講座」從龐雜的文法中去蕪存菁，重新詮釋，提出一套寫作導向的文法導引。這種將文法提升至寫作層次的教材教法，足以翻轉既有的文法學習，造就成功的寫作學習歷程。

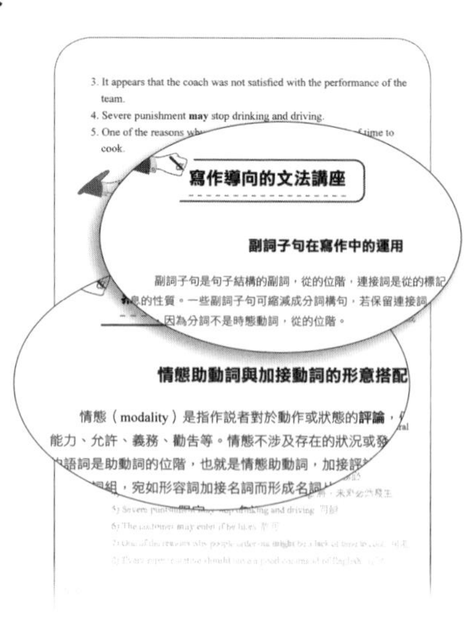

寫作技巧是文章的施工藍圖，按圖施工才能完成一篇頂標佳作

除了評分要項，不同題型呈現不同風格與架構，當然必須運用不同的寫作技巧，而技巧需要學習及操練才能熟能生巧，穩操勝券。熟習英文寫作 30 技巧，不論是看圖、說明、圖表、論說題型，都能寫出符合評分要項的頂標佳作。

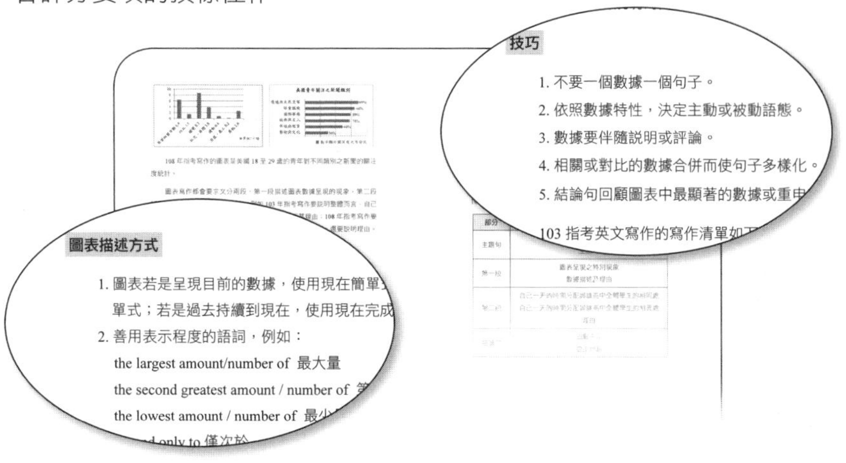

情境插畫活化寫作力，範文音檔多感官學習，搭配線上付費課程，學習如虎添翼

- 全書搭配數十幅作者精心原創手繪插圖，藉由視覺強化文字情境。
- 每一篇範文皆由美籍作家 Tony Coolidge 親自錄音，語料透過語音內化為寫作養分，語感也能自然提升。
- 全書內容製作成線上影音課程，並與國內知名線上課程平台 WÖRD UP 合作發行，學習更生動。

全書音檔雲端連結

因各家手機系統不同，若無法直接掃描，
仍可以至以下電腦雲端連結下載收聽。
（https://tinyurl.com/4udtkcxv）

Preface
前言

大多數英語學習者對於英文寫作感到生疏，甚至畏懼，有興趣的不多，文筆好的更少，究其原因就是缺乏動機：一般大眾的生活鮮少英文寫作需求，即使是簡單的訊息；青少年在學測之前，除非是參加英語能力測驗，否則幾乎都不須面對英文寫作。

當然，英語學習者也面臨諸多英文寫作的學習困境：

1. 英文寫作教導付諸闕如，學習歷程一片空白。
2. 入學型態導致學習意願減弱，遑論英文寫作。
3. 網路影響閱讀習慣，思考與表述能力明顯疲弱。

坊間雖然存在不少英文寫作出版品，但可惜的是，大多是針對特定測驗的寫作技巧而缺乏全方位的學習視角，往往造成強者恆強、弱者恆弱，甚至令弱者無所適從。以學測而言，高三才開始英文寫作，太晚，直接寫題目，太難，若只是破題、解題，成效仍是雙峰，畢竟中學生需要的是友善而有效的學習歷程。因此，吾等接受凱信出版集團的熱切邀請，擘劃並編寫《英文寫作 30 技巧》一書，由於以下特色，該書勢必成為英文寫作的良伴、良師、良方。

1. 針對內容、組織、文法、字彙等寫作評分要項提出容易入手的寫作技巧，內容涵蓋遣詞用字、句子結構、連貫銜接、語意鋪陳等要項。
2. 包含重要寫作原則與實用技巧，除了寫作測驗，還能運用於書信、課業筆記、生活隨筆、日常溝通。
3. 每一技巧搭配一篇「寫作導向的文法講座」，針對範文的文法熱點提出寫作導向的詮釋，引導讀者從寫作的視角看文法學習，提升英語文法學習的層次。

4. 全書搭配數十幅作者原創的手繪圖畫，幫助讀者藉由視覺融入文字情境，拉近與英文寫作的距離。
5. 每一篇範文皆由美籍作家 Tony Coolidge 親自錄音，語料透過語音輸入大腦而內化為寫作養分，語感也在過程中自然提升。
6. 除了學測寫作範文，全書羅列諸多適於差異化學習的語料，例如：國中會考題組文本、英檢初級或中級範文，落實友善而有效的學習歷程。
7. 為了激勵青少年動筆寫作，本書特別收錄多位試讀同學的生活隨筆、心得報告、測驗文章等優秀作品，本書不僅傳授英文寫作技巧，更是具備推動英文寫作教育的功能。
8. 全書內容製作成線上影音課程，並與國內知名線上課程平台 WORD UP 合作發行，英文寫作不再枯坐冥想，而是活力十足。

文字表達是重要的語言能力，古今中外，很多社會菁英或意見領袖於少年時期即開始探索文字並藉此展現自我。無庸置疑的是，英文是網路及科技領域主要的溝通語言，英文寫作已成為一種技能、素養、價值。大家若能在《英文寫作 30 技巧》的引領之下，戮力學習、殷勤操練、展現筆頭功夫，將是臺灣英文寫作教育可喜可賀的一樁好事。

蘇秦 王茹萱 解琪

學生試閱心得

試閱心得 1

升高三的暑假，儘管學校英文老師教到選擇題及閱讀的作答，還有英文簡報製作，但是對於「英文作文」還是一籌莫展，這使我面對即將到來的學測有一種沒有準備好的惶恐。

幸好，蘇秦老師的課程中，老師鼓勵我寫生活隨筆，就是寫生活中的一件事或一個想法，大約 100 個字，或許是親身經歷，所以總是能夠輕鬆下筆，讓我在面對學測時有了準備，不再那麼茫然。

讀到《英文寫作 30 技巧》時，我發現這本書將重要寫作技巧分門別類，提供有系統的歸納與學習，不僅說明考試的英文寫作策略，例如：讀題、列出寫作清單、從選擇題中找寫作材料，每一技巧還有範文、寫作導向的文法講座、練習，每一技巧都在音檔與插畫的陪伴下學習，這些都是學測英文作文的養分，幫助我的英文作文成長壯大。

曹祐誠／內壢高中

試閱心得 2

兩年高中生涯中，理組生的我，學校英文作文的教學少之又少，幾乎空白。如今要升高三，單字與文法算是熟練，英文作文卻非常陌生，對於學測非選部分非常擔心及迷惘：諸多的「如何」縈繞腦際一單字運用、語意連貫、文句順暢，還有最重要的一得到高分。這些未解的「如何」，使我學校的寫作考試都是憑感覺，分數慘不忍睹。

今年暑假，我和爸爸積極尋求英文寫作救星，終於遇見《英文寫作 30 技巧》這本書，真是幸運。因為說明和排版邏輯清晰、條理分明，我立即決定好好研讀。這本書簡單易懂，幫助我掌握英文寫作的技巧，補足我所欠缺的，例如：篇章的結構、句型運用的眉角、語氣、簡潔有力的寫法。熟悉寫作技巧之後，我寫了二篇歷屆試題，英文老師稱讚我的寫作進步許多，這燃起了我的自信，對於英文作文也不再感到焦慮。

學測前的一學期，我會努力熟悉英文寫作 30 技巧，相信《英文寫作 30 技巧》將助攻我的英文攀登頂標。

陳盈蓁／聖功女中

試讀心得 3

The book "The 30 Techniques of Writing" highlights the most practical and important ways of improving writing skills. First, it contains the unique tips to develop a writing strategy that will grab the attention of the examiner. Deciding the theme and the procedure are a critical factors that will determine your grade. Second, it coaches you on the principles of building a good structure of composition. This important information helps you to create a template with order and meaning. Third, it includes an understandable system to correct and improve the grammar and the word usage in every sentence and paragraph. This is an opportunity to have a completely different fabric and quality than other students' writing. Last but not least, it includes real themes from the exam, which makes the 30 techniques become more practical.

In my opinion, "The 30 Techniques of Writing" can really level up your ability and can make the examiner realize that you have a higher capacity than other students. I believe that this book will give you a wonderful writing learning experience and I sincerely recommend it to you all.

陳鼎鈞／政治大學附屬中學

試讀心得 4

高一時，我對英文寫作毫無概念、自信，幾近排斥，但在蘇秦老師以《英文寫作 30 技巧》教導寫作技巧，自己寫了幾篇文章之後，明顯感受到寫作能力提升了，寫作的自信和底氣增加了，走筆也敏捷多了。

本書收錄我的幾篇文章，包括影片觀後心得和生活隨筆。

寫阿滴的影片觀後心得時，下筆時感到訊息繁雜，不知從何著手，缺乏連貫及可讀性，文字像一盤散沙。蘇秦老師修潤，過程中學會運用連接詞銜接句子而使文章具有連貫性。還有，名詞加接修飾語而使文章瞬間生動而具有感力。

我認為生活隨筆是操練英文作文的好方式，因為篇幅不長，而且只寫一件事，不須枯坐冥想。另外，一天一篇適足以積沙成塔，累積實力，而且內容是自己的生活事，磨練筆頭功夫之餘，還能夠記錄生活點滴，真是珍貴的學習歷程。

陳玗呈／羅東高商

試讀心得 5

上了蘇秦老師的英文寫作 30 技巧課程，了解了一些寫作技巧和用法，使我對英文作文產生興趣。蘇秦老師叮嚀每天以三句話寫一段生活隨筆，他也會即時修正，例如：句型不到位，單字再升級。堅定持續地操練不僅可以抓手感，相信對學測作文會有很大的幫助。

蘇秦老師周日有英文寫作 30 技巧線上課程，評析同學的生活隨筆作品，清楚解說以少數句子寫出一篇合乎寫作眉角的文章，重點明確清晰，技巧容易上手，對於面臨學測英文寫作的我，真是及時的幫助。

英文寫作 30 技巧除了有書本學習外，還有教學影片可以隨時看，豐富而精采的教材讓我能隨時隨地充實英文，是很棒的學習體驗。

（鄭勝元／新北市石碇高中）

試讀心得 6

預備英檢寫作時，英文老師批改我的作文就是用紅筆圈幾個地方，頂多在旁邊寫一兩個字。每當我看到這樣的批改，除了文法疏漏，單字誤拼，無法看出我的寫作缺點在哪裡？要怎樣修正？

我也看了一些英文寫作教學視頻，大多是分享幾個小技巧，但是作文是一篇文章，幾個亮點還是無法點亮字裡行間的晦暗。我也看到教寫作架構的影片，但是，我知道題目要怎麼寫，但是寫的跟想的距離有些遙遠，好像看懂建築藍圖，但是缺少建材，還是無從施工，無法竣工。英文寫作就是且戰且走，寫一篇算一篇，但是千篇一律，分數依舊。

我與英文寫作的糾葛直到研讀《英文寫作 30 技巧》書稿才終於化解。我確信這是我需要的英文寫作教材。這本書針對各個評分要項提出寫作技巧，讓我對寫作有全盤的了解，當然也能全面提升我的寫作力。另外，書中的「寫作導向的文法講座」開啟我的英語學習的新視野，引導我上到寫作的制高點看文法，讓我看見寫作詮釋文法的嶄新面貌，還有寫作與文法之間的共同邏輯。另外，作者又強調寫作、閱讀、解題三者的關聯，平時的閱讀、解題都在吸取寫作的養分，積蓄寫作的能量，很新的英語學習概念與做法。

（劉孝安／台中市衛道高中）

英文寫作的成功學習歷程

聽與說可以先天習得，寫作必須後天學習，母語如此，外語更是如此。

英文寫作四大要素包括文字、文法、文理、義理，對應寫作評分要項：字彙、文法句構、組織、內容，寫作是英語能力與思考的產出，英語學習的巔峰。

寫作的學習歷程的三個面向：

學習：學習寫作技巧，包括文章架構、訊息組織、文法句式、遣詞用字等。

練習："write, write and write" 是練就筆頭功夫的過程，唯有堅定持續地練習，方能熟練寫作的方方面面。

熟習：練習中印證、熟悉寫作技巧，技巧透過練習而深化、拓化，進而熟習寫作的堂奧。

原則

1. 思考重於語料，翻譯只是將他人的想法轉變為文字，不是呈現自己的想法。
2. 從三句話一個段落開始，練習小篇幅表達一件小事。
3. 單圖描述開始，一篇三圖題可以分三次完成。
4. 簡單技巧開始，逐漸學習精細技巧。
5. 寫作與閱讀、題組息息相關，寫作導向的閱讀、解題即是預備寫作。

歷程

1. 三句話生活小梗

三句話講一段生活的梗，第一句講時間、地點、相關的角色，第二句講發生什麼事情，第三句話講感想或結果，例如：

This morning, I heard a kitten meowing beside the sidewalk on my way to school. It was cute but it looked sick and scared. I wanted to take care of it, but I could not because I had to go to school.

說明

1) 運用英文寫作 30 技巧：

15【進入故事山，故事架構穩如泰山】

26【名詞標記數目指涉，正確使用代名詞】

27【動詞標記時態及語態，時間及主被動要明確】

2) 合作學習：英文寫作同好共組群組，定期傳三句話隨筆，一起討論修潤。

2. 小段落生活隨筆

There are two confirmed COVID-19 cases in our class. We must stay at home and follow the epidemic prevention measures until next Thursday. We will have online classes as scheduled every day. We will have a big test on the day that we go back to school. Mr. Lin wants to ensure we will study as usual, even when classes are closed.

（出處：【技巧 16 主題必須一致，語意必須連貫】）

運用英文寫作 30 技巧：

9【融入生活經驗或經驗法則，直接入戲】

11【按照方向秩序描述空間，扮演稱職導遊角色】

20【片語起首，句首結構更多樣】

23【文字呈現感官知覺，描述更加生動鮮活】

28【修飾語如影隨形，語意擴增更精采】

3. 初級看圖題

- 不要一次寫完三圖，多寫一個圖，就多一些錯誤。
- 先寫第一圖，修潤之後寫第二圖，而後第三圖，每圖 50 字，共 150 字。
- 練習 5-8 篇初級程度看圖題之後再進入中級或學測寫作。

例如：

Yesterday, Cindy had her 15th birthday and she invited several of her friends over to her house for a celebration. They drank juice and chatted about their school life in the living room. They also enjoyed the music played on the CD player, which reminded them of their beautiful memories.

Then, Cindy and her friends sat around the coffee table, which had a birthday cake on it and gifts beside it. Cindy's friends sang the 'Happy Birthday' song for her. It sounded sweet. Filled with joy in her mind, she made a wish with her hands crossed on her chest.

After that, Cindy's friends gave her their gifts, which included a pretty hat, an elegant hand bag, and a cute stuffed panda. Cindy was very surprised to see all these birthday gifts, and she loved them so much. To Cindy, it was an unforgettable birthday full of happiness and friendship.

運用英文寫作 30 技巧：

6【遵照題目說明，適度展現創意】

7【描述圖片要精確，圖片無關的橋段要精簡】

17【除了連貫，還要銜接，敘述才能更順暢】

20【片語起首，句首結構更多樣】

4. 學測看圖題

控制式寫作是指遵循架構、組織提示而進行的寫作活動，內容受到控制，門檻較低，廣泛運用於基礎寫作的教學及練習。控制式寫作有諸多進行方式，其中以看圖寫作最為常見，而三圖式寫作更是國內英語能力檢定或入學考試作文重要題型。

練習順序

四框四圖 → 四框三圖 → 二圖 → 一圖

5. 二段式說明文

英檢中級寫作測驗都是二段式說明文，學測寫作則是常考該題型，英文寫作 30 技巧都用上了。

6. 圖表題

圖表判讀是大學入學考試中心精進素養導向命題的重點方向中的整合運用能力之一，圖表判讀應用在英文寫作就是圖表寫作，勢必成為學測英文寫作的熱門題型，一定要熟練寫作技巧。

運用英文寫作 30 技巧：

10【圖表寫作有技巧，數據要伴隨評論】

寫作自學方法

英文寫作 30 技巧線上課程，不僅是精湛的教材，還是寫作學習的必勝策略、戰略、戰術，寫作導向的英語學習，時時增添寫作量能。

語詞方面

1. 多閱讀線上英漢字典，尤其是 Cambridge Dictionary，閱讀定義及例句，了解用法。
2. 熟讀課本或雜誌文章，熟記寫作用得上的語詞，適時運用。
3. 依照寫作運用，建立自己的詞彙庫，例如興趣、志向、家庭背景。

文法方面

1. 知曉寫作導向文法學習的三個面向，從形意搭配與寫作運用層面學習文法。

   1) what- 句型是什麼

   2) why- 句型為什麼是這樣

   3) how- 如何運用在寫作

   知曉文法形意搭配與寫作語詞邏輯的二本必讀書籍：

閱讀方面

1. 閱讀課文、雜誌、題組時，預備二支筆，一支畫文法、一支畫優美的語詞，勤做筆記，時常複習，例如：

   On a warm spring morning, while walking in the park, Cindy heard a cat meowing beside the path. Out of curiosity, she walked up to the cat and found it cute and lovable, **with its eyes expressing such a strong message of affection.**

   "with its eyes expressing such a strong message of affection" 是足以融化人心的表達，記起來，好用，多用。

2. 除了單字、文法，還要知曉文章的篇章結構，這對閱讀及解題頗有助益。

生活方面

甘心樂意讓英文入侵生活，並且佔有一席之地。

1. 手機的語言調為英語，強迫暴露於英語媒介中。
2. 與一些好友約定操練以英文傳訊息，即使只有一個單字。
3. “Say what you see and what is happening”，以英語默想當下的情景。
4. 所有科目都收編為英文教材，地理的地名、歷史事件、數理生物的物質或現象，這些英文對照辭彙都要收入腦中，發揮在寫作或跨科目的素養題。
5. 操練以英文做數學筆記、表達數學，句型簡單，詞彙不多，只要願意，一定能做到，超前部署大學課業。
6. 與英文同好成立群組，每天以 3-5 句英文分享生活隨筆。
7. 讓手機成為電子書，Cambridge Dictionary 查過的連結、閱讀時畫的優美語詞的 Google 例句，都可傳到英文群組，時時複習。

生活隨筆

肯寫，就是踏出寫作的第一步，進而逐步邁向成功。寫作需要二大因素，一是語料，二是技巧，熟讀課本、雜誌、題組就是累積語料，搭配技巧，便能完成一篇佳作。

1.

Today, I ate cold noodles for dinner alone. Actually, I should have finished the food at lunchtime, but I didn’t because I lacked the appetite. After that, I played puzzles in my room while listening to my favorite music. Suddenly, I heard my mom yelling at me, urging me to make a reply to my teacher. I ended up having a day of boredom and depression.

新店高中 郭品倢同學

2.

It was just another typical day. Feeling bored and too lazy to go out, I chose to eat dinner at home. I ate a bowl of cheese ramen with pork, cabbage and carrots. It tasted delicious, but I really hoped to have something more delicious next time.

內壢高中 曹祐誠同學

3.

A few days ago, my youngest son had a fever of up to 38°C during the night. The next morning, I took him to the hospital for an exam. As expected, I was told to closely observe his condition and give him his fever medicine as scheduled.

4.

This weekend, I took a wonderful trip to Alishan with my family and several relatives. It is one of the most popular attractions in Taiwan, famous for its magnificent views and high-quality tea. It is also well-known for sunrise-watching, which is our must-do during the trip. On the second day, we got up around three o'clock and rushed to a specific viewing site, since the sunrise would never wait for procrastinators. Upon arrival at the destination, I saw a brilliant beam of sunshine emerge from the eastern horizon, splendid and marvelous. It was the most touching surprise I had ever experienced. Then, the golden sunrise gradually approached to my sight and the sky became brighter and brighter, with its shade changing as time passed. The view made me appreciate the greatness of Nature. It was such a fantastic experience!

台北市中崙高中 蘇恭煒同學

學測英文作文評分標準

英文作文依考生在內容、組織、文法句構、字彙拼字之表現評分，各項得分加總後給予一個整體分數（holistic score），再依總分 1 至 20 分，分為下述五等級：特優（19-20 分）、優（15-18 分）、可（10-14 分）、差（5-9 分）、劣（0-4 分）。閱卷委員在仔細評估考生的作答內容後，再依其內容是否切題、組織是否具連貫性、句子結構與用字是否能適切表達文意，以及拼字與標點符號使用是否正確等要項，進行評分；為確保評分之一致性，在試閱時，閱卷委員皆必須完全熟悉及理解各分項的評分標準（分項說明詳見表一）。字數嚴重不足者，扣總分 1 分；未分段者，亦扣總分 1 分；寫多段，不扣分。

項目＼等級	優	可	差	劣
內容	主題（句）清楚切題，並有具體、完整的相關細節支持。 （5-4分）	主題不夠清楚或突顯，部分相關敘述發展不全。 （3分）	主題不明，大部分相關敘述發展不全或與主題無關。 （2-1分）	文不對題或沒寫（凡文不對或沒寫者，其他各項均以零分計算）。 （0分）
組織	重點分明，有開頭、發展、結尾，前後連貫，轉承語使用得當。 （5-4分）	重點安排妥，前後發展比例與轉承語使用欠妥。 （3分）	重點不明、前後不連貫。 （2-1分）	全文毫無組織或未按提示寫作。 （0分）
文法、句構	全文幾無文法、格式、標點錯誤、文句結構富變化。 （5-4分）	文法、格式、標點錯誤少，且未影響文意之表達。 （3分）	文法、格式、標點錯誤多，且明顯影響文意之表達。 （2-1分）	全文文法錯誤嚴重，導致文意不明。 （0分）
字彙、拼字	用字精確、得宜、且幾無拼字、大小寫錯誤。 （5-4分）	字詞單調、重複，用字偶有不當，少許拼字、大小寫錯誤，但不影響文意之表達。 （3分）	用字、拼字、大小寫錯誤多，明顯影響文意之表達。 （2-1分）	只寫出或抄襲與題意有關的零碎字詞。 （0分）

資料出處：大考中心學科能力測驗英文考科評分標準說明

看圖寫作題型

圖片形式

1. 四個框，四張圖片，僅描述圖片。
2. 四個框，三張圖片，依據時間順序的圖片，留空的第四框依據圖片寫出可能的發展。
3. 二張圖片，文分二段，第一段要求描述圖片，第二段依題目書寫與圖片相關的說明。
4. 一張圖片，文分二段，第一段要求描述圖片，第二段依題目書寫與圖片相關的說明。

寫作要點

1. 詳實描述每一圖片，確實寫出人物、場景、結果等，完整呈現一個故事。
2. 著重名詞、動詞，形容詞、副詞等修飾語。

3. 善用轉折詞，標示故事發展的脈絡。
4. 創意須以圖片為依據，避免偏離題目說明，例如：96 學測英文作文題目說明即寫道「請注意，故事內容務必涵蓋四張圖意，力求情節完整、前後發展合理。」
5. 每一圖片或說明項目的份量儘量均衡，若以全文 300 字寫滿答案卷，各圖片形式的段落字數分配如下：

四框，四圖片		四框，三圖片		二圖片		一圖片	
框一	75 字	框一	75 字	圖一	75 字	圖片	150 字
框二	75 字	框二	75 字	圖二	75 字		
框三	75 字	框三	75 字	說明一	75 字	說明	150 字
框四	75 字	框四	75 字	說明二	75 字		

歷屆學測看圖寫作題目說明：

96 學測

請以下面編號 1 至 4 的四張圖畫內容為藍本，依序寫一篇文章，描述女孩與貓之間的故事。你也可以發揮想像力，自己選定一個順序，編寫故事。請注意：故事內容務必涵蓋**四張圖意，力求情節完整、前後發展合理**。

99 學測

請仔細觀察以下三幅連環圖片的內容，並想像第四幅圖片可能的發展，寫出一個涵蓋連環圖片內容並有完整結局的故事。

100 學測

請仔細觀察以下三幅連環圖片的內容，並想像第四幅圖片可能的發展，寫出一個涵蓋連環圖片內容並有完整結局的故事。

103 學測

請仔細觀察以下三幅連環圖片的內容，並想像第四幅圖片可能的發展，寫一篇涵蓋所有連環圖片內容且有完整結局的故事。

106 學測

請仔細觀察以下三幅連環圖片的內容，並想像第四幅圖片可能的發展，然後寫出一篇涵蓋每張圖片內容且結局完整的故事。

109 學測

請觀察以下有關某家賣場週年慶的新聞報導圖片，並根據圖片內容想像其中發生的一個事件或故事，寫一篇英文作文，文長約 120 個單詞。文分兩段，第一段描述兩張圖片中所呈現的場景，以及正在發生的狀況或事件；第二段則敘述該事件（或故事）接下來的發展和結果。

111 學測

不同的公園，可能樣貌不同，特色也不同。請以此為主題，並依據下列兩張圖片的內容，寫一篇英文作文，文分兩段。第一段描述圖 A 和圖 B 中的公園各有何特色，第二段則說明你心目中理想公園的樣貌與特色，並解釋你的理由。

98 學測

請根據右方圖片的場景，描述整個事件發生的前因後果。文章請分兩段，第一段說明之前發生了什麼事情，並根據圖片內容描述現在的狀況；第二段請合理說明接下來可能會發生什麼事，或者未來該做些什麼。

主題寫作題型說明

主題寫作屬於説明文，寫作方式是依照邏輯順序，客觀而明確地說明一個主題，或是提供主題有關的知識，同時以事實或證據支持論點，爭取讀者的認同。説明文的內容主要有四種類型，每一類型都見於學測題組：

1. 問題與解決
2. 因果關聯
3. 比較與對比
4. 過程順序

主題寫作是學測英文作文的題型之一，題目説明包括主題及二個段落的説明項目，寫作觀點是第一人稱。寫作時，首先要讀題，清楚了解題目有那些説明項目，也就是「寫作清單」，然後擬定寫作的內容，就是在題目説明中按圖索驥，寫作清單中按圖施工。

主題寫作要避免二個段落的份量不均衡，或是觀點區分不夠明確而造成組織不佳，語意邏輯不清楚。另外，每一段落必須充分闡述自己的觀點，內容力求充實。

歷屆學測主題寫作題目例示：

104 年學測

下面兩本書是學校建議的暑假閱讀書籍，請依書名想想看該書的內容，並思考你會選擇哪一本書閱讀，為什麼？請在第一段說明你會選哪一本書及你認為該書的內容大概會是什麼，第二段提出你選擇該書的理由。

這篇文章的寫作清單應該是：

主題句	學校建議二本暑假閱讀書籍
第一段	選擇哪一本書 該書的內容
第二段	選擇該書的理由一 選擇該書的理由二
結論句	

105 年學測

「你認為家裡生活環境的維持應該是誰的責任？請寫一篇短文說明你的看法。文分兩段，第一段說明你對家事該如何分工的看法及理由，第二段舉例說明你家中家事分工的情形，並描述你自己做家事的經驗及感想。」

主題是家裡生活環境的維持，第一段的重點有二，一是自己對於家事分工的看法，二是該看法的理由；第二段的重點有三，一是舉例說明自己家中的家事分工，二是描述自己做家事的經驗，三是感想。這篇文章的寫作清單應該是：

<table>
<tr><td>主題句</td><td>HOOK
家裡生活環境的維持</td></tr>
<tr><td>第一段</td><td>自己對於家事分工的看法
理由一
理由二</td></tr>
<tr><td>第二段</td><td>舉例說明自己家中的家事分工
描述自己做家事的經驗
感想</td></tr>
<tr><td colspan="2">結論句</td></tr>
</table>

圖表寫作題型說明

命題趨勢

圖表判讀是大學入學考試中心精進素養導向命題的重點方向中的整合運用能力之一，圖表判讀應用在英文寫作就是圖表寫作，勢必成為學測英文寫作的熱門題型，一定要熟練寫作技巧。

題目形式及歷屆試題

圖表寫作包括一個圖表及簡短文字說明，例如 103 年指考寫作的圖表是「美國某中學全體學生每天進行各種活動的時間分配」。

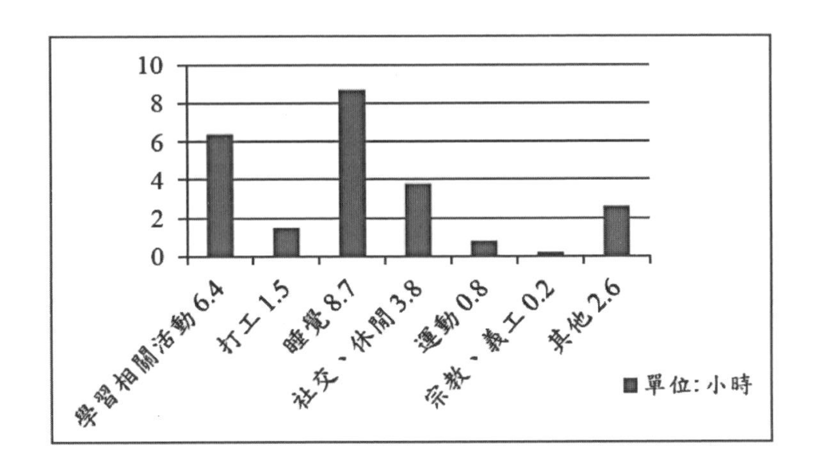

108 年指考寫作的圖表是「美國 18 至 29 歲的青年對不同類別之新聞的關注度統計」。

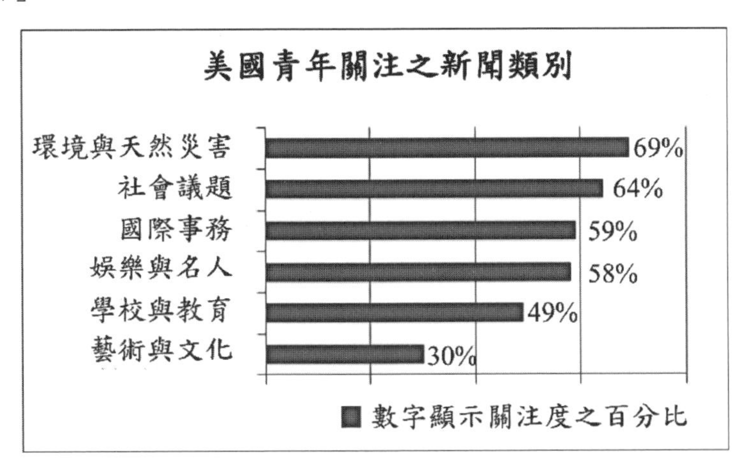

圖表寫作都會要求文分兩段，第一段描述圖表數據呈現的現象，第二段説明自己與該現象的對照及理由，例如 103 年指考寫作要説明整體而言，自己一天的時間分配與該高中全體學生的異同，並説明其理由；108 年指考寫作要描述六個新聞類別中，自己較為關注及較不關注的新聞主題，還要説明理由。

圖表描述要點

1. 圖表中每一數據項目都要提到，但不須每一數據都寫。
2. 若是六個數據項目，可分成前二數據、中間二數據、後二數據等三部分予以敘述。
3. 可以數據差距代替數據，避免只有數據的描述。
4. 說明前二數據及後二數據的原因或評論，通常二者具有因果關聯。
5. 題目若要求比較圖示數據與自己經驗的異同時，可用文氏圖增強解題概念，例如 103 年指考寫作要說明整體而言，自己一天的時間分配與該高中全體學生的異同，並說明其理由。

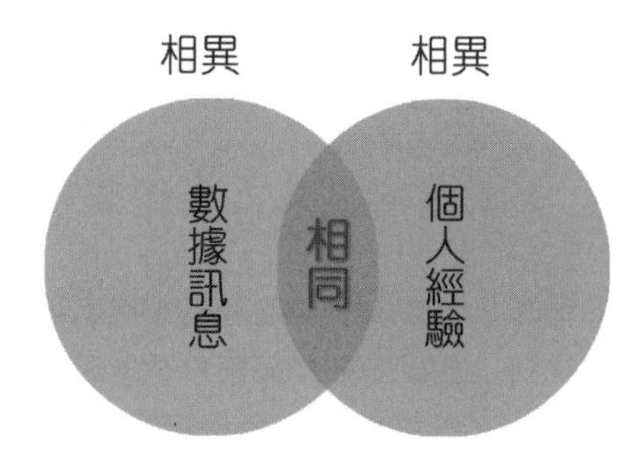

6. 善用表示程度的語詞說明數據，例如：
   the largest amount/number of 最大量
   the second greatest amount/number of 第二大量
   the lowest amount/number of 最少量
   second only to 僅次於

7. 常用的圖表説明轉折詞：

while

obviously

that is to say

for this reason

all overall

預備方法

1. 熟習圖表數據的慣用詞及句型。
2. 加強圖表數據統整及論述能力。
3. 加強描述自己生活經驗的能力。

技巧 1

一個單字，引爆一個段落，考試當下的應試戰略

學測英文科考試時間是 100 分鐘，選擇題作答時間可分配約 50-60 分鐘，翻譯及作文作答時間則分配約 40-50 分鐘。作文若以 40 分鐘書寫，在頭腦遭受長達 60 分鐘的折磨之後，要立即轉換頻道，從看到題目、構思到下筆，一鼓作氣寫完一篇內容、結構、文法、字彙面面俱到的文章，真的很不容易，對於英文能力與心理素質都是一大挑戰。

寫完選擇題及翻譯題之後才看到作文題目絕非上策，即使不能提早動手，總要及早動腦，蒐集語料，超前部署。

考試當下的作文戰略是就定位後，立刻翻閱考卷到非選擇題頁面，默念一遍作文題目、注視一下圖片或圖表，並且掃描到腦海中，然後回到選擇題作答。

寫作的超前部署就是寫選擇題時，從題目中蒐集寫作可能用上的語料或概念，用筆做記號。語料包括單字、片語，甚至句型，寫作時有現成的材料可用，何樂而不為？而更好的是，若是抓到概念的關鍵字，一個單字就能引爆一個觀點，寫出來就是一個段落，真是小兵立大功。

高分寫作應試戰略：

- **瀏覽作文題目**
- **寫選擇題**
- **蒐集語料**
- **寫作運用**

111 年學測英文，寫作題目：

提示：不同的公園，可能樣貌不同，特色也不同。請以此為主題，並依據下列兩張圖片的內容，寫一篇英文作文，文分兩段。第一段描述圖 A 和圖 B 中的公園各有何特色，第二段則說明你心目中理想公園的樣貌與特色，並解釋你的理由。

這篇作文的寫作清單如下：：

<table>
<tr><td rowspan="3">第一段</td><td>主題句</td></tr>
<tr><td>介紹公園 A</td></tr>
<tr><td>介紹公園 B</td></tr>
<tr><td rowspan="3">第二段</td><td>轉折語詞</td></tr>
<tr><td>說明一</td></tr>
<tr><td>說明二</td></tr>
<tr><td colspan="2">結論句</td></tr>
</table>

我們在選擇題中找到 60 多個可以用在寫作中的單字或片語，其中文意選填提到電影特技演員的表演，篇章結構提到日本盂蘭盆節的慶祝儀式，「表演、慶祝、文化」大可成為陳述自己理想的公園的特色。

↘ 主題句，呼應題目說明

A variety of styles and **characteristics form** our **image** of parks. **For example**, in my neighborhood, there are two parks with distinctive **features**, as the photographs **show** here.

↘ 公園 A

Park A is a featured park, **equipped** with several **public** recreational **facilities** for **children**, **including** slides, climbing frames, and walking nets. **Also**, the ground of the **play areas** is padded with a layer of soft **material** so that children can play there **safely**. **However**, there are no trees or flowers around the park.

↘ 公園 B

Park B, located in the **east** of the **town**, is characterized by a **natural** environment, where there are rows of **tall** and upright trees, a large circle of beautiful flowers, **green plants**, and a manicured lawn. It is a nice location to take a walk, take in the fresh **air** and relax one's eyes, and **therefore**, nearby residents enjoy **spending** some **time** there every **day**.

↘ 轉折語詞

These neighboring parks are both great, but, in my **mind**, they are not ideal **enough**.

↘ 說明一

An ideal park should be friendly to residents of all **ages**. Children can have a great time there since it is **clean** and **safe**. Teenagers can **find** their own **spot** among the pavilions to enjoy themselves **reading** or **talking**. Adults can stay there for a **while** to **rest** on the benches under the shade. Seniors can take **light exercise** in the relaxing environment.

↘ 說明二

In **addition**, an ideal park should be **functional**, with a spacious **stage** for **various performances**, so that **festivals**, **celebrations**, or local **events** could be **held** in the park. This would **make** it a **place** to bring locals or **visitors together** to **share pleasures** and **create** fond memories.

↘ 結論句

I cannot think of a **better** place for **people** to **gather** together. The green spaces of parks are **healthy** and it **helps** people to appreciate **Nature** more than ever.

各式各樣的風格與特色構成我們對公園的印象，例如在我家附近有二座各具特色的公園，就如這裡所顯示的。

A 公園是一特色公園，設置包括蹺蹺板、攀爬架及步行網道等數項兒童公共休閒設施，遊戲區地面還墊著一層安全材料，這樣孩童便可以在那裏安全地遊玩。然而，公園周圍都沒有樹木或花朵。

位於鎮東邊的公園 B 以天然環境為特色，那裏有好幾排的高聳樹木，一大圈的美麗花朵、綠色植物及修剪整齊的的草坪，是個散步、吸入新鮮空氣及放鬆眼睛的好地方。因此，附近的居民喜愛每天到那裏打發一些時間。

這些鄰接的公園都很棒，但是，我認為都不夠理想。

一座理想的公園應該對所有年齡的居民都是友善的，孩童能夠在那裏玩得開心，因為環境乾淨又安全；青少年能夠在涼亭之間找到他們自己的地方讀書、談話；成年人能夠待在那裏樹蔭下的長凳歇一會兒；老年人可以在這個休閒的環境中做些輕鬆的運動。

此外，一座理想的公園應該是具有功能性的，設置供各種表演使用的寬敞舞台，節慶、慶祝活動或當地活動都能在公園裡舉行，公園便成為一個將當地人或訪客聚在一起分享愉悅及創造歡樂回憶的地方。

我想不出一個讓人們聚在一起的更佳場所，公園綠意盎然的空間是健康的，有助於人們對於大自然更加地欣賞。

1. 各式各樣的風格與特色構成我們對公園的印象。
2. 位於鎮東邊的公園以天然環境為特色。
3. 一座理想的公園應該對所有年齡的居民都是友善的。
4. 一座理想的公園應該是有功能的，設置適合各種表演的寬敞空間的舞台。
5. 公園是一個將當地人或訪客聚在一起分享愉悅及創造歡樂回憶的地方。

參考答案

1. A variety of styles and characteristics form our image of parks.
2. The park located in the east of the town is characterized by a natural environment.
3. An ideal park should be friendly to residents of all ages.
4. An ideal park should be functional, with a spacious stage for various performances.
5. The park is a place to bring locals or visitors together to share pleasures and create fond memories.

寫作導向的文法講座

文字表達的核心概念－結構與訊息的形意搭配

寫作是藉由語詞表達訊息，主要的、重要的訊息置於主要子句，次要的、修飾的訊息置於片語或從屬子句，結構與訊息份量對稱－形意搭配是寫作非常重要的原則。

形容詞子句是從的部分，修飾功用，主要子句才是訊息焦點。

例如：Puli, **which is in the center of the island**, is famous for its Shaoxing Wine.

重點是埔里以紹興酒聞名。

比較：Puli, **which is famous for its Shaoxing Wine,** is in the center of the island.

重點是埔里位於島嶼中央。

分裂句是形意搭配的標本，強調訊息置於主要子句，非強調訊息置於從屬子句，從的標記大多是 that。

1) In this pandemic, it is **humans that** transmit COVID-19 to other humans.

→ In this pandemic, humans transmit COVID-19 to other humans.

2) It is **the vaccine that** can build immunity in the human body.

→ **The vaccine** can build immunity in the human body.

主從分明在翻譯解題的運用

例示 1

1. 大地震來襲時，孩童們迅速躲到桌子底下，然後用他們的手遮蓋頭部。

   關於「用他們的手遮蓋頭部」的翻譯：

   句子的主題是地震時的避難動作，「手遮蓋頭部」是主題相關的訊息，「用他們的手」是工具，修飾部分。

正確英譯

When the big earthquake hit, children quickly hid under the table and covered their heads **with their hands**.

說明 介係詞片語 with their hands（從）修飾動詞片語 covered their heads（主）。

錯誤英譯

*When the big earthquake hit, children quickly hid under the table and used their hands **to cover their heads**.

說明 「遮蓋頭部」應以限定動詞標記主的位階，「用他們的手」以非限定動詞標記從的位階。

例示 2

1) We will use this knife to cut meat, especially beef.

   我們將用這把刀切肉，尤其是牛肉。

說明 重點是刀的用途，meat 是泛指。

2) We cut the meat with this knife this morning.

   今天早上我們用這把刀切了那些肉。

說明 重點是切了那些肉，meat 是特指。

結構與訊息的形意搭配

技巧一範文中，許多句子搭配修飾功用的片語或從屬子句，藉由語詞結構呈現訊息的份量，結構與訊息主從分明，達到展延並豐富句子結構的效果。

1. **For example**, in my neighborhood, there are two parks with distinctive features, **as the photographs show here**.

◦ *For example* 介係詞片語

◦ *as the photographs show here* 形容詞子句

2. Park A is a featured park, **equipped with several public recreational facilities for children, including slides, climbing frames, and walking nets**.

◦ *equipped with several public recreational facilities for children* 分詞片語

◦ *including slides, climbing frames, and walking nets* 介係詞片語

3. **Also**, the ground of the play areas is padded with a layer of soft material **so that children can play there safely**.

◦ *Also* 轉折詞

◦ *so that children can play there safely* 副詞子句

4. **However**, there are no trees or flowers around the park.

◦ *However* 轉折詞

5. Park B, **located in the east of the town**, is characterized by a natural environment, **where there are rows of tall and upright trees, a large circle of beautiful flowers, green plants, and a manicured lawn**.

◦ *located in the east of the town* 分詞片語

◦ *where there are rows of tall and upright trees, a large circle of beautiful flowers, green plants and a manicured lawn* 形容詞子句

6. Children can have a great time there **since it is clean and safe**.

◦ *since it is clean and safe* 副詞子句

7. **In addition**, an ideal park should be functional, **with a spacious stage for various performances, so that festivals, celebrations, or local events could be held in the park**.

° *In addition* 轉折詞

° *with a spacious stage for various performances* 介係詞片語

° *so that festivals, celebrations, or local events could be held in the park* 副詞子句

寫作時的句子形式

1. 句子必須包括**不含連接詞的主要子句**。

Tom was sick and his mother was busy, so he didn't attend the class.

說明 Tom was sick 不包含連接詞，his mother was busy 包含連接詞 and。

We didn't enjoy the day because the weather was so awful.

→ **The weather was so awful**, so we didn't enjoy the day.

***Because** the weather was so awful, **so** we didn't enjoy the day.

說明

1. because、so 都是從的位階，全句缺乏主要子句。
2. 句子若含二從屬連接的標記，語意累贅，省略一從屬連接詞。

We've invited Mr. Lin, but he may decide not to come.

Although we've invited Mr. Lin, **he may decide not to come.**

***Although** we've invited Mr. Lin, **but** he may decide not to come.

說明 but 應合併**不含連接詞**的主要子句。

2. 主要子句相鄰時，必須以對等連接詞或分號合併。

Cindy remained silent, **for** she was in low spirits.

Cindy remained silent**;** she was in low spirits.

*Cindy remained silent, she was in low spirits.

說明 逗號不具連接句子的功用。

請標示出以下文章每一句子的片語或子句修飾語：

文章出處：109 國中會考題組

Kivalina, an island village in Alaska, USA, is known by only a few people. It cannot be found on most maps of Alaska because it is only 10 sq km. This small Arctic village is home to 400 Inuit people*. However, their home will become uninhabitable because the island could be covered by the Chukchi Sea by 2025. These Inuit people will have to leave their homes.

But life now is already difficult. Over the past twenty years, winters have become warmer, the Arctic ice has kept melting, and the sea has been rising. These changes have made it harder to live by hunting and fishing than before. What's worse, there is no Arctic ice thick enough to keep them safe from terrible wind and rain.

These Inuit people think it is the oil and power companies in Alaska that have brought all these troubles, but they are the ones who are paying the price. It would cost hundreds of millions to move their village, and they have no idea where to get the money. Groups like ReLocate are working together with the Inuit people to save Kivalina, but nobody is sure if their hard work will come to anything. All the Inuit people can do now is to pray the rising sea will not cover their homes too soon.

* The Inuit people are a group of people who live in the Arctic.

✐ 參考答案

Kivalina, **an island village in Alaska, USA**, is known by only a few people. It cannot be found on most maps of Alaska **because it is only 10 sq km**. This small Arctic village is home to 400 Inuit people*. **However**, their home will become uninhabitable **because the island could be covered by the Chukchi Sea by 2025**. These Inuit people will have to leave their homes.

But life now is already difficult. **Over the past twenty years**, winters have become warmer, the Arctic ice has kept melting, and the sea has been rising. These changes have made it harder to live by hunting and fishing than before. **What's worse**, there is no Arctic ice thick enough to keep them safe from terrible wind and rain.

These Inuit people think it is the oil and power companies in Alaska that have brought all these troubles, but they are the ones **who are paying the price**. It would cost hundreds of millions to move their village, and they have no idea where to get the money. Groups like ReLocate are working together with the Inuit people to save Kivalina, but nobody is sure if their hard work will come to anything. All the Inuit people can do now is to pray the rising sea will not cover their homes too soon.

* The Inuit people are a group of people **who live in the Arctic**.

主題寫作有技巧，讀題才能完勝解題

主題寫作屬於説明文，寫作方式是依照邏輯順序，客觀而明確地説明一個主題，或是提供主題有關的知識，同時以事實或證據支持論點，爭取讀者的認同。説明文主要有四種類型，每一類型都見於學測題組。

1. 問題與解決

02-1

Airline passengers may have noticed that all plane windows have rounded edges, instead of the hard corners commonly found in our house. The round windows are indeed pleasant to the eye, but they actually were designed for reasons contrary to aesthetics.

In the early days of aviation, plane windows used to be square in shape.

Then as commercial air travel became popular in the 1950s and airplanes began flying higher and faster, **three planes mysteriously broke apart in midair**. **The cause?** Square windows. Scientists found that sharp corners are natural weak spots where stress concentrates. **The problem** is intensified when airplanes fly at higher altitudes, where the difference between the inside and outside pressure increases, causing added stress. When subjected to repeated pressurization high in the sky, the four corners of a square window may spell disaster.

Curved windows, on the other hand, distribute stress around more evenly, reducing the likelihood of cracks or breaks. Circular shapes are also stronger and resist deformation, and therefore can tolerate extreme differences in pressure inside and outside of an aircraft.

Thus, round windows are a major safety innovation that keeps planes from disintegrating mid-flight. They are also used on ships and spacecraft for their greater structural integrity.

（111 學測）

2. 因果關聯

02-2

Many people like to drink bottled water **because** they feel that tap water may not be safe, but is bottled water really any better?

Bottled water is mostly sold in plastic bottles and **that's why** it is potentially health-threatening. Processing the plastic can **lead to** the release of harmful chemical substances into the water contained in the bottles. The chemicals can be absorbed into the body and **cause** physical discomforts, such as stomach cramps and diarrhea.

Health risks can also **result from** inappropriate storage of bottled water. Bacteria can multiply if the water is kept on the shelves for too long or if it is exposed to heat or direct sunlight. **Since** the information on storage and shipment is not always readily available to consumers, bottled water may not be a better alternative to tap water.

Besides these safety issues, bottled water has other disadvantages. It **contributes to** global warming. An estimated 2.5 million tons of carbon dioxide were generated in 2006 by the production of plastic for bottled water. In addition, bottled water produces an incredible amount of solid waste. According to one research, 90% of the bottles used are not recycled and lie for ages in landfills.

（99 學測）

3. 比較與對比

02-3

Fans of professional baseball and football argue continually over which is America's favorite sport. Though the figures on attendance for each vary with every new season, certain arguments remain the same. To begin with, football is a quicker, more physical sport, and football fans enjoy the emotional involvement they feel while watching. Baseball, **on the other hand**, seems more mental, like chess, and attracts those fans that prefer a quieter, more complicated game. In addition, professional football teams usually play no more than fourteen games a year. Baseball teams, **however**, play almost every day for six months. Finally, football fans seem to love the half-time activities, the marching bands, and the pretty cheerleaders. **On the contrary**, baseball fans are more content to concentrate on the game's finer details and spend the breaks between innings filling out their private scorecards.

（95 學測）

✎ 4. 過程順序

🎧 02-4

A stunt person is a man or a woman who performs dangerous acts, usually in the television or movie industry. In this line of work, the person is paid to do daring actions that are deemed too risky for the regular actor to perform, including jumping from heights, crashing cars, or fighting with weapons.

Stunt work emerged out of necessity over time. **In the early days of the film industry**, actors themselves shot acrobatic acts and dangerous scenes, until they began to get injured. There were, however, no professional crew members to perform impressive stunts at that time. If something dangerous needed to be done for a scene, the producers would hire anyone crazy or desperate enough to do it. These people were not trained to perform stunts, so they often tried out things for the first time during the actual shooting. They had to learn from their own mistakes, which cost some their lives, and almost all suffered light or severe injuries.

Beginning around 1910, audiences developed a taste for serial action movies, which called for the use of dedicated stunt people to perform in dangerous scenes. Such demand increased with the rise of western movies, and many cowboys with masterful skills on horseback found a new career as a stunt person. Tom Mix and Yakima Canutt were among the most famous. **The 1960s and '70s** witnessed the development of most modern stunt technology, like air rams and bullet squibs. That technology has continued to evolve into the present.

Today, CGI (computer-generated imagery) is widely used in filmmaking, and it is now possible to create very lifelike scenes without using real stunt people. However, CGI has difficulties of its own, and there will always be a demand for the realism and thrilling sensation of an actual stunt. So, the stunt industry is probably in no immediate danger of dying off.

111 學測

主題寫作是學測英文作文的題型之一，題目說明包括主題及二個段落的說明項目，寫作觀點是第一人稱。寫作時，首先要**讀題**，清楚了解題目有那些說明項目，也就是**「寫作清單」**，然後擬定寫作的內容，也就是在題目說明中按圖索驥，在寫作清單中按圖施工。

104 年學測英文作文題目：

下面兩本書是學校建議的暑假閱讀書籍，請依書名想想看該書的內容，並思考你會選擇哪一本書閱讀，為什麼？請在第一段說明你會選哪一本書及你認為該書的內容大概會是什麼，第二段提出你選擇該書的理由。

這篇作文的寫作清單如下：

主題句	學校建議二本暑假閱讀書籍
第一段	選擇哪一本書 該書的內容
第二段	選擇該書的理由一 選擇該書的理由二
結論句	

105 年學測英文作文題目：

「你認為家裡生活環境的維持應該是誰的責任？請寫一篇短文說明你的看法。文分兩段，第一段說明你對家事該如何分工的看法及理由，第二段舉例說明你家中家事分工的情形，並描述你自己做家事的經驗及感想。」

主題是家裡生活環境的維持，第一段的重點有二：一是自己對於家事分工的看法，二是該看法的理由；第二段的重點有三：一是舉例說明自己家中的家事分工，二是描述自己做家事的經驗，三是感想。

這篇作文的寫作清單如下：

主題句	HOOK 家裡生活環境的維持
第一段	自己對於家事分工的看法 理由一 理由二
第二段	舉例說明自己家中的家事分工 描述自己做家事的經驗 感想
結論句	

我們可以用 **OREO**（**Opinion – Reason – Example – Opinion**）統整這篇文章的寫作架構：

Opinion	贊成的立場
Reason	分攤父母的辛勞 培養孩子勤奮性格及責任感 增進生活技能
Example	自己做家事的經驗及感想
Opinion	呼應贊成家事分工的立場

範文參考

02-5

↘ HOOK

As the saying goes, "Unity is strength."

↘ 家裡生活環境的維持

Every single family member should make an effort to maintain their household living environment by taking up the responsibility of doing chores.

↘ 理由一

Especially in a family with children, parents are always busily engaged in their work to support the family, and therefore, to relieve their hardship, children should do some light household chores. They can sweep the floor, take out the trash or do the dishes after dinner. In my mind, children should be thankful for what their parents have done for them through actual deeds in their daily lives.

↘ 理由二

Moreover, doing chores will enable children to develop their character of diligence and sense of responsibility and improve their daily living skills at an early age so that, one day, they will act as someone with virtue as well as usefulness among peers. It is what they can benefit from getting involved in doing housework.

↘ 舉例說明自己家中的家事分工

I have a nuclear family, including my parents, my sister and I, and we all share the household chores. My mother, a bilingual secretary, shoulders the most important chores, cooking and doing the laundry, and my sister usually acts as her assistant, doing the dishes after meals and hanging out the laundry. My father, a computer technician, tends to deal with the technical duties, maintaining mechanical or electrical devices in our house, which saves my family a lot of work to preserve our living environment.

↘ 描述自己做家事的經驗

As for me, I am actually a neat freak, so I am willing to clean the house and remove dust from home at theeast once a week. Last Sunday, I even spent almost one hour scrubbing the floor, walls, and ceiling in the bathroom because I found there were mold stains growing there, which made the bathroom look dirty and smell bad.

↘ 感想

After removing the mold, I felt refreshed and delighted because I had completed a wonderful chore to maintain a pleasant and healthy living environment for my dear family.

↘ 結論句

I strongly believe that sharing chores is the most meaningful and rewarding thing in my daily life, and, certainly, I will do more whenever I am available.

如同諺語所說，「團結就是力量」。

每一位家庭成員都應該藉由負起做家事的責任而努力維持他們的家庭生活環境。

尤其在有孩子的家庭，父母總是忙著從事工作以維持家計。因此，為了減輕他們的辛勞，孩子應該做一些輕便的家務，他們可以掃地、倒垃圾或晚餐後洗碗。我認為孩子應該藉由日常生活中的實際行為對父母為他們所做的表示感謝。

還有，做家務將使孩子能夠培養他們的勤奮性格及責任感，早年時就增進日常生活技巧，有一天，他們將在同儕之間成為具有德行及用處的人，這是他們自參與做家事所能獲益的。

我擁有一個小家庭，包括我父母、我妹妹和我，我們都分擔家務。我母親是一名雙語秘書，她肩負最重要的家務，就是烹飪及洗衣服，而我妹妹經常充當她的助手，飯後洗碗及曬衣服。我父親是一名電腦技術員，他會處理技術的工作，就是維修家裡的機械或電子設備，這讓家裡省去一大堆維護起居環境的擔子。

至於我，自己是個不折不扣的潔癖咖，因此願意一周至少整潔房子及打掃灰塵一次。上周日，我甚至花了將近一小時用力擦洗浴室地板、牆壁及天花板，因為我發現有霉漬在那裏擴大，這使浴室看起來髒，聞起來又臭。

除完霉漬，我感到舒暢又愉快，因為我做了一件美妙的家務，就是為親愛的家人維護一個令人愉快又健康的生活環境。

我堅信分擔家務是我日常生活中最有意義而有益的事，而且確定的是，我一有空就會多做一些家事。

1. 每一位家庭成員都應該負起做家事的責任。
2. 為了減輕父母的辛勞，孩子應該做一些輕便的家務。
3. 做家務將使孩子能夠培養他們的勤奮性格及責任感。
4. 我父親會處理技術的工作，就是維修家裡的機械或電子設備。
5. 我堅信分擔家務是我日常生活中最有意義而有益的事。

參考答案

1. Every single family member should take up the responsibility of doing chores.
2. To relieve their parents' hardship, children should do some light household chores.
3. Doing chores will enable children to develop their character of diligence and sense of responsibility.
4. My father tends to deal with the technical duties, maintaining mechanical or electrical devices in our house.
5. I strongly believe that sharing chores is the most meaningful and rewarding thing in my daily life.

寫作導向的文法講座

形意搭配原則中的句子主從分明

句子構成一個段落，段落構成一篇文章，知曉句子是練習寫作的第一要務。

1. 什麼是句子

句子是以敘述、疑問、指示等形式表達一個想法的一群字。

1) 敘述：I have a nuclear family.

2) 疑問：What size shoes do you wear?

3) 指示：Turn to page 100 in your textbook.

這些獨立存在的句子稱為獨立子句或主要子句，包括**直述句、疑問句、祈使句**。

2. 句子的基本成分

句子必須包含主詞及時態動詞，就是標記時態的動詞，因為表明句子所述事件的時間是英語溝通的必要成分。

1) We all share the household chores.

share 是時態動詞，表示常態、泛時。

2) Last Sunday, I even spent almost one hour scrubbing the floor in the bathroom.

spent 是時態動詞，表示過去發生。

3. 情態助動詞加接動詞原形是因為情態助動詞評論動作，動作不存在，無對應時間，不須標記時態。

1) Children should do some light household chores.

should 評論動作是「義務」。

2) They can sweep the floor, take out the trash or do the dishes after dinner.

can 評論動作是「可以」。

3) Doing chores will enable children to develop their character of diligence and sense of responsibility.

評論動作是「將發生」。

4. 祈使句

祈使句省略主詞，因為主詞是指涉明確的聽話者；句首搭配動詞原形，因為動作是訊息焦點且尚未執行，無對應的時態。

5. 疑問句

wh- 詞（what, which, who, when, where, why, how）移至疑問句首，wh- 詞是訊息焦點，疑問句中，be 動詞或助動詞移至主詞前面，詞序標記要求聽者回答的溝通訊息。

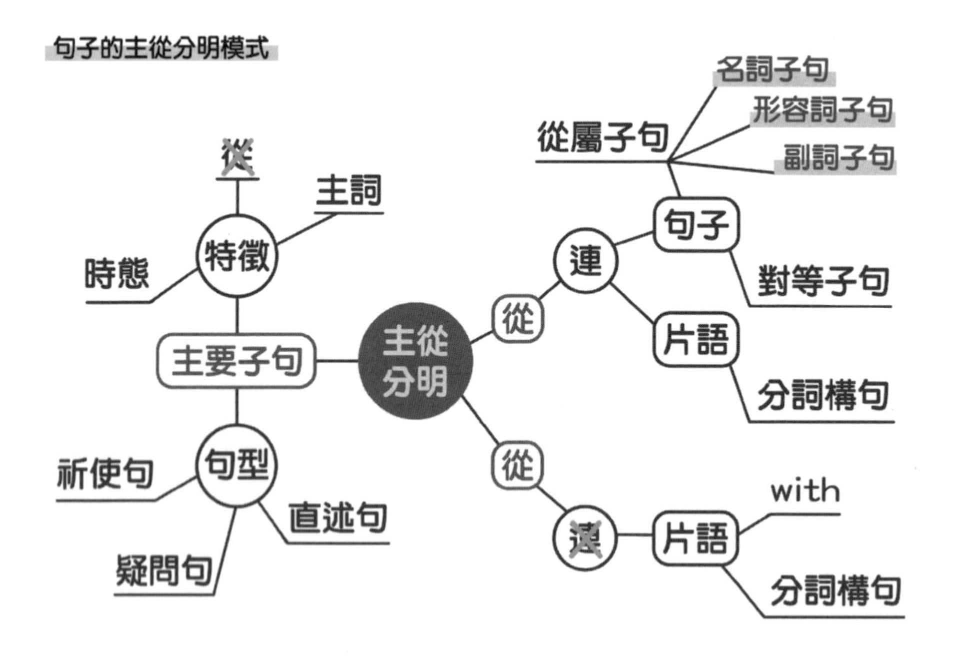

6. 從屬子句

無法獨立存在的句子是從屬子句，搭配從屬連接詞標記從的位階以維持一個句子只有一個主要子句的原則，這就是名詞子句、形容詞子句、副詞子句等句首必須出現連接詞的原因。

1) I strongly believe **that** sharing chores is the most meaningful and rewarding thing in my daily life.

   that 標記名詞子句是從的位階。

2) Children should be thankful for **what** their parents have done for them through actual deeds in their daily lives.

   what 標記間接問句是從的位階。

3) I found mold stains were growing there, **which** made the bathroom look dirty and smell bad.

   關係代名詞 which 標記形容詞子句是從的位階。

4) As the saying goes, “Unity is strength.”

   從屬連接詞 as 標記副詞子句是從的位階。

這是 107 年國中會考題組文章，包含三種名詞子句的類型，請找看看。

When we get wet, we need a towel to get ourselves dry. When a dog gets wet, all it needs is to shake its body. A study in 2010 showed that a wet dog can throw off half the water on its body by shaking for less than a second. This common act of dogs works better than a washing machine. The study found that animal shaking begins with the head and ends with the tail. During a shake, the animal's head, body, and skin all move. Smaller animals must shake faster than bigger animals to get water off. For example, in one second, a rat can shake 18 times, a dog 6 times, and a bear 4 times. Bigger animals can get their bodies dry with fewer shakes. For animals, shaking is not just about getting themselves dry. It is also about saving their lives. Being wet makes animals heavier, and that makes it harder to run. In the animal world, how fast an animal can run often decides whether it will live or not. Maybe that's why the "wet-dog shake" has become a common habit of many animals.

參考答案

1. that 子句

   that a wet dog can throw off half the water on its body by shaking for less than a secondthat animal shaking begins with the head and ends with the tail

2. wh- 間接問句

   how fast an animal can run

3. if/whether 間接問句

   whether it will live or not

技巧 3

下筆有掛鉤，釣出寫作靈感，勾住看官的眼珠子

無論是看圖寫作、主題寫作或是圖表寫作，往往找不到下筆的梗，第一個句子就束手無策。怎麼辦？總不能寫 “This article will be about⋯.” ，這是文章千萬不能出現的寫法。

還好，寫作有一稱為掛鉤—HOOK 的技巧，置於主題句前面作為開頭段落的第一句，目的是為釣出自己的寫作靈感，勾起讀者閱讀文章的興致，是足以使文章錦上添花的筆頭功夫。

時下新聞標題或商品文宣處處可見聳動的釣魚式標題（clickbait）可說是 HOOK 的應用，總是語不驚人誓不休，不達目的不罷休，因此掀起 “News hook, think before click. ” 的呼聲，提醒人們點閱前要三思，以免浪費時間。

快去加油！汽油明起調漲 0.5 元，95 無鉛升破 35 元大關
驚呆！幼兒園發生火災，幼童直接從二樓被扔下
3C 成癮？! 2021 年兒少每周上網 42.7 小時，年增快一倍網路安全誰把關？

言歸正傳，以下是產生掛鉤 HOOK 的四種方式：

1. Question：拋出一個與主題相關的簡短問題。

2. Facts or Statistics：陳述一個與主題相關的事實或數據。

3. Quotation：引用一段與主題有關的俚語或名人語錄。

4. Surprise：運用驚嘆語詞或擬聲字。

一般而言，Question 及 Surprise 較容易上手，考試時容易下手，而事實、數據、引用名言得靠平時的累積才不會「辭」到用時方恨少。

不同的題目適合不同的 HOOK，而例如 107 年學測英文作文就是四種 HOOK 都能派上用場。

題目說明是「排隊雖是生活中常有的經驗，但我們也常看到民眾因一時好奇或基於嘗鮮心理而出現大排長龍（form a long line）的現象，例如景點初次開放或媒體介紹某家美食餐廳後，人們便蜂擁而至。請以此種一窩蜂式的『排隊現象』為題，寫一篇英文作文。第一段，以個人、親友的經驗或報導所聞為例，試描述這種排隊情形；第二段，說明自己對此現象的心得或感想。」

我們的 HOOK 運用如下：

Question

03

Is it really worthwhile to join a long line for a bestseller or a promotional product? My answer is, "Never!"

↗ 這段自問自答表達對於排隊購買暢銷或促銷商品的否定立場，揭開負面的排隊經驗的序幕。

I will never forget my painstaking experience of waiting in a long line for a taste of Japanese ramen in a newly-opened Japanese restaurant in Taipei last month.

Facts or Statistics

Americans spend about 13 hours annually waiting for service in a restaurant.

↗ 以美國人在餐廳等候服務的時間數據對比文中排隊經驗的痛苦指數。

Whereas, two weeks ago, I used up the same amount of time to do the same thing just within a day. I was stupid enough to spend so much time waiting in a long line for a taste of Japanese ramen in a newly-opened Japanese restaurant in Taipei last month.

Quotation

As the saying goes, where there is a will, there is a way,

↗ 以俚語「有志者，事竟成」反諷文中排隊經驗需要強大的意志，當然這是一段沮喪的過程。

and a strong will may give us a way to move on. Accordingly, we need a strong will while waiting in a long line, and I am amazed that I had such a strong will while waiting for a taste of Japanese ramen in a newly-opened Japanese restaurant in Taipei last month.

Surprise

"Oh shit, there is still a long line ahead of me!

↗ 以聳動的驚人之語透露排隊當下的痛苦感受，當然這也是一段不好受的經驗。

"How long will I have to stand here like an idiot? " I will never forget my painstaking experience of waiting in a long line for a taste of Japanese ramen in a newly-opened Japanese restaurant in Taipei last month.

為了一本暢銷書或促銷商品而加入長長排隊行列真的值得嗎？

我的答案是，絕不。

我絕不會忘記上個月為了嚐一口位於台北新開幕日本拉麵店的日本拉麵而在長長隊伍中等候的痛苦經驗。

美國人一年花費大約 13 小時等候餐廳服務。

然而，二周前我僅僅一天之內就用光了相同時間量去做相同的事，自己真夠愚蠢，上個月為了嚐一口位於台北新開幕日本拉麵店的日本拉麵而花這麼多時間在長長隊伍中等候。

如同諺語所說，「有志者，事竟成。」一個強大的意志能夠給我們繼續往前的道路，同樣地，我們在長長隊伍中等候時也需要一個強大的意志。當我上個月為了嚐一口位於台北新開幕日本拉麵店的日本拉麵時，很訝異自己竟然有如此強大的意志。

「噢，該死，還有一長排在我前面！」

「我還得像個白癡在這裡站多久？」我絕不會忘記上個月為了嚐一口位於台北新開幕日本拉麵店的日本拉麵而在長長隊伍中等候的痛苦經驗。

1. 一個強大的意志能夠給我們繼續往前的道路。
2. 美國人一年花費大約 13 小時等候餐廳服務。
3. 我絕不會忘記上星期為了嚐一口日本拉麵而在長長隊伍中等候的痛苦經驗。
4. 我僅僅一天之內就用光了相同時間量去做相同的事。
5. 為了一本暢銷書或促銷商品而加入長長排隊行列真的值得嗎？

參考答案

1. A strong will may give us a way to move on.
2. Americans spend about 13 hours annually waiting for service in a restaurant.
3. I will never forget my painstaking experience of waiting in a long line for a taste of Japanese ramenlast week.
4. I used up the same amount of time to do the same thing just within a day.
5. Is it really worthwhile to join a long line for a bestseller or a promotional product?

寫作導向的文法講座

副詞子句在寫作中的運用

副詞子句是句子結構的副詞，從的位階，連接詞是從的標記，同時標記訊息的性質。一些副詞子句可縮減成分詞構句，若保留連接詞，則形成從的雙重標記，因為分詞不是時態動詞，從的位階。

1. 時間，常縮減為分詞構句。

We need a strong will **while waiting in a long line**.

2. 地方

Where there is a will, there is a way.

3. 原因

I am feeling frustrated **because there is still a long line ahead of me**.

4. 結果

The chef used up all the salt **so that he could not make a bowl of Japanese ramen**.

5. 條件

In case the janitor comes back, let me know immediately.

6. 讓步

Though it usually takes a long while to wait in line, many people choose to join it.

7. 對比

My cousin chose to order ramen, **while I ordered beef noodles**.

8. 限制

As long as you keep waiting in line, you will be able to enjoy a taste of Japanese ramen in this restaurant.

9. 作法

As the saying goes, where there is a will, there is a way,

10. 比較

The ramen in that restaurant costs less **than I expected**.

請將提示的副詞子句號碼填入正確的空格：

（文章出處：109 政大附中特招試題）

A. Not long after her arrival

B. When she first arrived

C. When you first move to a new place

D. when the honeymoon stage begins

E. as time goes by

F. Although how long it lasts depends on the individual

題目

Mei-Fang was new to New York City. __1__, she was over the moon with everything. __2__, though, the way the city operated was driving her crazy. She had to try hard to get used to the environment and become a New Yorker. Like Mei-Fang, many people have similar experiences of struggling to fit into a new place. Their up-and-down feelings are considered culture shock, a developmental process in which newcomers go through changes in feelings toward their new environment. __3__, culture shock generally moves through four stages: honeymoon, frustration, adjustment, and acceptance. __4__, everything seems extremely positive. This is__5__. It is all about a sense of freshness and excitement, which makes you feel an ideal life journey is just about to start. Unfortunately, the frustration stage creeps in at some point. Major disappointments like being unable to communicate with the locals make you panic; what is worse, tiny things like missing the bus also upset you. With the pressure increasing, you wish for a place like home, with hometown dishes, your mother tongue, and friends. Luckily, __6__, you will become less uncomfortable with the culture, language, people, and food of the new environment. Rather than blaming these differences for causing you inconvenience, you start to see them as routine. This means the adjustment stage has taken over, gradually easing the stress that has bothered you. Finally, you will reach the acceptance stage, which means building a sense of belonging. You take an active role in stepping outside your comfort zone and are willing to adopt new customs. Perhaps you have not yet mastered everything about the new place, but you have reasoned out ways to make yourself feel at ease. At this point, you will realize that cross-cultural experiences are not about judging differences but about understanding and showing respect.

1. _____ 2. _____ 3. _____ 4. _____ 5. _____ 6. _____

1. B 2. A 3. F 4. C 5. D 6. E

技巧 4 句子結構富有變化，變形與擴增是工法

學測英文作文依照內容、組織、文法句構、字彙拼字等項目的表現評分，其中「文句結構富變化」的方法就是句子儘量變形與擴增。

句子變形就是詞序或語氣改變，常用的寫作技巧如下：

1. 被動語態

This movie was made in Michigan.

2. 倒裝句型

Never put off until tomorrow what you can do today.

3. 強調句型

It is the coronavirus pandemic that led to lockdowns in many countries in 2021.

4. 祈使語氣

My dear Ken, please put away all of your video games, pick up your books and make a comeback.

5. 假設語氣

If I had had some time last weekend, I would have tidied up my room.

句子的擴增就是加接修飾語、從屬子句、對等子句而使結構擴大，常用的寫作技巧如下：

1. 加接修飾語

1) **Having gained EUA**, the vaccine is allowed to be used in non-clinical settings.

2) Jack would come to the party **if invited**.

2. 加接對等子句，形成對等連接的合句

The couple rushed to the hospital, **but** they were too late.

3. 加接從屬子句，形成從屬連接的複句

Puli, **which is in the center of the island**, is famous for its Shaoxing Wine.

4. 加接從屬子句及對等子句，形成對等連接與從屬連接的複合句

The pufferfish is a type of fish **that** is usually found in warm or tropical seas, **and** it can make itself larger by filling its stomach with water or air.

句子若是擴增，承載的訊息也就增加，那麼，怎樣增添訊息而使句子擴增呢？

wh- 詞 -what, which, who, when, where, why, how 的問題提供絕佳的線索。

例如：

I like to read storybooks.

↘ 增添地方、時間、原因等訊息，同時將句子擴增為複句。

I like to read storybooks at home in my free time because it usually makes me relaxed.

↘ 加上閱讀近況，常態的習慣延伸至特定的活動，構成一個段落。

I like to read storybooks at home in my free time because it usually makes me relaxed. This week, I have been reading a new storybook "American Crime Stories." It is so exciting.

除了 wh- 詞，我們可以將相關的訊息藉由語詞合併，使句子結構豐富多變，這是一篇佳作應該呈現的風格與文采。

例如這篇說明「是否贊成大學教授以英語授課及個人看法」的段落，語詞合併之後，句子結構豐富，且由於訊息集中而使個人觀點更具說服力。

04

Recently, a number of universities have encouraged their professors to lecture in English. Concerning this trend, I totally agree with it.

To begin with, English is a lingua franca. It has been widely used in the technology age. To keep up with this global advance, it is essential to have a good command of English. The younger generation needs to improve their English skills.

Furthermore, in Taiwan, the number of college students from other countries has been increasing in recent years. Certainly, they will benefit much more from classes where professors lecture in English. Likewise, we local students will benefit from interacting with these foreign students.

Therefore, I strongly believe that the trends follow opportunities. If we want to capitalize on the opportunities available, we should embrace English lectures in Taiwan's universities.

✎ 句子合併

Recently, a number of universities have encouraged their professors to lecture in English. Concerning this trend, I totally agree with it.

To begin with, English is a lingua franca, **which has been widely used in the technology age, and to keep up with this global advance, it is essential to have a good command of English, especially for the younger generation**.

Furthermore, in Taiwan, the number of college students from other countries has been increasing in recent years, **and certainly, they will benefit much more from classes where professors lecture in English**. Likewise, we local students will benefit from interacting with these foreign students.

Therefore, I strongly believe that the trends follow opportunities, **and if we want to capitalize on the opportunities available, we should embrace English lectures in Taiwan's universities**.

近來，許多大學鼓勵他們的教授以英語授課，關於這一趨勢，我完全贊同。

首先，英語是通用語，已在科技時代中廣泛使用，為了趕上這個全球進展，擅長英語是必要的，尤其是年輕世代。

此外，在臺灣，近年來，來自其他國家的大學生數量一直增加，確定的是，他們將從教授英語講授的課程中更加受益，同樣地，我們當地學生也將從與這些外國學生的互動中受益。

因此，我堅信趨勢衍生機會，若想要藉著手中的機會獲益，我們應當欣然接受在臺灣的大學以英語授課。

1. 我堅信趨勢衍生機會。
2. 我們當地學生將從與這些外國學生的互動中受益。
3. 在臺灣，近年來，來自其他國家的大學生數量一直增加。
4. 他們將從教授英語講授的課程中更加受益。
5. 為了趕上這個全球進展，擅長英語是必要的。

✐ 參考答案

1. I strongly believe that the trends follow opportunities.
2. We local students will benefit from interacting with these foreign students.

3. In Taiwan, the number of college students from other countries has been increasing in recent years.
4. They will benefit much more from classes where professors lecture in English.
5. To keep up with this global advance, it is essential to have a good command of English.

對等連接與從屬連接產生的訊息擴增

選字、詞綴、詞序、句構等皆與語意息息相關，這是英文「形意搭配」的原則。另一方面，藉由語詞的合併統整相關訊息，達到句式簡潔、語意充實的效果，這是「形意搭配」的應用，也是基要的筆頭功夫，應當熟習勤練。

1. **對等連接形成合句**

對等的訊息合併一個句子，訊息緊湊、易於辨識及理解。

I strongly believe that the trends follow opportunities.

If we want to capitalize on the opportunities available, we should embrace English lectures in Taiwan's universities.

合併 I strongly believe that the trends follow opportunities, and if we want to capitalize on the opportunities available, we should embrace English lectures in Taiwan's universities.

2. 從屬連接形成複句

主從位階的句子集中於複句，主從相鄰，語意緊湊，簡潔傳達訊息。

1) 形容詞子句

English is a lingua franca.

It has been widely used in the technology age.

合併 English is a lingua franca, which has been widely used in the technology age.

They will benefit much more from classes.

Professors lecture in English in the classes.

合併 They will benefit much more from classes, where professors lecture in English.

2) 副詞子句

We want to capitalize on the opportunities available.

We should embrace English lectures in Taiwan’ s universities.

合併 If we want to capitalize on the opportunities available, we should embrace English lectures in Taiwan’s universities.

3) 名詞子句

I strongly believe something.

The trends follow opportunities.

合併 I strongly believe that the trends follow opportunities.

3. 對等連接與從屬連接形成複合句

In Taiwan, the number of college students from other countries has been increasing in recent years.

Certainly, they will benefit much more from classes.

Professors lecture in English in the classes.

合併 In Taiwan, the number of college students from other countries has been increasing in recent years, and certainly, they will benefit much more from classes, where professors lecture in English in the classes.

4. **搭配副詞性質的語詞，增添訊息，語意更完整**

1) **Recently**, a number of universities have encouraged their professors tolecture **in English**.
2) **Concerning this trend**, I **totally** agree with it.
3) **To begin with**, English is a lingua franca, which has been widely used **in the technology age**, and **to keep up with this global advance**, it is essential to have a good command of English, **especially for the younger generation**.
4) **Furthermore**, **in Taiwan**, the number of college students from other countries has been increasing **in recent years**, and **certainly**, they will benefit **much more** from classes where professors lecture in English.
5) **Likewise**, we local students will benefit from interacting with these foreign students.
6) **Therefore**, I **strongly** believe that the trends follow opportunities, and if we want to capitalize on the opportunities available, we should embrace English lectures **in Taiwan's universities**.

請將提示的語詞填入文章的空格內：

A. Suddenly

B. Last Sunday

C. for a drink

D. To my surprise

E. After getting off the bus

F. After a drink of fruit tea

G. a town in the north of the Tainan area

H. a nice place familiar to me

I. one hour earlier than the appointment

J. my homeroom teacher in my senior high school

題目

__1__, I went to Jiali, __2__, to visit Mr. Lin, __3__. I took a bus and arrived at the town __4__. __5__, I looked around and hoped to find a coffee shop nearby __6__, but there was none in sight. It was a little frustrating! __7__," Siri" came to my mind, and therefore, I picked up my iPhone and said, "Hey Siri." I asked her to show me a coffee shop in the neighborhood. __8__, there was one just a five-minute walk away from the bus station. It was Louisa Coffee, __9__. __10__, I headed for Mr. Lin's house and had a long joyful talk with him.

1. B 2. G 3. J 4. I 5. E 6. C 7. A 8. D 9. H 10. F

技巧 5

寫清楚講明白，避免以偏概全

陳述事實是寫作的主要任務，知曉真相，據實陳述是作者的責任，而最常見的偏離真相是過度概化，不是百分百的寫成百分百，百分之五十寫成百分之八十，解套的技巧就是運用不定代名詞、頻率副詞、情態助動詞等語詞。

避免以偏概全的寫作技巧

✎ 1. 搭配表示數量的不定代名詞或程度的副詞

1) Teenagers eat too much fast food.

這句話表示 100% 的青少年都吃太多的速食，但事實是：

→ **Many** teenagers **tend to** eat too much fast food.

2) English is **the most** important **language** in the world.

→ English is **one of the most important languages** in the world.

説英文是全世界最重要的語言應該有很多人會抗議。

3) In Taiwan, all the high school students have got vaccinated twice.

→ In Taiwan, **almost** all the high school students have got vaccinated twice.

少數持有醫師證明的青少年未施打疫苗，almost 不是修飾語，而是表達真實的必要語詞。

4) Convenience stores can be found everywhere in Taiwan.

→ Convenience stores can be found everywhere in Taiwan, **except for several remote villages**.

台灣還有幾個偏遠或離島鄉鎮沒有便利商店。

5) Mrs. Lee walks her dog in the late afternoon **every day**.

→ Mrs. Lee walks her dog in the late afternoon **almost every day**.

戶外遛狗不會風雨無阻每天進行。

about 也有 almost 的意思，搭配 about，客觀而準確表達數據。

6) It took me four hours to produce this video.

→It took me **about** four hours to produce this video.

四小時整，不太可能，大約四小時，切合事實。

7) People order out because they are too busy to cook.

太忙而無法煮飯是叫外送的唯一原因，過度概化。

→ **One of the reasons** why people order out **might be** a lack of time to cook.

叫外送的其中一個原因可能是沒時間煮飯。

2. 搭配頻率副詞

1) In Taiwan, English should be used in the classroom.

→ In Taiwan, English should be used in the classroom **more often**.

目前國高中階段無法做到全英語教室，只能說儘量。

2) People spend too much time on their cellphone.

→ People **usually** spend too much time on their cellphone.

3. 搭配情態助動詞

情態助動詞有助於準確呈現真相或使語意婉轉，是寫作不可或缺的語詞。

1) Severe punishment **will** stop drinking and driving.

→ Severe punishment **may** stop drinking and driving.

will 表示必然發生，但是酒駕無法在嚴罰之下杜絕。

2) Every high school student should study English well.

→ High school students **had better try to** study English well.

只能勸告中學生努力讀好英文，不能成為一種責任或義務。

4. 運用 appear、seem，語氣不致武斷。

1) Polly is at the age of 42, but she often seems to be younger.

2) I seem to know more about Tom than anyone else.

說明 「我似乎」表示還有其他人。

3) It appears as if / as though my partner got me wrong.

說明 appear as if / as though 避免主觀認定我的夥伴錯怪我。

4) It appears that the coach was not satisfied with the performance of the team.

5) My grandfather appears to like the stray dog, which I find incredible.

6) It would appear that everyone got vaccinated for the third time against COVID-19.

7) It would seem that those who are bilingual may experience more advantages.

說明 appear、seem 搭配情態助動詞是正式寫法。

寫作不該出現語意模擬兩可的句式，例如「我的父母不都是老師。」，中文很清楚，但是 “Both of my parents are not teachers.” 是「我的父母都不是老師。」的意思，以下二句才是「我的父母不都是老師。」清楚的寫法：

1) Not both my parents are teachers.

2) Only one of my parents is a teacher.

青少年吃太多速食。

→ 許多青少年傾向吃太多速食。

英語是世界上最重要的語言。

→ 英語是世界上最重要的語言之一。

在臺灣，所有中學生已打兩次疫苗。

→ 在臺灣，幾乎所有中學生已打兩次疫苗。

在臺灣，到處都可找到便利商店。

→ 在臺灣，到處都可找到便利商店，除了幾個偏遠鄉村。

林太太每天傍晚溜她的狗。

→ 林太太幾乎每天傍晚溜她的狗。

製作這影片花我四小時。

→ 製作這影片花我大約四小時。

人們因為太忙而無法煮飯，所以叫外送。

→ 人們叫外送的其中一個原因可能是太忙而無法煮飯。

在臺灣，英語應該在教室中使用。

→ 在臺灣，英語應該在教室中使用更頻繁。

人們花費太多時間在他們的手機上。

→ 人們經常花費太多時間在他們的手機上。

嚴厲處罰將阻止酒駕。

→ 嚴厲處罰可能阻止酒駕。

每一中學生都應該讀好英文。

→ 中學生最好能夠努力讀好英文。

Polly 42 歲，但她常常似乎更年輕些。

我似乎比任何其他人更了解 Tom。

好像是我的夥伴錯怪我了。

教練好像不滿意球隊的表現。

我祖父顯得喜歡那隻流浪狗，我覺得難以置信。

似乎每個人都打了第三劑 COVID-19 疫苗。

雙語人士似乎能夠體驗到較多的優勢。

我的父母不都是老師。

我的父母只有其中一位是老師。

1. 在臺灣，幾乎所有中學生已打兩次疫苗。
2. 在臺灣，到處都可找到便利商店，除了幾個偏遠鄉村。
3. 教練好像不滿意球隊的表現。
4. 嚴厲處罰可能阻止酒駕。
5. 人們叫外送的其中一個原因可能是太忙而無法煮飯。

參考答案

1. In Taiwan, almost all the high school students have got vaccinated twice.
2. Convenience stores can be found everywhere in Taiwan, except for several remote villages.

3. It appears that the coach was not satisfied with the performance of the team.
4. Severe punishment may stop drinking and driving.
5. One of the reasons why people order out might be a lack of time to cook.

寫作導向的文法講座

情態助動詞與加接動詞的形意搭配

情態（modality）是指作說者對於動作或狀態的評論，例如可能、確定、能力、允許、義務、勸告等。情態不涉及存在的狀況或發生的事件，表示情態的語詞是助動詞的位階，也就是情態助動詞，加接評論的事件，構成一個動詞組，宛如形容詞加接名詞而形成名詞片語。

形容詞	**限定**	**名詞**
情態助動詞	**評論**	**動詞**

情態助動詞不是動作或狀態，沒有人稱、單複數的變化。搭配情態助動詞的動詞未對應時態，保留原形，這是情態助動詞搭配動詞原形的原因。

1) Convenience stores **can** be found everywhere in Taiwan, except for several remote villages. 可以
2) It **must** have rained last night. 對過去肯定推測
3) Individuals **must** not smoke inside a smoke-free vehicle. 務必
4) Severe punishment **will** stop drinking and driving. 將，未來必然發生
5) Severe punishment **may** stop drinking and driving. 可能
6) The customer **may** enter if he likes. 許可
7) One of the reasons why people order out **might** be a lack of time to cook. 可能
8) Every representative **should** have a good command of English. 義務

情態助動詞加接的動詞結構

1. be V-ing，標示說話當下正進行或強調。
   1) Tom **must be sleeping** now. 推測當下正進行。

      比較 Tom is sleeping now. 當下的事實，不搭配情態助動詞。
   2) You **should be wearing** your seatbelt now. 強調現在應該正進行。

2. have 過去分詞，評論過去的動作或狀態。

   情態助動詞不加接過去式動詞，以「have 過去分詞」標示說話之前較早發生。
   1) My partner **must have got** me wrong.

      說明 參考時間是現在，對於過去肯定的猜測，確定的語氣。
   2) The coach **might have not been** satisfied with the performance of the team.
   3) Tom **cannot have gone** out because the light was on!

      說明 may, might, could + have 過去分詞，表示對過去不確定、存疑，參考時間是現在。

3. have been V-ing，過去某時正在進行或強調。
   1) Mrs. Lin **must have been walking** her dog in the park at that time.
   2) You **should have been wearing** your seatbelt at the time the plane took off.

情態助動詞與加接動詞的形意搭配		
情態助動詞	V	評論現在
	be V-ing	評論現在進行
	have pp	評論過去
	have been V-ing	評論過去進行

請修正以下句子以使語意明確、合乎邏輯。

1. Dogs do not eat fruit or vegetables.

2. People tend not to answer cellphone calls from unknown numbers.

3. Tom looks sleepy. He stayed up late last night.

4. In Taiwan, four is not a lucky number.

5. At the party, that woman talked a lot, and she knew a lot about fashion.

6. Mr. Lin called a client in Kaohsiung.

參考答案

1. Some dogs eat fruit or vegetables.
2. Most people tend not to answer cellphone calls from unknown numbers.
3. Tom looks sleepy. He might have stayed up late last night.
4. In Taiwan, for most people, four is not a lucky number.
5. At the party, that woman talked a lot, and she seems to know a lot about fashion.
6. Mr. Lin called a client who was in Kaohsiung.
   Mr. Lin called a client when he was in Kaohsiung.

技巧 6

遵照題目說明，適度展現創意

寫作測驗依照內容、組織、文法句構、字彙拼字等表現予以評分，內容必須切題，遵照題目說明，適度展現創意，千萬不要想太多或扯太遠，畢竟考試時間有限，每一文字都要切合主題。

106 年學測英文作文題目「請仔細觀察以下三幅連環圖片的內容，並想像第四幅圖片可能的發展，然後寫出一篇涵蓋每張圖片內容且結局完整的故事。」，這是典型的「遵照題目說明，適時展現創意」。首先依據三幅連環圖片詳實描述，而後想像第四幅圖片可能的情節，完成一篇完整的故事。就看圖寫作而言，應該避免杜撰圖片沒有的角色。但是，圖片若是細節不多或不易描述，為了故事完整或段落分量均衡，我們就得循著情節展現創意，填補細節，就是 “outside the picture” 的部分。

06

Last Saturday was the first day of spring break, and it was a sunny day. Tina's father, humming a song with joy, placed a bag and a big suitcase into their van. Now Tina and her family were ready to go on a trip.

↗ Last Saturday was the first day of the spring break 增添故事背景訊息，適時展現創意。

Unfortunately, there was a serious traffic jam all along the way, and all the vehicles were moving bumper to bumper at a slow speed. Tina's parents were getting impatient and depressed because their van was stranded in traffic. However, Tina was still in a good mood and looked forward to the journey.

↗ impatient and depressed 從交通狀況揣摩情緒反應，是生活經驗，也是創意。

At last, they got to their destination—Happyland, a popular theme park in the area. To their shock, another tragedy happened. A sea of faces came into their sight and stopped them from getting access to the entrance, which made Tina upset and burst into tears.

↘ 看圖題應先聚焦圖片而充分描述，不貿然杜撰情景，例如以下粗體部份。

At last, they got to their destination—Happyland, a popular theme park in the area. To their shock, another tragedy happened. A sea of faces came into their sight and stopped them from getting access to the entrance. **Suddenly, a middle-aged man in a wheelchair approached Tina's family and asked them to buy a pack of chewing gum from him, which made them more upset and annoyed.**

Not to waste time there, they decided to leave and choose to head for another attraction—the beach to the west of town. Though there were a lot of people there, too, the beautiful beach was a good place for them to enjoy an exciting time on such a nice day.

↗ 為了完整描述全家旅行這一故事，依照圖片情節而發揮創意，將第四框寫好寫滿。

上周六是春季假期的第一天，也是一個晴朗天。緹娜的父親，愉悅地哼著一首歌，將一個袋子及一只大行李箱放入他們的廂型車。現在，緹娜及她的家人預備好要去旅行了。

不幸地，沿途一路嚴重塞車，所有車輛都一輛挨著一輛慢速移動。緹娜的父母漸漸變得不耐煩又沮喪，因為他們的廂型車陷在車流中，然而緹娜仍是好心情，期待這趟旅程。

終於，他們抵達目的地，Happyland，是該地區的一處熱門主題公園。令他們驚愕的是另一悲劇發生了。人山人海的景象盡入眼簾而使他們無法接近入口，這讓緹娜難過而突然哭了。

不要浪費時間在那裏，他們決定離開而選擇前往另一景點，鎮西邊的海灘。雖然那裏也有很多人，美麗海灘是他們在這麼美好的一天享受一段令人興奮的時光的絕佳去處。

1. 緹娜的父親，愉悅地哼著一首歌，將一個袋子及一只大行李箱放入他們的廂型車。
2. 所有車輛都一輛挨著一輛慢速移動。
3. 緹娜的父母漸漸變得沒有耐心又沮喪，因為他們的廂型車陷在車流中。
4. 人山人海的景象盡入眼簾而使他們無法接近入口。
5. 不要浪費時間在那裏，他們決定離開而選擇前往另一景點。

✎ 參考答案

1. Tina's father, humming a song with joy, placed a bag and a big suitcase into their van.
2. All the vehicles were moving bumper to bumper at a slow speed.
3. Tina's parents were getting impatient and depressed because their van was stranded in traffic.
4. A sea of faces came into their sight and stopped them from getting access to the entrance.
5. Not to waste time there, they decided to leave and chose to head for another attraction.

寫作視角下的冠詞－指涉

為使訊息明確而達成溝通目的，名詞必須標記指涉的對象是特指或是泛指，而冠詞是最重要的指涉標記。

1. 定冠詞 the

 1) 標記共同認知的指涉對象

 The street was familiar to me.

 那條街對我很熟悉。

 I'll pick you up at **the** airport.

 我會在機場接你。

 There is a new refrigerator in **the** kitchen.

 廚房有一台新冰箱。

2) 標記多數中特指的對象

This coat is **the** more expensive of the two.

這件外套是二件中較貴的。

The lawyer is **the** most intelligent person I know.

那名律師是我認識的最聰明的人。

3) 標記前述的名詞

I am raising a cat and a dog. **The** cat usually bullies **the** dog.

我養一隻貓及一隻狗，貓經常欺負狗。

4) 宇宙唯一的物體

The moon orbits **the** Earth once every 27.322 days.

月亮每 27.322 天沿著軌道繞地球一圈。

The sun rises in **the** east and sets in **the** west.

太陽從東邊升起，從西邊落下。

說明 方向是明確指涉，搭配定冠詞。

5) 泛指一類的地方

We spent all day at **the** beach.

我們一整天都在海灘度過。

Let's go to **the** movies this weekend.

這周末我們去看電影。

說明 the movies 是指電影院。

I need to go to **the** bank at lunchtime.

中餐時間我需要去銀行。

I had a light lunch in **the** restaurant.

我在餐廳吃一份輕便中餐。

I had a light lunch in **a** restaurant.

我在一家餐廳吃一份輕便中餐。（針對餐廳會有後續的描述。）

I had a light lunch in **a** restaurant, and **the** restaurant owner is from Turkey.

我在一家餐廳吃一份輕便中餐，那家餐廳老闆來自土耳其。

2. 不定冠詞 a/an

1) 首次提及而未特指的對象

I heard **a** child crying.

我聽見一名孩子在哭。

She is **a** friend of mine.

她是我的一位朋友。

There was **a** sudden loud noise.

突然來了一聲巨響。

2) 同類的總稱

A dog is man's best friend.

狗是人類最好的朋友。

說明 human's 是舊式用法。

An orchid is a blooming plant with waxy leaves.

蘭花是擁有蠟一樣光澤葉子的開花植物。

A dictionary is a book of words with their meanings.

字典是一本提供字詞語義的書。

說明 名詞下定義時搭配不定冠詞。

3) 泛指一類對象中的一例

He is such **an** idiot.

他真是個白癡。

You're just **a** big bully!

你就是個大惡霸！

Do you have **a** smartphone?

你有一支智慧型手機嗎？

3. 冠詞只標記特指的單數、複數、不可數名詞，泛指的單數名詞，因此，泛指的複數及不可數名詞不搭配冠詞（零冠詞）。另外，複數可以表示泛指的同類總稱。

Time is **money**.

時間就是金錢。

Bats have small eyes with very sensitive vision.

蝙蝠有非常敏銳視力的小眼睛。

Human beings are a social species that relies on cooperation to survive.

人類是依賴合作存活的群居物種。

這是一篇三圖寫作，請閱讀後想像圖片內容，然後找出一處可能因圖片內容不足而增補的動作。

Last Friday, I went to my uncle's for a three-day visit. I arrived at Pingtung Train Station around 2 p.m. The moment I got to the entrance of the station, I saw my uncle and cousins waiting for me there. They greeted me with warm smiles and I felt happy.

On Saturday, because it rained heavily, my cousins and I couldn't help but stay indoors. We sat on the floor and played card games. At first, my little cousin lost and she was a little upset. After I shared some tips with her, she started to win and became happy.

On Sunday, it was sunny and we went to the beach. My first cousin and I swam and played with beach balls in the water happily. My little cousin didn't join us but just played by herself nearby. We all had fun, and I had a joyful ending to my vacation.

參考答案

At first, my little cousin lost and she was a little upset. After I shared some tips with her, she started to win and became happy.

技巧 7

描述圖片要詳實，圖片無關的橋段要精簡

寫作著重開門見山，一開始便揭曉主題，表明立場。梁啟超在他的《飲冰室文集》中提及：「寫文章要令人一望而知其宗旨之所在，才易於動人。」寫文章時，最好將要點開篇便提出。

看圖寫作首重詳實描述圖片，圖片的主題是動作，呈現的是動作的終點，動作之前的過程不可著墨太多，即使是能夠信手拈來，恣意發揮，主題優先是寫作的準則，必須遵守。

範文 1

圖片的場景是家中廚房，情節從男孩到家的時候開始描述。

🎧 07-1

After a tiring day at school, my stomach started to rumble as I got to my house. The smell of food overcame me, which made me even hungrier since my mom was cooking my favorite dish, fried rice and fried vegetables. Therefore, I rushed to the kitchen and was immediately greeted by our dog.

↘ 返家的交通過程屬於臆測，應該略去，畢竟人已到家，若還說「搭捷運、轉公車，走路十分鐘才到家」，就是累贅而離題。

After a tiring day at school, **I rushed to the MRT station and squeezed into the crowded train. After a twenty-minute ride, I left the MRT station and walked toward my home as fast as possible, like a marching soldier.** Finally, I arrived home. As I opened the door of my house, a smell came to me that made me even hungrier. My mom was cooking my favorite dish, fried rice with my favorite side dish, fried vegetables. Walking to the kitchen, the dog barked at me happily.

（國立政治大學附屬中學 陳鼎鈞同學）

範文 2

例如題目是「上周六 Patty 與父母到動物之家領養一隻小狗」，故事必須開門見山，主題句依照題目說明直接破題 --"Last Saturday, Patty and her parents visited an animal shelter in town"，至於寵物店與動物之家的比較，雖然言之有物，但與主題無關，仍應割捨。

07-2

A pet store exists to sell animals and make a profit from them, and animals there might come from illegal breeding grounds, where various problems exist.

However, the purpose of an animal shelter is to take care of animals and find them home, where they are treated as a family member. Therefore, in order to adopt a dog as their pet, last Sunday, Patty and her parents visited an animal shelter in town. After a short talk with a staff member in the office, they were guided to the dog section behind the office. While looking around there, Patty noticed a Chihuahua casting a loving glance at her with its tail wagging, which drew her to move to this cute dog and touch its head gently.

範文 3

看圖題的目的是測驗描述圖片的能力，不同級次測驗的圖片必然不同。詳實描述圖片是切題的基本要求，也是看圖寫作的首要任務，切勿略過圖片而天馬行空、恣意發揮。

例如 98 學測英文作文題目是「請根據下方圖片的場景，描述整個事件發生的前因後果。」圖片是一間破損嚴重、沒有家當的空屋，前半部屋頂、牆壁倒塌，樑柱裸露，前面一片瓦礫殘骸，我們可以這樣描述：

Unfortunately, this deserted old house, located on an empty plain, was severely damaged. The walls and roof on the southern side fell, beam-columns collapsed and bricks scattered. Now, it is totally a ruin.

範文 1

在學校疲累的一天之後，到家時我的肚子開始發出轆轆聲，食物的味道征服了我，讓我更加飢餓，因為我母親正在做我最愛的一道菜，炒飯及炒青菜。因此，我趕緊到廚房，也立刻受到我家毛孩的歡迎。

範文 2

寵物店是為了販售動物並從中獲取利潤而存在，那裏的動物可能來自非法養殖場，裡面有各式各樣的問題。

然而，動物之家的目的是要照顧動物及為牠們找到家，在那裡牠們是以家庭成員受到對待。因此，為了領養一隻狗作為他們的寵物，上周日帕迪及她的父母造訪市區一處動物之家。與一名職員在辦公室簡短談話之後，他們被引導至辦公室後面的狗狗區域。帕迪在那裏四處張望時，注意到一隻吉娃娃帶著鍾愛的眼神看了她一下，還搖擺著尾巴，這吸引她過去這可愛的小狗那裏輕撫牠的頭部。

範文 3

不幸地，這棟廢棄的舊房子，位於一片空曠的平地上，遭到嚴重損壞，南側牆壁及屋頂掉落，樑柱倒塌，磚頭散落一地，現在是一片廢墟。

1. 這棟廢棄的舊房子，位於一片空曠的平地上，遭到嚴重損壞。
2. 南側牆壁及屋頂掉落，樑柱倒塌，磚頭散落一地，現在是一片廢墟。
3. 帕迪注意到一隻吉娃娃帶著鍾愛的眼神看了她一下，還搖擺著尾巴。
4. 動物之家的目的是要照顧動物及為牠們找到家。
5. 在學校疲累的一天之後，到家時我的肚子開始發出轆轆聲。

參考答案

1. This deserted old house, located on an empty plain, was severely damaged.
2. The walls and roof on the southern side fell, beam columns collapsed and bricks scattered.
3. Patty noticed a Chihuahua casting a loving glance at her with its tail wagging.
4. The purpose of an animal shelter is to take care of animals and find them home.
5. After a tiring day at school, my stomach started to rumble as I got to my house.

寫作導向的文法講座

鋪陳訊息時應該知道的上層字與下層字

1. 上層字（hyperonymy）是知識類別的字，例如 color, animal, building 等；下層字 hyponymy）是上層字細項的字，例如 red, yellow, green, blue 等是 color 的下層字，wolf, fox, dog 等是 canine（犬科動物）的下層字。

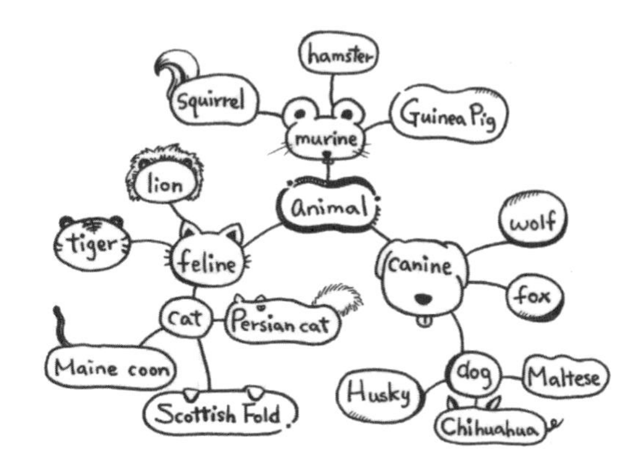

A wild canine, such as a wolf, dingo, or coyote, would not make for a good house pet.

2. 下層字可再分出其下層字，構成多層單字連結，形成知識系統，適合以心智圖呈現，例如 plant 的下層字可以包括 flower, tree, grass, fern 等，而 flower 又有 rose, carnation, lily 等下層字。

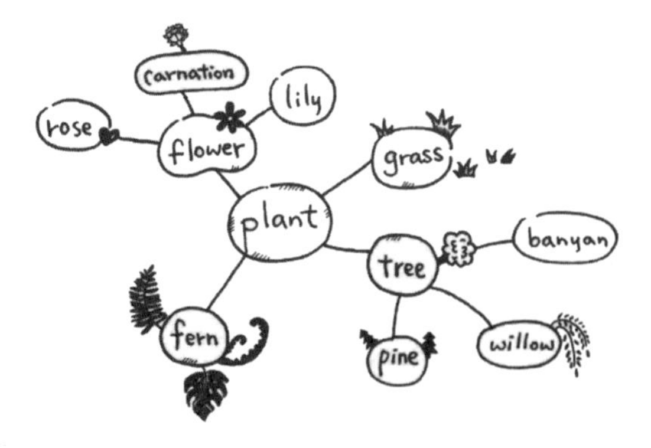

3. 上層字與下層字的關聯可以運用在寫作上，上層字是 general 的主題，下層字是 specific 的細節，二者構成連貫的發展形式，例如：

My neighbor, Mrs. Lin, loves animals very much. She is raising three dogs. One is a Husky, another is a Chihuahua, and the other is a Maltese.

這是一篇三圖寫作，請閱讀後想像圖片內容，然後找出三處可能與圖片內容無關的部分。

Last Sunday afternoon, Brian went to the park with his dog, Lucky. Brian sat on a bench and read his favorite novel. Lucky was quietly sitting by Brian's side. Several gardeners were trimming bushes and mowing the lawn around the lake. Suddenly, a squirrel appeared in front of Lucky, and out of curiosity, it followed the squirrel wherever it moved, but Brian was totally unaware of Lucky's encounter.

All of a sudden, Brian noticed Lucky was not around. He put down his book, stood up, and looked around, but he did not see his beloved dog. Then, he looked for Lucky everywhere around the park, calling "Lucky" over and over again. Brian approached two people who were walking by, inquiring about his dog. At last, he quit and left the park, tired and depressed.

To Brian's surprise, the moment he got home, he saw Lucky sitting by the door and eating raw beef in a bowl. The dog was looking at Brian, its tail wagging with excitement as usual. It filled him with a sense of relief and delight, and he felt not only thankful but lucky.

參考答案

1. Several gardeners were trimming bushes and mowing the lawn around the lake.
2. Then Brian approached two people who were walking by, inquiring about his dog.
3. and eating raw beef in a bowl

技巧 8

說明觀點有原則，數量、均衡、宏觀都要講究

說明文的細節針對主題提出說明、證明、舉例，是全文份量最重的部分，寫作時必須遵守一些原則。

數量原則：至少提出二個，至多三個說明。

均衡原則：每一說明的份量力求均衡，宛如一個圓周分為二或三個同樣大小的圓弧，彼此明顯差異，甚至具有相對性。

宏觀原則：觀點要一致，避免宏觀中穿插微觀的細節而造成語意不連貫，宛如原本開車在高速公路，突然鑽進鄉間小路。

例如題目是「全世界選擇素食的人越來越多，請說明素食受到青睞的原因及個人對於素食的看法。」

這是常見的說明文題型，針對一個議題提出二個問題，作答方式是主題句起首，呼應議題，接著針對二個問題分別提出二至三個說明，每一說明必須力求份量均衡，宏觀程度一致。

這篇文章的寫作清單如下：

主題句	HOOK 主題句	蛋白質的重要 全世界選擇素食的人越來越多
素食流行的原因	原因一 原因二	for health reasons to respect life
素食的個人看法	看法一 看法二	in terms of health Human beings are omnivores.
結論句	呼應主題，重申立場	

🎧 08

↘ HOOK

It is essential to consume enough protein on a daily basis and we can get protein from many food sources, including plants and animals.

↘ 主題句

However, more and more people all over the world choose to become vegetarians and eat mostly vegetables.

↘ 引介素食流行的二個原因

In my mind, there are two main reasons for this type of diet.

↘ 原因一

First, for health reasons, vegetarianism has become more common, and some people tend to abandon meat because they think meat is high in animal fat and oil, which will cause a negative or harmful impact on their health. Compared with meat, they believe vegetables can be digested and absorbed more easily, and therefore, their body can function more properly and get sick less often.

↘ 原因二

Second, to respect life, they would rather not eat meat from killing animals. They especially want to avoid letting animals be treated in cruel ways. In addition, to obtain meat products at a low cost, human beings may mistreat animals. To show mercy to these living things, vegetarians will avoid eating meat.

↘ 個人對素食的立場

Personally, I am against vegetarianism.

↘ 看法一

In terms of health, human beings need certain elements from animals, such as protein and fat. Also, a proper amount of meat will not cause obesity but offer our body sufficient energy and strength.

↘ 看法二

Naturally, human beings are omnivores, and not only are vegetables supposed to be our natural food sources, but meats are as well. Therefore, we don't need to feel guilty if we eat meat from animals, even though some people choose to avoid meat in their diet.

↘ 結論句

Fresh fruit and vegetables form an important part of our daily diet, but with the lack of meat, the nutrition in our body would not be balanced.

每日攝取足夠的蛋白質非常重要，我們可自包括植物及動物等許多食物來源獲取蛋白質。

然而，全世界越來越多的人選擇成為素食者，並且大多食用蔬菜。我認為這種特定飲食型態有二主要原因。

首先是健康的原因。素食主義已變得越加普遍，而且一些人傾向放棄肉類，因為他們認為肉類富含動物性脂肪及油脂，這對他們的健康將造成負面或有害的影響。相較於肉類，他們相信蔬菜能夠較容易消化吸收，因此，他們的身體能夠更加順暢地運作，而且較不常生病。

其次，為了尊重生命，他們寧願不食用殺生而來的肉品，尤其要避免讓動物受到殘忍及不人道對待。此外，為了低成本獲得肉類產品，人類可能虐待動物。為了展現對這些生物的憐憫，素食主義者會避免吃肉。

個人來說，我反對素食主義。

就健康來說，人類需要某些來自動物的元素，例如蛋白質及油脂，而且，適量的肉類不會導致肥胖，反而會提供我們人體足夠的能量及力量。

就天然條件而言，人類是雜食動物，不僅蔬菜，各種肉類也應該是我們的天然食物來源，因此，如果食用來自動物的肉類，我們不需要感到愧疚，即使一些人選擇在他們的飲食中避免肉品。

新鮮蔬果構成我們日常飲食的一個重要部分，但是，若是缺乏肉類，我們身體的營養將不平衡。

1. 每日攝取足夠的蛋白質非常重要。
2. 為了健康的原因，素食主義已變得越加普遍，而且一些人傾向放棄肉類。
3. 素食主義者尤其要避免讓動物受到殘忍及不人道對待。
4. 若是缺乏肉類，我們身體的營養將不平衡。
5. 為了低成本獲得肉類產品，人類可能虐待動物。

參考答案

1. It is essential to consume enough protein daily.
2. For health reasons, vegetarianism has become more common, and some people tend to abandon meat.
3. Vegetarians especially want to avoid letting animals be treated in cruel and inhumane ways.
4. With the lack of meat, the nutrition in our body would not be balanced.
5. To obtain meat products at a low cost, human beings may mistreat animals.

描述人物的利器－連綴動詞

連綴動詞是將主詞與描述部分聯繫起來的動詞，主詞是描述的對象，稱為描述主詞。主詞的描述部分是主詞補語，除了形容詞，一些其他語詞也可充當主詞補語。

最常見的連綴動詞是 be 動詞，搭配不同結構的主詞補語，例如：

1. 名詞

My parents have been **vegetarians** for almost ten years.

2. 形容詞片語

Meat is **high** in animal fat and oil.

3. 現在分詞

Some animals have been **suffering** from mistreatment.

4. 過去分詞

Those animals will be **delivered** to the slaughterhouse.
Vegetables can be **digested and absorbed** more easily.
With the lack of meat, the nutrition in our body would not be **balanced**.
Not only vegetables but meats are **supposed** to be our natural food sources.

5. 不定詞

A good way to alleviate the stress on our environment is **to consume** less meat and dairy.

6. 副詞

These wild animals have been **away** from their habitat for a long time.

7. 介係詞片語

My sister has been **on a diet** for several months.

8. 名詞子句

The fact is **that we can get protein from many food sources**, including plants and animals.

9. 間接問句

That is **why people choose to avoid meat in their diet**.

10. 副詞子句

It is **because they want to avoid letting animals be treated in cruel ways**.

連綴性質常是動詞基本語意的引伸

1. appear 原意是 “come into view”（進入眼簾），引申為「顯得怎樣」。

The dog appeared to enjoy eating raw meat.

2. get 原意是「獲得物品」，引申為「處於某種狀態」。

Some vegetarians believe that they get sick less often.

3. come 原意是「為了目的而移動」，移動至某種狀態就是「變成」。

Tom’s dream finally comes true.

4. become 是 come 黏接強調字首 be，來到某種狀態就是變成。

Vegetarianism has become more common.

More and more people all over the world choose to become vegetarians.

5. grow 原意是 “become green”，與 green, grass 同源，「變成綠色」衍伸為「變成某種狀態」，gradually become 的意思。

Some vegetarians grow bored of vegetarian diets.

6. go 原意是「前進」，前進至某種狀態就是「變成」。

I have decided to go green. From now on, I am going to consume less meat.

7. turn 原意是「轉動方向」，轉動至某種狀態就是「變成」，become, change into 的意思。

The weather has suddenly turned cold.

8. fall 原意是 “drop from a height”，掉落至某種狀態就是「變成」。

She fell asleep during the movie.

9. feel 感覺

We don’t need to feel guilty if we eat meat from animals

10. stay 字源是 stand，從站立譬喻為停留，衍伸為「保持某種狀態」。

To stay healthy, my brother eats less and less processed food.

11. keep 字源是 hold（握住），握住某種狀態也就是「保持」。

Keep left at the traffic lights.

連綴動詞搭配形容詞呈現完整語意，與句子結構、語意轉折或邏輯無關，學習上，不須整理那些單字是連綴動詞，更不須記憶「連綴動詞加接形容詞」的規則，只須知道連綴動詞的字源語意，例如 taste 嚐、sound 聲音、smell 氣味，閱讀時見招拆招，寫作時借字用字，不擔心詞窮或誤用。值得一提的是，連綴動詞與中文的語意及詞序一致，寫作時，依循中文轉換為英文即可正確表達，例如：The chef tasted the food before serving. 主廚端上食物之前先嚐過，taste the food 當然不是嚐起來怎樣，而是「嚐食物」。

說明文常提到數個人物或是物品，彼此份量均等，敘述便要力求均衡，避免厚此薄彼，例如描述家庭成員時，可以先提父母，而後兄弟或姊妹，父母之間、兄弟或姊妹之間的敘述儘量均衡，內容儘量一致，猶如填寫同一份履歷格式一樣。

以下這篇文章介紹 Joshua 的家人，敘述的順序是父母、姊妹、兄弟，內容都是職業為主，搭配專長及生活動態，請試著找出各個敘述的段落。

Joshua is an exchange student visiting from Jerusalem, Israel. He is from a large Jewish family, which includes his parents and four siblings. Joshua's parents are pediatricians at a children's hospital, and they specialize in treating children's rare diseases. Joshua has two sisters, Esther and Levana. Esther is serving in the Israeli army and she doesn't like young girls' wear. Levana is an art major in college, and she will become an intern in a museum in the neighborhood of the Western Wall. By the way, Esther's and Levana's boyfriends are both from Taiwan. Is that a strange coincidence? Joshua has two brothers, Asher and Lavi. Asher is an expert in the field of women's studies, and he is going to visit Taiwan for a conference this summer. Lavi has a Ph.D. degree in biotechnology, and now he is a director of the vaccine department in a national medical institute. Asher and Lavi's godfather is an unofficial government representative stationed in Taiwan. Joshua is studying in Taiwan now, which makes his family more familiar with it. Sooner or later, perhaps his entire family will be connected to Taiwan in some way.

參考答案

主題句

Joshua is an exchange student visiting from Jerusalem, Israel. He is from a large Jewish family, which includes his parents and four siblings.

介紹 Joshua 的父母

Joshua's parents are pediatricians at a children's hospital, and they specialize in treating children's rare diseases.

介紹 Joshua 的姊妹

Joshua has two sisters, Esther and Levana. Esther is serving in the Israeli army and she doesn't like young girls' wear. Levana is an art major in college, and she will become an intern in a museum in the neighborhood of the Western Wall. By the way, Esther's and Levana's boyfriends are both from Taiwan. Is that a strange coincidence?

介紹 Joshua 的兄弟

Joshua has two brothers, Asher and Lavi. Asher is an expert in the field of women's studies, and he is going to visit Taiwan for a conference this summer. Lavi has a Ph.D. degree in biotechnology, and now he is a director of the vaccine department in a national medical institute. Asher and Lavi's godfather is an unofficial government representative stationed in Taiwan.

結論句

Joshua is studying in Taiwan now, which makes his family more familiar with it. Sooner or later, perhaps his entire family will be connected to Taiwan in some way.

技巧 9

融入生活經驗或經驗法則，直接入戲

圖片或題目呈現故事的綱要，提示發生了什麼事、要發表什麼看法，至於情緒、起因、影響等橋段若要順暢、生動，最好的方法是直接入戲，發揮自己的生活經驗或是經驗法則，身歷其境、現身說法，這樣便能循著經驗檔案而言之有物。

例如這篇半夜 Jack 被鄰居打麻將的聲音吵得難以入睡的情節，不忍了、質問、責難都是受害者的正常情緒反應，而吵到鄰居的林太太感到尷尬、連連道歉應該是可預期的回應，這樣的內容，入戲才能掰得輕鬆、寫得流暢。

09

What was happening this late at night?

It was one o'clock in the morning, but Jack was lying in bed awake and anxious because of the noises of a mahjong game coming from upstairs, which sounded like hundreds of machine guns were shooting at him. "It must be Mrs. Wang, who is playing mahjong with her friends. What a lousy neighbor!" he thought.

Not willing to tolerate it any longer, Jack got up, went upstairs, and knocked on the neighbor's door. "How come you are still playing mahjong and making noisesso late at night? It is high time to sleep." Scolded by Jack, Mrs. Wang was so embarrassed that she apologized to him by saying sorry over and over again.

Mrs. Wang and her friends stopped playing mahjong and turned off the lights. The night became silent. Jack finally fell asleep at two o'clock, one hour after he asked Mrs. Wang to stop disturbing him. For him, it took a long time to get a good night's sleep.

註解

- awake and anxious 半夜被吵到睡不著的情緒，同時營造上樓抗議的氛圍。
- coming from upstairs 將聲音與位置連結起來，鋪陳事件的空間動線。
- like hundreds of machine guns were shooting at him 比喻手法誇飾麻將聲音，提升衝突的強度，增加解決衝突的必要性。

- who is playing mahjong with her friends 臆測鄰居與朋友打麻將是經驗法則，同時交代事件的人物角色。
- Not willing to tolerate it any longer 不忍了，要解決衝突了！就生活經驗而言，半夜被吵到睡不著是無法忍受的，這是採取行動前的心理狀況。
- 不忍了，產生 how come—責備的語氣，若是 tell, ask，口氣不到位，與前述醞釀的情緒不符。
- 依照經驗法則，how come 與 scold 的語氣相稱，自知理虧的一方就是 apology。
- apology 之後就是改進，行動是 stopped playing mahjong，讓夜晚恢復平靜。

夜晚這麼晚了發生什麼事？

現在是早上一點鐘，但是傑克正躺在床上，醒著又焦慮，因為來自樓上的麻將聲聽起來像幾百支機關槍一直射向他。「一定是王太太，她在跟朋友打麻將，多麼差勁的一位鄰居！」他想著。

不願意再容忍了，傑克起床、上樓，然後敲鄰居的門，「晚上這麼晚了你怎麼還在打麻將，還製造噪音？該睡覺了。」遭到傑克責備，王太太好尷尬，一再向他道歉，連聲說對不起。

王太太和她的朋友停止打麻將，隨後關燈。夜晚變得安靜，傑克在二點鐘，就是要求王太太停止打擾他之後一小時終於睡著了。對他來說，花好長時間才得以睡一晚好覺。

1. 早上一點鐘，但是 Jack 正躺在床上，醒著又焦慮。
2. 不願意再容忍了，Jack 起床、上樓，然後敲鄰居的門。
3. 遭到傑克責備，王太太好尷尬，一再向他道歉，連聲説對不起。
4. 傑克在二點鐘，就是要求王太太停止打擾他之後一小時終於睡著了。
5. 王太太和她的朋友停止打麻將，隨後關燈。

參考答案

1. It was one o'clock in the morning, but Jack was lying in bed awake and anxious.
2. Not willing to tolerate it any longer, Jack got up, went upstairs and knocked on the neighbor's door.
3. Scolded by Jack, Mrs. Wang was so embarrassed and apologized to him by saying sorry over and over again.
4. Jack finally fell asleep at two o'clock, one hour after he asked Mrs. Wang to stop disturbing him.
5. Mrs. Wang and her friends stopped playing mahjong and turned off the lights.

增添訊息、活化結構的非限定動詞

謹守主從分明原則，限定動詞搭配非限定動詞便是輕鬆事，尤其是分詞構句，更是足以化繁為簡，語意及結構雙向破解句型。

1. 以 want, remember 為例，非限定動詞與限定動詞的主詞一致時，非限定動詞主詞省略，若是不一致，非限定動詞主詞保留。

    1) I want to come back soon.
    該句原是 I want / I to come back soon.
    "to come back soon" 是非限定動詞，主事者是 I，與 want 的主詞一致，省略。

    2) I want Tom to come back soon.
    該句原是 I want / Tom to come back soon.
    受詞與受詞補語是一事件，受詞是主事者，受詞補語是動作。
    "to come back soon" 的主事者與 want 的主詞不一致，Tom 保留。

    3) I remember turning off the light when I left the office.
    該句原是 I remember / I turning off the light when I left the office.
    限定動詞（remember）與非限定動詞（turning off the light）的主詞一致，非限定動詞的主詞 I 省略。

    4) I remember Tom turning off the light when he left the office.
    該句原是 I remember / Tom turning off the light when he left the office.
    限定動詞與非限定動詞的主詞（Tom）不一致，Tom 保留。

2. 分詞構句是非限定動詞組，與主要子句主詞一致，分詞構句的主詞省略。

1) Sometimes, giraffes sleep while standing.

→ Sometimes, giraffes sleep while they are standing.

2) United we stand, divided we fall.

→ If we are united, we stand; if we are divided, we fall.

3. 分詞構句搭配從屬連接詞以使語意明確，雙重標記從的位階。

1) Jack would come to the party if invited.

→ Jack would come to the party if he was invited.

2) Even though studying hard, John still failed his math test.

→ Even though John studied hard, he still failed his math test.

說明 even though 搭配分詞構句的用法較正式，但口語不常用。

4. 完成式非限定動詞表示較限定動詞早發生。

Having gained EUA, the vaccine is allowed to be used in non-clinical settings.

→ After the vaccine gained EUA, it is allowed to be used in non-clinical settings.

5. 分詞構句改寫為限定動詞、副詞子句或主要子句乃依事件而定。

1) 限定動詞

Tim closed the door, locking himself out.

→ Tim closed the door and locked himself out.

2) 副詞子句

Injured in the accident, the operator was rushed to the hospital.

→ Because he was injured in the accident, the operator was rushed to the hospital.

3) 主要子句

Standing still at the entrance, the dog was waiting for its owner shopping in the store.

→ The dog was standing still at the entrance, and it was waiting for its owner shopping in the store.

說明 分詞構句改寫為主要子句，表示方式。

以下文章空格有二選項，請選出其中一個符合生活經驗或經驗法則的選項。

1. out of pity / out of curiosity
2. sad and speechless / calm and effortless
3. Tina took the boy to the nearby police station / Tina and the boy went to the nearby police station
4. he called his mother / he gave the policewoman his mother's phone number
5. The boy's tears turned into smiles. / What a narrow escape!

Last Tuesday afternoon, on her way home from school, Tina saw a little boy crying by the roadside, with a teddy bear in his arms. __1__, she went up to the boy and asked him if he needed any help. However, he just kept crying, __2__.

Then, __3__, and told the policewoman what happened to him. The policewoman comforted the sobbing boy and tried to help him get home soon because it was getting dark. The boy was still crying as __4__.

It was six o'clock, one hour after their long wait. The boy's mother showed up. When he saw his mother, the boy ran toward her, calling "Mom" loudly. They both opened their arms wide, hugged and looked at each other. __5__ At this heartwarming sight, Tina and the policewoman felt relieved and delighted.

参考答案

1. out of pity
2. sad and speechless
3. Tina took the boy to the nearby police station
4. he gave the policewoman his mother's phone number
5. The boy's tears turned into smiles.

技巧 10

圖表寫作有技巧，數據要伴隨評論

命題趨勢

圖表判讀是大學入學考試中心精進素養導向命題的重點方向中的整合運用能力之一，圖表判讀應用在英文寫作就是圖表寫作，勢必成為學測英文寫作的熱門題型，一定要熟練寫作技巧。

題目形式及歷屆試題

圖表寫作包括一個圖表及簡短文字說明，例如 103 年指考寫作的圖表是美國某中學全體學生每天進行各種活動的時間分配。

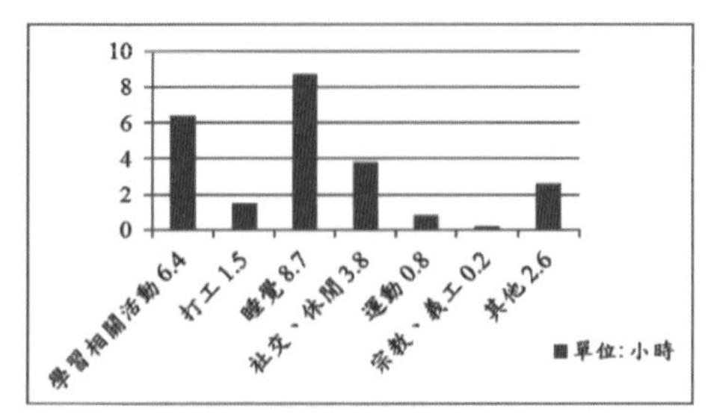

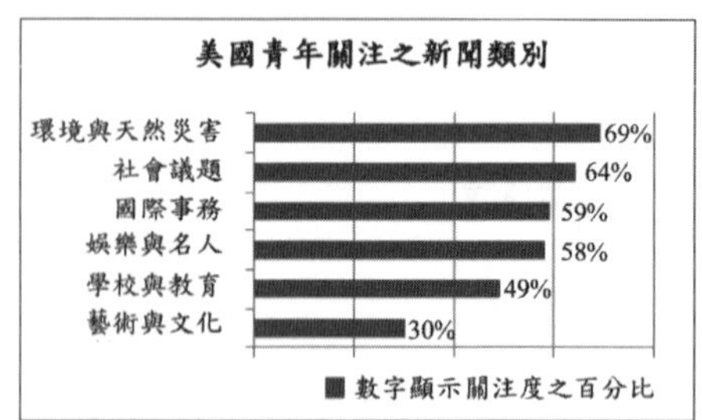

108 年指考寫作的圖表是美國 18 至 29 歲的青年對不同類別之新聞的關注度統計。

圖表寫作都會要求文分兩段，第一段描述圖表數據呈現的現象，第二段說明自己與該現象的對照及理由，例如 103 年指考寫作要說明整體而言，自己一天的時間分配與該高中全體學生的異同，並說明其理由；108 年指考寫作要描述六個新聞類別中，自己較為關注及較不關注的新聞主題，還要說明理由。

圖表描述方式

1. 圖表若是呈現目前的數據，使用現在簡單式；若是過去，使用過去簡單式；若是過去持續到現在，使用現在完成式。
2. 善用表示程度的語詞，例如：

   the largest amount/number of 最大量

   the second greatest amount/number of 第二大量

   the lowest amount/number of 最少量

   second only to 僅次於
3. 常用的圖表說明轉折詞

   while

   obviously

   that is to say

   for this reason

4. 具備主題句、細節、結論句架構

技巧

1. 不要一個數據一個句子。
2. 依照數據特性，決定主動或被動語態。
3. 數據要伴隨說明或評論。
4. 相關或對比的數據合併以使句子多樣化。
5. 結論句回顧圖表中最顯著的數據或重申其現象。

103 指考英文寫作的寫作清單如下：

部分	功用
主題句	HOOK 主題句
第一段	圖表呈現之特別現象 數據描述及理由
第二段	自己一天的時間分配與該高中全體學生的相同處 自己一天的時間分配與該高中全體學生的相異處 理由
結論句	回顧主題 提出總結

🎧 10

↘ 感嘆句作為 HOOK

How much I envy those high school students in America!

↘ 主題句，依照題目說明美國某高中的全體學生每天進行各種活動的時間分配

The bar chart clearly indicates how all the students of a high school in the U.S. allot their time daily among seven activities.

↘ 第一段，圖表呈現之特別現象

The activity with the largest amount of time spent on it is sleeping, with up to 8.7 hours a day, while the activity with the second largest amount of time spent on it is learning. This means that during the daytime, high school students allot the greatest amount of time to learning. Meanwhile, they tend to take a break from their studies by interacting with peers, and therefore, they spend a lot of time on social and recreational activities, second only to learning. For this reason, high school students spend much less time on part-time jobs, sports and, especially volunteer work.

Obviously, for these students each day, sleeping accounts for the largest allotment of time. However, doing voluntary work seems to be the last option they would choose, for it is the least related to their health, studies, or friendship.

↘ 第二段，自己一天的時間分配與該高中全體學生的異同及理由

Compared to the time allotment of daily activities indicated above, my time allotment is quite similar to it. First of all, getting sufficient sleep is important to me, but I tend not to spend that much time on it, getting eight hours a day or so. Second, as a high school student in Taiwan, I have to spare no effort to perform well at school. I go to school early in the morning and have seven classes until late afternoon. After school, I usually rush to attend math and English intensive classes, since I desire to get good grades on tests. On weekdays, studies account for almost all the daytime, and, needless to say, there is very little time for social and recreational activities, let alone other activities. In fact, I enjoy doing sports and voluntary work, and the weekend is the only time I can engage in them. What a pity!

↘ 結論句

However, I am clear that I am living a substantial life despite my simple time allotment.

我好羨慕這些美國中學生喔！

這長條圖清楚顯示美國一所中學所有學生如何每日在七項活動中分配他們的時間。

花費最大量時間的活動是睡覺，一天達 8.7 小時，而花費次大量時間的活動是學習，這意指白天期間，中學生分配最大量時間在學習。同時，他們傾向藉由與同儕互動從課業中稍作休息。因此，他們花費很多時間在社交及休閒活動，僅次於學習。因著這理由，中學生花費在兼差工作、運動，尤其志願工作的時間就少多了。

明顯地，對這些學生來説，每天睡覺佔最多分配時間，然而，從事志願工作似乎是他們最後選擇的項目，因為與他們的健康、課業或友誼最不相關。

比較以上顯示的每日活動時間分配，我的時間分配相當相似。首先，獲得足夠睡眠對我是重要的，但是我不會花費那麼多時間。大約一天八小時。第二，身為一名在臺灣的中學生，我必須在學校不遺餘力表現良好，一大早上學，上七節課直到傍晚。放學後，我經常趕去上數學及英文加強課程，因為我想要得到好的考試成績。在周間日，學習佔了幾乎所有的白天時間，不消說，幾乎沒有社交及休閒活動的時間，其他活動就不用説了。事實上，我喜愛運動及志願工作，而周末是我唯一能夠參與的時間，好可惜！

然而，我很清楚自己正過著充實的生活，儘管我簡單的時間分配。

1. 花費最大量時間的活動是睡覺，一天達 8.7 小時。
2. 白天期間，中學生分配最大量時間在學習。
3. 中學生傾向藉由與同儕互動從課業中稍作休息。
4. 身為一名在臺灣的中學生，我必須在學校不遺餘力表現良好。
5. 不消說，幾乎沒有社交及休閒活動的時間，其他活動就不用說了。

參考答案

1. The activity with the largest amount of time spent on it is sleeping, with up to 8.7 hours a day.
2. During the daytime, high school students allot the greatest amount of time to learning.
3. High school students tend to take a break from their studies by interacting with peers.
4. As a high school student in Taiwan, I have to spare no effort to perform well at school.
5. Needless to say, there is very little time for social and recreational activities, let alone other activities.

寫作一定要知曉的非限定動詞

非限定動詞不受主詞人稱及數目的限定，不標記事件的時間或態貌，搭配限定動詞，從的位階，包括不定詞、動名詞、分詞。動名詞是名詞性質，扮演主詞、受詞、補語等必要成分；不定詞、分詞常扮演修飾或附帶角色，簡潔結構，增添訊息，豐潤描述內容。非限定動詞以從的位階呈現一個動作，與限定動詞形成結構與語意的主從對應，是結構縮減，訊息緊湊的重要寫作技巧。

1. 搭配各種時態就是沒有時態。

   1) Tom likes to play basketball.
      Tom liked to play basketball before.

   2) Mark was tired this morning.
      The film is interesting.

2. 非限定動詞扮演結構及語意的必要成分

   1) Reading comic books is a great way to share the joy of reading with children.
      說明 Reading comic books 是動名詞，主詞角色，reading with children 也是動名詞，介係詞的受詞角色。

   2) We're not planning to stay here much longer.
      說明 現在分詞 planning 是主詞補語，不定詞 to stay 是 planning 的受詞。

   3) *We not planning to stay here much longer.
      說明 主格格位的主詞不與非限定動詞構成句子。

3. 對等連接詞合併結構相同的非限定動詞，形成平行結構。

1) I am planning to take a trip to Israel and visit the Western Wall.

2) You have to collect things, put prices on them, put them out on tables and then wait for people to come.

109 國中會考

3) Drinking and smoking are highly associated behaviors.

說明 二件事情，搭配複數動詞。

4) Tom was listening to music and talking on the phone then.

說明 同時進行動作。

4. 不定詞

不定詞的標記 “to” 源自介係詞，“in the direction of ” 的意思，從空間的目標衍伸至時間、感官投射、話題的方向，乃至事件的發展一不定詞，具有「要去做、未完成、不存在」的意涵，表示目的、結果、事實。

1) 修飾全句，與句子結構無關

To be honest with you, I don’ t think it will be possible.

To change the subject, have you been vaccinated yet ？

To make a long story short, we will be receiving our new carpet next week.

說明 未來進行式表示預定發生。

Two of our players were ill, and to make matters worse, our goalie had broken his ankle.

2) 不定詞常搭配形容詞，評論句子所述的內容

Sad to say, the smartphone was never found.

→ It is sad to say that the smartphone was never found.

Needless to say, the clerk will be off work for a while.

→ It’s needless to say that the clerk will be off work for a while.

3) 表示目的，常伴隨手段

This tool is used to measure the diameter.

Bill Gates will spend a lot of money to fight climate change.

4) 表示結果

It's never too late to mend relationships.

My brother is tall enough to change the bulb without getting on a chair.

5) 表示完成的事實

Neil Armstrong is the first astronaut to walk on the moon.

Tom was made to complete the extensive training course.

6) come、go 帶有邀請、請求、命令等意涵時，常加接省略 to 的不定詞以強調該動作。

Come collect your gift by entering your "BeautiMed Friend" card number at e-BeautiMed before 8/31.

110 國中會考

Go stand in the corner.

I'll go take a shower now.

5. 動名詞

1) 主詞

Getting sufficient sleep is important to me.

Doing voluntary work seems to be the last option they would choose.

2) 受詞

I enjoy doing sports and voluntary work.

They tend to take a break from their studies by interacting with peers.

3) 補語

The activity with the largest amount of time spent on it is sleeping.

6. 分詞

1) 現在分詞具有主動、持續、進行、存在等意涵，過去分詞具有完成、被動的意涵。分詞置於限定動詞右側，與限定動詞主事者一致，表示附帶或接續的動作。

主動搭配現在分詞

Mr. Lin died two years ago, leaving three children.

→ Mr. Lin died two years ago and left three children.

The janitor left the office, taking the keys with him.

→ The janitor left the office and took the keys with him.

The man was seen by the pedestrian breaking into the building.

Please come to the gym wearing your mask and leave it on during your time in the gym.

被動搭配過去分詞

Hank glanced at his semester report card, pleasantly surprised to get an A for history.

The famous entertainer was posing for photos in the lobby, surrounded by a huge crowd of fans.

→ The famous entertainer was posing for photos in the lobby, and she was surrounded by a huge crowd of fans.

2) 搭配位置動詞

現在分詞是主詞補語，表示主詞於該動作時的狀態。動詞加接副詞，副詞修飾該動詞；動詞加接分詞，分詞修飾主詞，連綴動詞加接的形容詞是主詞補語。

They sat drinking beer at an outdoor table.

→ They sat and drank beer at an outdoor table.

The agent stood taking a survey of his surroundings.

→ The agent stood and took a survey of his surroundings.

I was lying looking at the amazing sky full of bright stars.

→ I was lying and looking at the amazing sky full of bright stars.

3) 搭配移動的動詞，表示主事者移動的樣貌。

A rabbit came hopping through the meadow.

The boy went jumping to open the door.

The instructor approached running to find out what was going on.

4) go 搭配動詞黏接 ing，表示從事戶外活動。

go camping

go hiking

go mountain-climbing

go bird-watching

go roller-skating

5) 一些副詞搭配現在分詞 speaking，表達作說者對於事件的意念或評論。

Frankly speaking, it's a big dilemma for me.

Generally speaking, men are stronger than women.

Relatively speaking, it is a low-risk investment option.

Strictly speaking, Great Britain consists of England, Scotland, and Wales, and the United Kingdom consists of Great Britain and Northern Ireland.

6) with/without 的受詞加接非限定動詞或其他語詞（受詞的敘述部分），共同描述事件的附帶狀況。with/without 僅接受詞不足以構成附帶狀況，加接非限定動詞或其他語詞才能提供充分訊息。

Your book must be in good shape, without any page missing.

（106 國中會考題組）

It's impossible to carry on a conversation with all this noise going on.

Last Christmas, when Monica was jogging in the park, the old man came up to her with a large bag on his shoulder.

（100 北北基）

Duncan also surprised the people of her time by dancing in comfortable clothes and without shoes on.

請閱讀以下文章，然後畫出第一段的圖表及第二段的題目說明。

The line graph indicates three facilities on high school campuses used most often by students in Taiwan. As we can see, in 2019, the Gym had the highest visit frequency, with up to 60 percent, followed by the Study Center/Library, with 10 percent less, and the Club Office, with 40 percent less. In 2020, the Gym and Club Office both increased by 10 percent of visit frequency, while the Study Center/Library lost 10 percent. In 2021, the Gym and Club Office also increased visit frequency, but the former just 5 percent, and the latter up to 15 percent. As for the Study Center/ Library, unfortunately, repeated the decreasing tendency.

The graph above is consistent with my experience on campus. I go to the gym whenever I am free from study because I need to relax and reduce my stress from my heavy homework and tiring exams by participating in exciting sports, like volleyball or badminton.

I have been a member of the choir simply the first year in high school because singing is my favorite hobby, and therefore, even under heavy stress from my studies, I will occasionally visit the club office to refresh myself by singing alone or with other members. As for the study center, I visit it less often because I prefer to study at home, where I find it much easier for me to focus on my studies.

技巧 11

按照方向秩序描述空間，扮演稱職導遊角色

敘述故事大多是依照時間順序，開始、發展、結束依序連貫，清晰而合乎邏輯。描述空間必須擬定描述的秩序，從遠而近或從近而遠、從上而下或從下而上、從左而右或從右而左，清楚勾勒場景，若是能夠提及人物，場景將更為生動。

例如這篇描述公寓的段落，主題句介紹公寓的位置，發展部分先描述與人有關的室內格局，轉折語詞 However 將鏡頭轉換至室外，但仍提及人物而使空間產生與人的連結，增添場景的人文氣息。

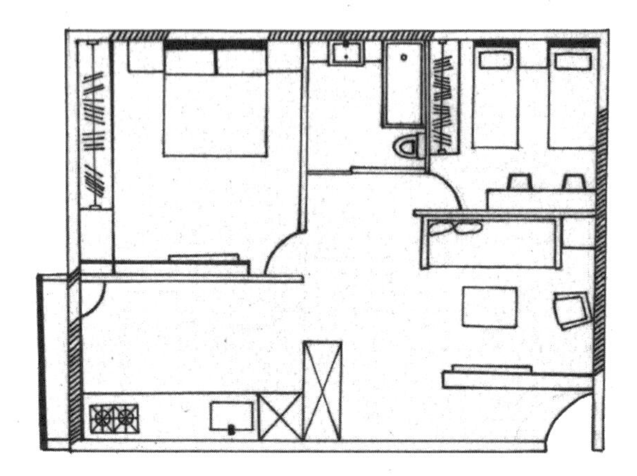

範文 1

11-1

Tom's family lives in an apartment in a suburb of Taipei. It is elegant but small, with a living room, a kitchen, a bathroom and two bedrooms. They eat meals in the living room because there is no dining room. In addition, Tom and his brother share a smaller bedroom, where they sleep and study together. However, the apartment is well-managed since there is a security guard at the entrance of the apartment building all the time. Across from the entrance is a courtyard with bushes, flowers, and several marble benches. Tom's parents usually take a walk there after dinner.

註解

- Tom's family lives in an apartment in a suburb of Taipei.
  標示情景的位置，提供地理上的訊息。
- It is elegant but small
  傳達公寓的印象。
- with a living room, a kitchen, a bathroom and two bedrooms
  室內格局呼應 small 的描述。
- They eat meals in the living room because there is no dining room.
  室內空間產生的作息影響。
- In addition, Tom and his brother share a smaller bedroom, where they sleep and study together.
  引介人物在空間中的活動。
- However
  轉折語詞將鏡頭移至室外。
- the apartment is well-managed
  說明公寓大樓的整體評價。
- since there is a security guard at the entrance of the apartment building all the time.
  舉例證明。
- Across from the entrance is a courtyard.
  從公寓大樓入口而至大樓內部的庭院。
- with bushes, flowers, and several marble benches.
  庭院的景物，由外而內，逐漸詳細描述空間。
- Tom's parents usually take a walk there after dinner.
  空間與人物的生活連結，產生動態的場景感力。

範文 2

以下這篇文章以第一人稱的觀點敘述到附近新開幕的全聯福利中心的經驗，空間的秩序是從外而內，由右而左，描述商品區域中流露個人敏銳觀察及飲食特性。

11-2

I went to a new PX Mart store in my neighborhood yesterday, which looked familiar to me because I have been to a number of PX Mart stores in many other locations.

After scanning the QR Code at the entrance and checking my body temperature, I entered the store. The moment I stepped into the store, a variety of fresh fruits of different sizes and colors appeared in front of me, like a warm welcome for a special guest. Then I started my visit from the right side, where there was an entire aisle of fruits, vegetables and dairy products. The bright lights made each item look fresh and attracted me to take a look at them more.

At the backside opposite to the entrance was a long wall of raw meat and seafood. I just walked by quickly and took a quick glance because I had no idea what I would do with any of them if I bought them. The moment I turned to the left side, a wide selection of desserts immediately caught my eye, urging me to get closer and, under the influence of my sweet tooth, I picked up a container of strawberry ice cream. I am sure the dessert section is always my favorite area in a PX Mart store.

To my surprise, when I got to the cashier counter in the left corner of the store, the clerk told me that I could get another container of strawberry ice cream for free that day! Right away, I went hopping back to get one more container of my favorite dessert. It was the happiest and luckiest visit to this familiar store.

註解

- I went to a new PX Mart store in my neighborhood yesterday
  文章起首即標示地點及時間。
- which looked familiar to me because I have been to a number of PX Mart stores in many other locations
  人對空間的記憶與印象。
- After scanning the QR Code at the entrance and checking my body temperature, I entered the store.
  依照生活經驗據實描述，拉近人與空間的連結。
- The moment I stepped into the store, a variety of fresh fruits of different sizes and colors appeared in front of me, like a warm welcome for a special guest.
  呈現商品擺設與人的關聯。

- Then I started my visit from the right side.
  情景從入口轉至右側。
- At the backside opposite to the entrance was a long wall of raw meat and sea food. I just walked by quickly and took a quick glance because I had no idea what I would do with any of them if I bought them.
  入口作為空間投射的原點，先是右側，再來是正前方，就是全聯店面的正後方。
- The moment I turned to the left side,
  再來是左側。
- a wide selection of desserts immediately caught my eye, urging me to get closer and, under the influence of my sweet tooth, I picked up a container of strawberry ice cream. I am sure the dessert section is always my favorite area in a PX Mart store.
  藉由甜點凸顯空間與人的互動，空間拓化至人物。
- To my surprise, when I got to the cashier counter in the left corner of the store the clerk told me that I could get another container of strawberry ice cream for free that day! Right away, I went hopping back to get one more container of my favorite dessert.
  情景移至左前方收銀櫃臺，在此布局人的空間的強烈互動。
- It was the happiest and luckiest visit to this familiar store.
  人的感受作為空間描述的總結。

範文 1

湯姆家住在台北郊區的一棟公寓裡，雅致但不大，有一間客廳、一間廚房、一間浴室及二間臥室。他們在客廳用餐，因為沒有飯廳。此外，湯姆和他弟弟共用一間較小的臥室，他們一起在那裏睡覺、讀書。然而，這棟公寓管理良好，因為公寓大樓入口隨時都有一名警衛。入口對面是一庭院，裡面有矮灌木叢、花卉及幾座大理石長凳，湯姆的父母經常晚餐後在那裡散步。

範文 2

昨天我去附近的一家新開幕全聯福利中心，看起來蠻熟悉的，因為我去過許多其他地方的幾家全聯福利中心。

入口掃描實聯制及量體溫之後，我進到店裡。一踏進店裡，各式各樣不同大小及顏色的新鮮水果呈現在我前面，像是一份提供給特別來賓的溫馨歡迎。然後我從右方開始逛，那裏有一整走道水果、蔬菜及乳製品，明亮的燈光使每一品項看起來新鮮，並且吸引我多看一下。

入口對面的後方是一長長牆壁的生肉及海鮮，我只快走過去時很快看一眼，因為如果買了，自己也不知道怎麼處理。我一轉到左邊，種類齊全的甜點立刻引起我的注意，催促我靠近一點，在嗜甜的作用下，我拿起一盒草莓冰淇淋。我確定甜點區永遠是全聯福利中心裡我最喜愛的地方。

令我驚訝的是，我到了店左邊角落的收銀櫃檯之後，店員告訴我那天我可以免費獲得另一盒草莓冰淇淋，我立即跳著回去再拿一盒我最喜愛的甜點，這是我逛這家熟悉的商店最開心、最幸運的一趟。

1. 這棟公寓管理良好，因為公寓大樓入口隨時都有一名警衛。
2. 入口掃描實聯制及量體溫之後，我進到店裡。
3. 我從右方開始逛，那裏有一整走道水果、蔬菜及乳製品。
4. 我一轉到左邊，種類齊全的甜點立刻引起我的注意，催促我靠近一點。
5. 店員告訴我那天我可以免費獲得另一盒草莓冰淇淋。

參考答案

1. The apartment is well-managed since there is a security guard at the entrance of the apartment building all the time.
2. After scanning the QR Code at the entrance and checking my body temperature, I entered the store.
3. I started my visit from the right side, where there was an entire aisle of fruits, vegetables and dairy products.
4. The moment I turned to the left side, a wide selection of desserts immediately caught my eye, urging me to get closer.
5. The clerk told me that I could get another container of strawberry ice cream for free that day.

重新認識形容詞子句

形容詞子句具有添增訊息、擴展結構的功用，是非常重要的寫作句式，應當熟習。

形容詞子句包括限定形容詞子句、補述形容詞子句、條件形容詞子句等三類型。

限定形容詞子句

1. 限定形容詞子句不可省略，否則先行詞指涉不清楚。
   先行詞 限定形容詞子句
2. 中譯：限定形容詞子句 **的** 先行詞
   的常作為限定標記，判斷限定或補述的重要依據。

1) a great achievement that impresses modern people
   令現代人印象深刻**的**偉大成就
   比較 a great achievement → 不清楚偉大成就是什麼

2) It was built to remember people who died in the war.
   建造的目的是為紀念死於戰爭**的**人。
   比較 It was built to remember people. → 不清楚指誰

3) Any food I cook is always tasty and perfectly cooked.
   任何我烹煮**的**食物都很美味，煮得很棒。
   比較 Any food is always tasty and perfectly cooked.
   任何食物都很美味，煮得很棒 → 不合理
   any 沒有指定，必須搭配限定形容詞子句。

補述形容詞子句

1. 補述形容詞子句僅補充說明先行詞，省略時不影響先行詞的辨識。
   先行詞 補述形容詞子句

2. 中譯：先行詞 補述形容詞子句
   補述用法中譯沒有**的**，不以**的**標記補述。

3. 補述形容詞子句不搭配 that，that 不用於逗號之後。
   1) Mr. Chen, who lives next door, is a little sloppy.
      陳先生，住在隔壁，他有點邋遢。
      比較 The man who lives next door is a little sloppy.
      住在隔壁**的**男子有點邋遢。
   2) Mrs. Lin has three daughters, who are all working for TSMC.
      林太太有三個女兒，都在台積電工作。
      比較 Mrs. Chen has three daughters who are working for TSMC.
      陳太太有三個在台積電工作**的**女兒。→ 還有其他女兒。
   3) He is Terry Fox, who had a strong will to support cancer research.
      他是 Terry Fox，懷抱支持癌症研究的堅強意志。
      說明 人名標示明確指涉對象，形容詞子句僅是補充說明。
   4) Mr. Yung, who specializes in morphology, gave a lecture in the library yesterday.
      楊先生，專攻構詞學，昨天在圖書館發表演講。
      比較
      1. The Mr. Yung who comes from Pingtung talked with me during the lunch break.
         來自屏東**的**那位楊先生午休時間與我聊了一下。
         姓名搭配 the，標記特指，搭配限定形容詞子句。

2. A Mr. Yung called you when you were in the meeting.

一位楊先生在你會議時打電話給你。

不定冠詞 a 標記不特定指涉對象「某一位楊先生」。

3. Miss Lin called you when you were in the meeting.

林小姐在你會議時打電話給你。

共同認知的姓名指涉，不須搭配冠詞。

4. 年份是共同的時空背景，不須限定，搭配補述形容詞子句。

Tom was born in 2003, when SARS broke out in Taiwan.

湯姆出生於 2003 年，台灣爆發 SARS 的時候。

5. when, where, why 等關係副詞引導限定或補述形容詞子句。

1) This is one of the oldest tea houses in Kyoto where we can enjoy traditional sweets.

這是京都我們能夠享受傳統甜食**的**最悠久茶室之一。

2) This is one of the oldest tea houses in Kyoto, where we can enjoy traditional sweets.

這是京都最悠久的茶室之一，我們能夠在那裏享受傳統甜食。

6. 補述形容詞子句常以前面句子做為先行詞，評論該句子所述內容。

One of the boys kept laughing, which annoyed Miss Lin intensely.

條件形容詞子句

1) Men **who wear** beards look masculine.

→ If men wear beards, they look masculine.

男子留鬍子，看起來有男子氣概。

說明 先行詞是泛指。

2) A son who is treated as a man early will be a man soon.

→ If a son is treated as a man early, he will be a man soon.

及早以一名男子對待的兒子將很快成為一名男子。

說明 a son 是非特定，泛指。

3) Anyone who can answer this in ten minutes will get a thumbs up from me.

→ If anyone can answer this in ten minutes, I will give a thumbs up.

→ Whoever can answer this in ten minutes, I will give them a thumbs up.

任何在十分鐘之內回答這問題**的**人，我就按一個讚。

說明

1. 複合關係代名詞 whoever ＝ anyone who。
2. 條件形容詞子句的先行詞是複數或單數名詞，泛指。
3. 條件形容詞子句等同於表示條件的副詞子句。
4. 同位語子句提供一些需要說明內容的名詞訊息，結構上不同於形容詞子句的是沒有主詞或受詞的空缺。

 1) The CEO issued a denial of the report that he is about to resign.

 執行長針對他即將辭職的報導發佈一份否認聲明。

 2) It is a well-known fact that new cars lose a lot of their value in the first year.

 新車在第一年嚴重折價是眾所周知的事實。

請寫出以下粗體名詞的修飾語及其結構：

文章出處：109 政大附中特招試題

As the owner of Wolf House, I have been trying very hard to make my pub not merely **a place** to have fun, but also **a community pub** where locals can build connections with each other. However, it was not until the pub-goers and I offered support to **Chuck**, an elderly man living nearby, that the existence of Wolf House as a community pub was finally realized.

Each day, I greeted every customer, hoping they would enjoy themselves in Wolf House. One of my frequent customers was **Chuck**, who was always the one to bring up topics in an attempt to chat with other customers but was unable to keep conversations going. **Our conversations** with him lasted only a few sentences before there was dead silence.

One Friday night, he did not show up, and **those** who had tried to talk to him also noticed this. At that moment, I felt uneasy about his absence and decided to go to Chuck's place to check on him. Upon arrival, I was terrified to see him lying on the floor. Without a second thought, I took him to the hospital, feeling afraid that my sixth sense had led me there.

Several days later, when I took some fruit to the hospital, I found him surrounded by many of Wolf House's customers. "How are you today?" I asked Chuck. "I'm good. I haven't had so many **visitors** for such a long time. Wolf House has been the only place I meet people, but when I am with people, I run out of **words** to express myself…" he admitted. "Don't worry," I replied, "I want everyone to feel at ease and stay connected at Wolf House. That's **the spirit** of a community pub, isn't it?" I saw Chuck wink at me with a smile. I knew right away that he recognized my effort to run Wolf House as **a pub** that bonds locals together.

參考答案

1. **a place** to have fun 不定詞
2. **a community pub** where locals can build connections with each other 形容詞子句
3. **Chuck**, an elderly man living nearby 同位語
4. **Chuck**, who was always the one to bring up topics in an attempt to chat with other customers but was unable to keep conversations going 補述形容詞子句
5. **Our conversations** with him 介係詞片語
6. **those** who had tried to talk to him also noticed this 限定形容詞子句
7. so many **visitors** 形容詞片語
8. **the only place** I meet people 限定形容詞子句
9. **words** to express myself 不定詞
10. **the spirit** of a community pub 介係詞片語
11. **a pub** that bonds locals together 限定形容詞子句

技巧 12 一片 OREO，一篇好文

作者寫作的目的（Author's Purpose）有三，一是說服（persuade），說服讀者認同文章的觀點，二是告知（inform），告知讀者一些事實或知識，三是娛樂（entertain），敘述一個有趣的故事，這三個單字開頭字母拼在一起正好是 PIE。

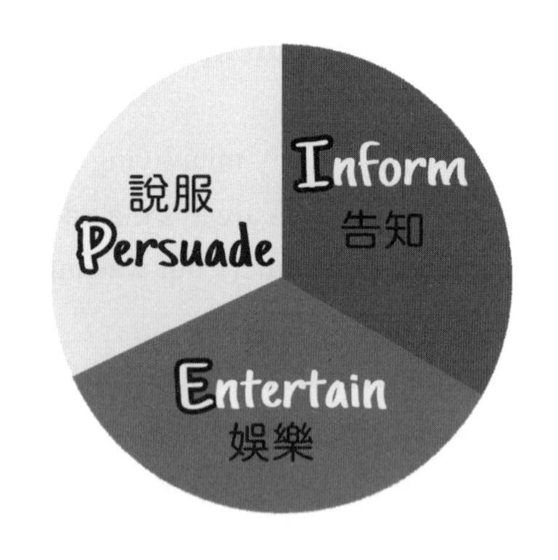

意見不同於事實（fact），表達意見的目的是說服他人認同自己的觀點，過程常包含意見（Opinion）、原因（Reason）、舉例（Example）及重申意見（Opinion），Opinion、Reason、Example、Opinion 這四個單字組成的頭字詞是 OREO，與一款知名餅乾同名。

學測英文作文鮮少出現論說文體，但常搭配其他題型要求表達意見，例如 105 年學測英文作文題目第一段要求說明你對家事該如何分工的看法及理由，107 學測年英文作文題目第二段要求說明自己對於排隊現象的心得或感想，111 年學測英文作文題目搭配圖片，第二段要求說明你心目中理想公園的樣貌與特色，並解釋你的理由。

一個理由的說服力當然不足，二個理由較為充實，三個理由是最佳的意見表達方式。當然，不論是二或三個理由，彼此的差異必須明顯，舉例才會多樣化，一個簡單的檢視方式就是細節不重疊。另外，每一理由的份量儘量均衡，這樣的篇章架構才是上乘。三個份量均衡的理由及其舉例宛如弧度相同的賓士汽車標誌，這樣的段落架構就稱為「OREO 的思考賓士圖」。

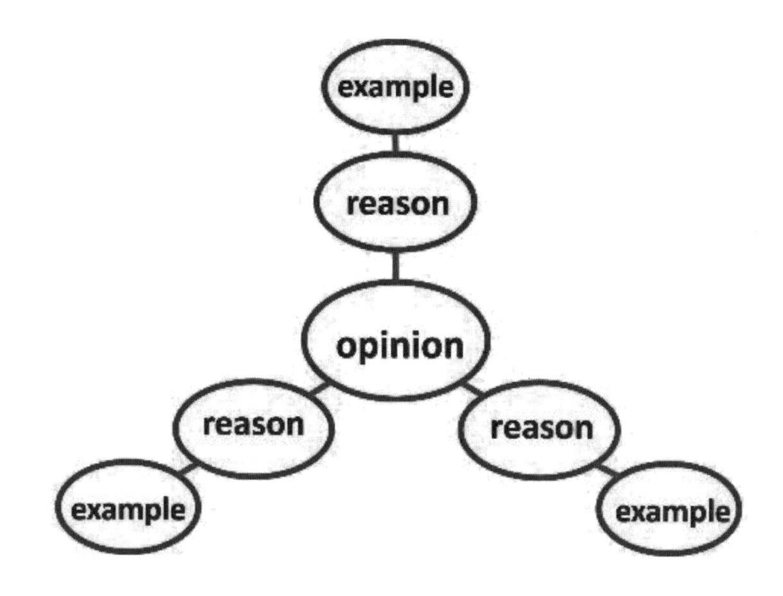

現在我們就以說明對於排隊現象的心得或感想為例，OREO 架構的寫法如下：

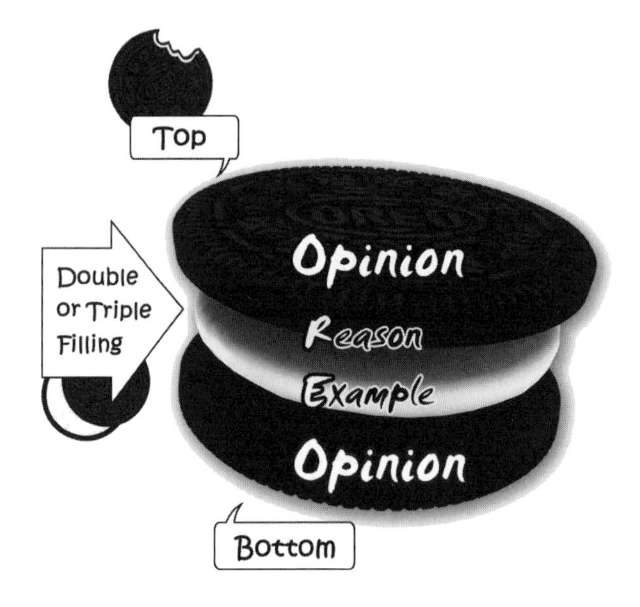

12

↘ **Opinion**

I think the phenomenon of queueing in long lines seems ridiculous.

↘ **Reason1**

Undoubtedly, it is certainly an energy-consuming waste of time for any of the followers.

↘ **Example 1**

For example, they have to arrive at the scene a few hours earlier than scheduled and then spend a substantial amount of time standing with strangers, which will consume their energy and make them tired and bored.

↘ **Reason 2**

What's worse, a long line of people will cause a negative impact on public space or even endanger the pedestrians.

↘ **Example 2**

Since the sidewalk is fully-crowded with those in line, pedestrians cannot help but take a detour or move off the sidewalk, which will make the public space not only chaotic but also risky.

↘ **Opinion 呼應文章起首的意見，具有結論的功用。**

In my opinion, lining up should be the last thing I choose to do in my daily life, and I will try to avoid it. There are few things in the world worth waiting for in a very long line.

OREO 架構常搭配一些慣用的語詞或句型，例如：

<table>
<tr><td rowspan="5">Opinion</td><td colspan="2">In my opinion</td></tr>
<tr><td colspan="2">My opinion is</td></tr>
<tr><td colspan="2">I think</td></tr>
<tr><td colspan="2">I feel</td></tr>
<tr><td colspan="2">I believe</td></tr>
<tr><td rowspan="4">Reason
Example</td><td>One reason</td><td>For example</td></tr>
<tr><td>First of all</td><td>For instance</td></tr>
<tr><td>Another reason</td><td>Another example</td></tr>
<tr><td>Also</td><td>In fact</td></tr>
<tr><td rowspan="2">Opinion</td><td colspan="2">This is why I think / believe / feel</td></tr>
<tr><td colspan="2">For these reasons I think / believe / feel</td></tr>
</table>

我認為大排長龍的現象似乎是荒謬的。無疑地，對於任何排隊的人來說，這一定是消耗體力而浪費時間。例如，他們必須較預定的時間提早幾小時抵達現場，然後花費大量時間與陌生人站在一起，耗掉他們的體力且令他們疲累又枯燥。

更糟的是，一長隊伍的人將對公共空間造成負面衝擊，甚至對行人造成危險，因為人行道擠滿了排隊人潮，行人只好繞道或從人行道走開，這將使公共空間不僅混亂，還會具有危險。

我認為排隊應該是我日常生活中最不願意做的事，我會盡力避免。世界上很少事情是值得大排長龍地等待的。

1. 我認為大排長龍的現象似乎是荒謬的。
2. 無疑地，對於任何排隊的人來說，這一定是消耗體力而浪費時間。
3. 一長隊伍的人將對公共空間造成負面衝擊，甚至對行人造成危險。
4. 行人只好繞道或從人行道走開，這將使公共空間不僅混亂還會具有危險。
5. 世界上很少事情是值得大排長龍地等待的。

✐ 參考答案

1. I think the phenomenon of queueing in long lines seems ridiculous.
2. Undoubtedly, it is certainly an energy-consuming waste of time for any of the followers.
3. A long line of people will cause a negative impact on public space or even endanger the pedestrians.
4. Pedestrians cannot help but take a detour or move off the sidewalk, which will make the public space not only chaotic but also risky.
5. There are few things in the world worth waiting for in a very long line.

寫作導向的文法講座

洗鍊的寫作力從語詞合併開始

語詞合併可使結構簡潔、訊息緊湊。以下合併功能的連接語詞都形成平行結構，合併的語詞結構相同。

1. both...and

1) Both the sample and the catalog have been sent to the client.

2) After four weeks of treatment, I felt both physically and mentally better.

2. not...but 不……而

1) We should not accept any form of bribe, but refuse it on the spot.

說明 but 是明確的轉折，引介訊息焦點，莎士比亞的名劇 “The tragedy of Julius Caesar” 中的一句台詞即是耳熟能詳的例子：

***Not** that I loved Caesar less, **but** that I loved Rome more.*

我愛凱薩，我更愛共和。

3. not only...but also 不僅……而且

also 是副詞，可以省略。中譯「不僅……而且」，「不僅」加接的是已知的舊訊息，不是溝通焦點，「而且」加接的是未知的新訊息，溝通焦點，與動詞單複數一致，這是語意與結構的形意搭配。

1) Not only the manager but also the staff members were pleased with the sales figures.

4. either...or 不是……就是

1) You can add one slice of apple to your tea.

You can add two slices of apple to your tea.

→ You can add either one or two slices of apple to your tea.

2) We can choose French fries.

We can choose baked potato.

We can choose mashed potatoes.

→ We can choose either French fries, baked potato or mashed potatoes.

5. neither...nor 既不……也不……，……和……都不

1) The device is not safe.

The device is not accurate.

→ The device is neither safe nor accurate.

2) Tom's father doesn't speak Chinese.

His mother doesn't speak Chinese.

→ Neither Tom's father nor his mother speaks Chinese.

說明 正式寫作中，neither of 組成的複數名詞片語搭配單數動詞，複數動詞是非正式用法。

Neither of the answers **is** correct.

6. rather than 而不

I'd like to stay at home this weekend.

I'd prefer not to go out this weekend.

→ I I'd like to stay at home this weekend rather than go out.

→ I I prefer staying at home this weekend to going out.

這是一篇有關穆斯林學生 Aafiya 的故事，請依照敘述填寫 and, but 等合併語詞的字在空格裡。

Aafiya is a Muslim student from Southeast Asia. She always wears a headscarf, worships toward Mecca five times a day, _____1_____ never eats pork. She is religious, _____2_____ outgoing and sweet-tempered.

Aafiya is homesick ____3______ misses her grandparents, who brought her up since her childhood. She wants to pay her way through college, ____4______ she is working two part-time jobs on the weekend; one is in a department store downtown, _____5_____ the other in a restaurant. She is ____ 6____ self-confident, ____7______ hard-working.

Last Sunday was her 22nd birthday. It was not her day, ____ 8____ she didn't think so, because she believed it was Allah's will. She overslept, got to work late, ____9______ made mistakes in the restaurant. She mistook mangosteens for passion fruit, recommended high-calorie food to a lady who was on a diet, ____ 10____ served red wine to customers who ordered a seafood meal. She was scolded severely, ____11_____ not depressed at all. She was so strong-minded.

1. and 2. but 3. and 4. so 5. and 6. not only 7. but 8. but 9. and 10. and 11. but

技巧 13

PEEL －剝去論述障礙，展露筆頭功夫

表達意見首重陳述清楚，立論足以令人信服，結論呼應主題，除了 OREO 的寫法，還有一種段落架構 － PEEL，以下單字構成的頭字詞：

- Point 主題，或是 Purpose 目的、Position 立場
- Explanation 說明，或是 Elaboration 詳細闡述
- Evidence 證明
- Link 連結

Point，就是主題，一個段落只有一個主題，這是一致的原則。

Explanation，說明的原則是從普遍、大範圍談到具體、小範圍（from general to specific，G to S），當然也可以反過來 from specific to general（S to G），但都要邏輯清晰，直截了當，言之有理，以理服人。

Evidence，證明的目的是增強觀點的正確性或正當性，證明的方式包括引用專家的話或統計數據，提及真實事件等，這是段落最重要的部分。

Link，結論必須連結主題，避免出現新的論點，而最佳的結論是提出劍及履及的行動，說服讀者響應自己的觀點。

表達意見的寫作技巧有三：

1. 切合題目，結論呼應主題。
2. 立論扣合主題，立場一致。
3. 提升至精神層次，超越論理的範疇。

PEEL 的段落結構如下：

主題句	Point 主題
段落發展	Explanation 說明 Evidence 證明
結論句	Link 連結

101 學測英文寫作題目

你最好的朋友最近迷上電玩，因此常常熬夜，疏忽課業，並受到父母的責罵。你打算寫一封信給他 / 她，適當地給予勸告。

這份題目是以書信的形式表達自己對打電玩的意見，適合以 PEEL 的架構書寫，我們先讀題並列出寫作清單。

<table>
<tr><th>開頭</th><th>問候</th></tr>
<tr><td rowspan="4">第一段
寫信的緣由</td><td>最近迷上電玩</td></tr>
<tr><td>常常熬夜</td></tr>
<tr><td>疏忽課業</td></tr>
<tr><td>受到父母的責罵</td></tr>
<tr><td>第二段
勸告</td><td>立場
説明
證據—醫學、課業、舉例</td></tr>
<tr><td>第三段
結尾</td><td>行動
鼓勵</td></tr>
</table>

13

↘ 問候

Dear Ken,

I hope you are doing well.

↘ 遵照題目說明，陳述勸告的緣由

I really enjoyed our talk at Starbucks last Sunday, and I value our friendship so much. You are my best friend. However, I was really upset to hear that you became addicted to playing video games. I heard you often stay up late playing them and consequently, you are ignoring your schoolwork. What's worse, you have been severely scolded by your parents many times for your "NEW HOBBY."

↘ 勸告的主題及說明

Ken, it is my sincere advice that you make a decision to turn off the gaming console video games and turn to books as soon as possible, because playing video games has led you astray, far from the life where you can maintain a normal daily routine and concentrate on your studies.

↘ 科學證據證明勸告的必要

It is clear that indulging in the virtual world may lead to a gaming disorder, which will hijack the brain and hinder it from thinking normally. This can give rise to certain symptoms of attention deficit disorder, which causes insomnia and anxiety. This is what you are suffering from now.

↘ 共同的課業挑戰加強勸告的必要

However, in a few months, you are going to be a high school senior, facing severe challenges from your preparation for the GSAT. During this tough time before the big test, only a sober mind and a healthy body are able to support you to survive this competition and guide you to the desired result. Under the spell of addiction from playing video games, your youth will be lost in the shadows. It is something I never want to see.

↘ 以同儕的經驗作為正面例子

By the way, do you remember our senpai, Brian? On the first day of the summer vacation before the GSAT, he gave his own tablet computer to his cousin and canceled the Internet service on his smartphone, which forced him to escape from video games and focus on his studies. Now, he is a medical student in National Taiwan University. I am sure you will achieve your goal successfully like Brian as long as you pull yourself together from now on.

↘ 呼喚好友立即行動

My dear Ken, please put away all of your video games, pick up your books and make a comeback. I will always be there to back you up.

Love,

Jack

親愛的肯恩

希望你一切順利。

我很享受我們上周的談話，非常珍惜我們的友誼，你是我最好的朋友。然而，聽到你打電動成癮，我感到非常不安，也聽到你常熬夜玩遊戲，結果就一直忽略學校課業，更糟的是，因著「新嗜好」，你已多次受到父母的嚴厲責難。

肯恩，這是我誠摯的勸告，該下定決心關掉遊戲機電玩，儘快轉向書本。因為打電玩已讓你偏離正軌，遠離能夠維持每日常規及專心課業的生活。

清楚的是，沉溺於虛擬世界可能導致遊戲行為失調，它將控制大腦並阻礙其無法正常思考，產生注意力缺失症的某些症狀，造成失眠及焦慮，這是你目前遭受到的。

然而，幾個月之後，你將成為高三學生，面對來自預備學測的嚴厲挑戰，大考前的這段艱辛的期間，只有清明的心思及健康的身體才能支撐你在這場競爭中生存並引導你到想望的結果。打電動成癮的魔咒之下，你的年輕歲月將迷失在陰影之中，這是我絕不要看見的事。

順道一提，記得我們的學長，Brian 嗎？他在學測前暑假的第一天就將平板電腦送給表弟，取消手機網路服務，強迫自己逃離電玩並專注課業，現在他是台大醫學生。我確信你只要從現在起振作，一定能像 Brian 一樣成功達成自己的目標。

我親愛的肯恩，請收起你的電玩，拾起你的書本，反敗為勝，我會永遠支持你。

傑克

1. 聽到你打電動成癮，我感到非常不安。
2. 你常熬夜玩遊戲，結果就一直忽略學校課業。
3. 因著「新嗜好」，你已多次受到父母的嚴厲責難。
4. 這會產生注意力缺失症的某些症狀，造成失眠及焦慮。
5. 只有清明的心思及健康的身體才能支撐你在這場競爭中生存。

✎ 參考答案

1. I was really upset to hear that you became addicted to playing video games.
2. You often stay up late playing them and consequently, you are ignoring your schoolwork.
3. You have been severely scolded by your parents many times for your “NEW HOBBY.”

4. This can give rise to certain symptoms of attention deficit disorder, which causes insomnia and anxiety.
5. Only a sober mind and a healthy body are able to support you to survive this competition.

寫作導向的文法講座

寫作需要的時態大不同

句子描述事件，事件的核心是動作，動詞語意的必要成分（受詞、補語）必須完整。句子所述事件必須標記時間及態貌，就是時態，這是英語的溝通要項，也是寫作必須遵守的。時態標記在動詞，標記時態的動詞稱為時態動詞。

寫作時的時態要點：

1. 句子必須包含時態動詞，若是提及數個時態動詞，連接詞連接，這是句子與片語的差別。
   1) I value our friendship so much.
      現在簡單式表示泛時、常態。
   2) On the first day of the summer vacation before GSAT, he gave his own tablet computer to his cousin and canceled the Internet service on his smartphone, which forced him to escape from video games and focus on his studies.
2. 助動詞標記時態，加接動詞原形。
   1) do、does、did 加接原形動詞，時態標記在助動詞而不重複標記。
      Do you remember our senpai, Brian?

2) 情態助動詞評論動作或標記未來，動作不存在，不標記時態。

It is clear that indulging in the virtual world may lead to a gaming disorder, which will hijack the brain and hinder it from thinking normally. This can give rise to certain symptoms of attention deficit disorder.

3. 現在簡單式，第三人稱單數主詞具有針對性，動詞必須標記。

My father walks two miles to work every morning.

4. 現在完成式是結算的概念，標記截至說話時是否完成。

1) What's worse, you have been severely scolded by your parents many times for your "NEW HOBBY."

2) Playing video games has led you astray, far from the life where you can maintain a normal daily routine and concentrate on your studies.

5. 表示未來的方式

1) 情態助動詞

will

單純的未來（正式用法）

I am sure you will achieve your goal successfully.

意願

I've asked her but she won't come.

If you will vote for me, I will work for you.

= If you are willing to vote for me, I will work for you.

預測

They won't run out of fuel.（future prediction）

She won't respond to the news.

她不會回應這消息。（future prediction）

她不要回應這消息。（future volition）

要求

Will you give me her LINE ID?

能力

The car won't start.

可能

As you all will know, election day is next week.

should

建議

Where should we meet tonight?

將、會

My dry cleaning should be ready this afternoon.

may

或許

Indulging in the virtual world may lead to a gaming disorder,

許可

A reader may borrow up to five books at any one time.

can

能夠

If the party is awful, we can leave earlier.

許可

You can park over there.

可能

This can give rise to certain symptoms of attention deficit disorder.

2) 未來意涵的語詞

1. **be going to**：go 搭配進行式，「正前往」譬喻為事件即將發生。

   將要

   In a few months, you are going to be high school seniors.

   預計要發生（現在的原因即將產生的結果）

   I must hurry. I'm going to be late for the interview.

2. **be about to** 正要

字源上，about 表示 on the outside，衍生為 on the move，後來出現 be about to 的用法，about 是形容詞，「剛要……的」，不搭配表達時間量的語詞，on the point of、to be going to do something very soon。

I was about to leave when Tom arrived.

3. **be bound to** 勢必

to be very likely to do or feel a particular thing，口語用法，書寫用法是 certain to、it is inevitable that。

Mistakes are bound to happen.

= It is inevitable that mistakes will happen.**be to**

4. **to** 動詞原形

正式的安排

The Prime Minister is to visit Taiwan next week.

應該

You are not to smoke in this building.

可能

Street children are to be found in the largest cities.

3) 現在簡單式：現在簡單式表示恆常為真，進而表示未來必然為真。

排定而難以改變

Today is Monday. Tomorrow is Tuesday.

The first day of Fall 2023 begins the day after tomorrow.

根據自然規律必然發生，可以 will 代換，未來發生如同現在，現在式表示未來。

Oil floats on water.

= Oil will float on water.

4) 現在進行式

方位移動或停止的動作常以現在進行式表示即將發生。

Ladies and gentlemen, we are landing in five minutes.

Another typhoon is approaching to Japan this weekend.

I'm taking my pet dog to the vet tomorrow morning.

A. 請以 Tom 作為主詞，do the work 作為動詞，依照提示時態寫出正確結構：

1. 過去簡單式
2. 過去進行式
3. 過去完成式
4. 過去完成進行式
5. 現在簡單式
6. 現在進行式
7. 現在完成式
8. 現在完成進行式
9. 未來簡單式
10. 未來進行式
11. 未來完成式
12. 未來完成進行式

參考答案

1. Tom **did** the work.
2. Tom **was doing** the work.
3. Tom **had done** the work.
4. Tom **had been doing** the work.
5. Tom **does** the work.
6. Tom **is doing** the work.
7. Tom **has done** the work.
8. Tom **has been doing** the work.
9. Tom **will do** the work.
10. Tom **will be doing** the work.
11. Tom **will have done** the work.
12. Tom **will have been doing** the work.

B. 請寫出空格提示動詞的形式

文章出處：110 國中會考試題

Dear Diary,

I ____1____ (be) very sad to hear what ____2____ (happen) to Woollie yesterday. Woollie ____3____ (be) my favorite sheep. I ____4____ (have) a storybook about Woollie. It ____5____ (say) when Woollie ____6____ (be) four, he ____7____ (run) away from Mr. Armstrong's farm, and it ____8____ (take) Mr. Armstrong six years to find Woollie. But Woollie ____9____ (grow) so much fleece that he didn't even ____10____ (look) like a sheep. Mr. Armstrong ____11____ (decide) to cut his fleece on TV so everyone could ____12____ (see). Daddy ____13____ (say) this ____14____ (happen) on the day I was born. Woollie's fleece ____15____ (weigh) 27 kg, and could ____16____ (make) clothes for 20 large men. I ____17____ (ask) Daddy if his favorite vest was made from Woollie's fleece. Daddy ____18____ (say) no, because Woollie's fleece was sold to collect money for sick kids. In the storybook, Woollie was taken to see Ms. Stella Clark, the leader of our city then. They even ____19____ (have) tea together. Daddy ____20____ (say) Woollie did ____21____ (meet) Ms. Clark, but he wasn't sure if they ____22____ (have) tea. Daddy ____23____ (say) Woollie was put down because he ____24____ (be) too sick and there ____25______ (be) no way to help him. I ____26____ (cry). I ____27____ (hope) Woollie ____28____ (be) happy up there in the sky.

1. was 2. happened 3. was 4. have 5. says 6. was 7. ran 8. took 9. had grown 10. look 11. decided 12. see 13. said 14. happened 15. weighed 16. make 17. asked 18. said 19. had 20. said 21. meet 22. had 23. said 24. was 25. was 26. cried 27. hope 28. will

技巧 14

一篇文章二段落，一個段落三部分

數個句子組成的一個段落，而段落是展現寫作技巧的單位，英文寫作大多是一個議題分為二個段落，每一段落都要遵照說明書寫。

段落包含三部分：

主題句，主題句就是段落的摘要，前面可以放一個 HOOK 而使段落有一精彩的開始。

細節，陳述細節的句子是支持句，目的是說明主題，常搭配理由、舉例、證據以陳述主題的真實性或重要性。就著段落的擴展而言，說明文主要有問題與解決、因果關聯、比較與對比、過程順序等類型，其他還有分類與部分、概括與例示、特點與細節等。

結論句，段落結尾的句子，目的是回顧主題或提出總結，不應提供新的細節，但可以不同的語詞重複主題或提出寓意。

一個段落的組成如下：

部分	功用	內容
主題句	段落的摘要	主題
細節	陳述主題 支持句	說明 舉例 證據
結論句	回顧主題 提出總結	不提供新的細節 以不同的語詞重複主題 提出寓意

但是以學測英文寫作而言，整篇文章起首出現主題句，結尾出現結論句即可，也就是將全文視為一個段落。

108 年指考英文寫作題目：

下表顯示美國 18 至 29 歲的青年對不同類別之新聞的關注度統計。請依據圖表內容寫一篇英文作文，文長至少 120 個單詞。文分二段，第一段描述圖表內容，並指出關注度較高及偏低的類別；第二段則描述在這六個新聞類別中，你自己較為關注及較不關注的新聞主題分別為何，並說明理由。

讀題之後列出寫作清單如下：

部分	內容
主題句	美國 18 至 29 歲的青年對不同類別之新聞的關注度統計
第一段	圖表內容 關注度較高的類別 關注度偏低的類別
第二段	自己較為關注的新聞主題 說明理由 自己較不關注的新聞主題 說明理由
結論句	回顧主題 提出總結

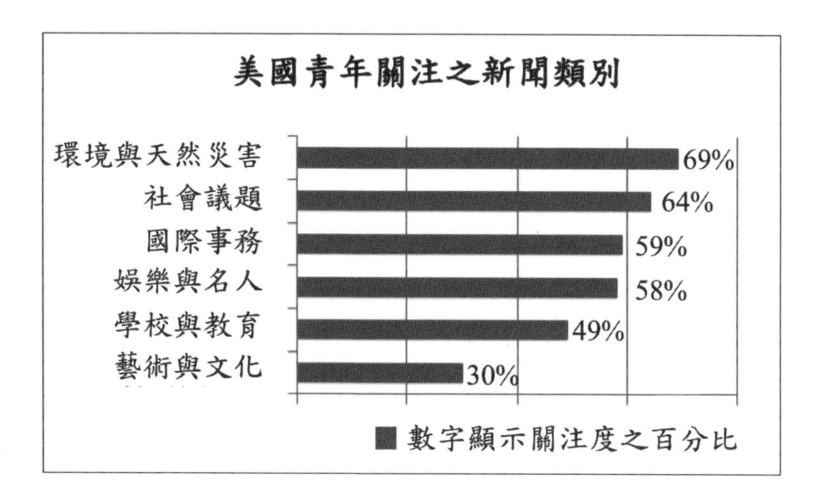

14

↘ 以令人驚奇的語詞作為 HOOK

Wow! The younger generations of Americans have changed.

↘ 遵照題目說明寫出主題句

This bar chart clearly illustrates the statistics for American younger (ranging from 18 to 29 years old) generations' concern toward various categories of news.As can be seen, the attention level toward various news topics seems to be consistent with that of what impacts their life.

↘ 關注度較高的類別及理由

In recent years, due to climate abnormality, most parts of America have been suffering from severe damage caused by floods, hurricanes and polar vortexes. This has increased young people's awareness of the environment and natural disasters and their concerns for this issue increased to 69%. Second only to the news category of environment and natural disasters is the social issue, with merely 5% of difference. This reflects that some problems are severely impacting American society, such as campus shootings, drug abuse and the widening wealth gap.

↘ 關注度偏低的類別及理由

In comparison, the category of art and culture is the least fascinating to the youth of today, accounting for only 30%, up to 19% less than the category of school and education. Obviously, for younger generations in America, humanities no longer play an important role. In addition, in between them are international affairs and recreation and celebrities, which account for 59% and 58% respectively, with almost the same attention level.

↘ 第二段

自己較為關注的新聞主題及理由

At the present time, among these news categories is that of school and education, which draws my attention most simply because, as a high school student, I have to focus on learning-related information like the GSAT trends and notice news about the college admissions process. I strongly believe that only substantial knowledge will enable me to make a distinguished contribution to society.

↘ 自己較不關注的新聞主題及理由

Consequently, the category of recreation and celebrities, which ranks fourth in the bar chart, is the last news category to draw my attention. It neither has anything to do with my studies nor has any significant influence on the quality of my daily life. To tell the truth, I deem it as a waste of time to concern myself about what is happening to a celebrity.

↘ 以年輕世代應該知曉新聞事件作為結論句

In my opinion, the younger generations are playing a critical role in this world, which is changing all the time, and therefore, being knowledgeable about what is happening in the world seems to be quite important.

哇！美國年輕世代變了。

這個長條圖清楚描繪美國年輕世代對於各種類型的新聞的關注統計（範圍從 18 至 29 歲）。就如我們所見，各種新聞主題的關注程度似乎與對他們的生活影響程度一致。

最近幾年，由於氣候異常，美國大部分地區持續遭受洪水、颶風及極地氣旋引起的嚴重損害，增加了年輕人對環境及天然災害的體認，而他們對這議題的關切也增加至69%。僅次於環境及天然災害新聞類型的是社會議題，僅有5%的差距，這反映了一些問題正嚴重衝擊美國社會，例如校園槍擊、毒品濫用及持續擴大的貧富差距。

相較之下，藝術文化類對當今年輕人最不具吸引力，僅占 30%，較學校教育類少了 19%，明顯地，對於美國年輕世代，人文學科不再扮演重要的角色。此外，介於前述二者的是國際事務及休閒名人新聞，分別佔 59% 及 58%，關注程度幾乎相同。

目前，這些新聞中就學校教育類別最吸引我的注意，僅是因為身為一名中學生，我必須專注在像學測趨勢的學習相關訊息，注意有關大學入學過程的新聞。我堅信只有充實的知識能使我對社會做出卓越的貢獻。

結果，長條圖排在第四的休閒及名人是最後吸引我注意的新聞類別，既與我的課業無關，對我的日常生活品質又無任何顯著影響。老實說，我將關注某位名人現在怎麼了視為一種浪費時間。

我認為年輕世代在這個一直在改變的世界中扮演至關重要的角色，因此，知曉世界正發生什麼似乎相當重要。

1. 這個長條圖描繪美國年輕世代對於各種類型的新聞的關注統計。
2. 各種新聞主題的關注程度似乎與對他們的生活影響程度一致。
3. 最近幾年，由於氣候異常，美國大部分地區持續遭受洪水、颶風及極地氣旋引起的嚴重損害。
4. 僅次於環境及天然災害新聞類型的是社會議題，僅有 5% 的差距。
5. 休閒及名人類既與我的課業無關，對我的日常生活品質又無任何顯著影響。

✎ 參考答案

1. This bar chart illustrates the statistics for American younger generations' concern toward various categories of news.
2. The attention level toward various news topics seems to be consistent with that of what impacts their life.
3. In recent years, due to climate abnormality, most parts of America have been suffering from severe damage caused by floods, hurricanes and polar vortexes.
4. Second only to the news category of environment and natural disasters is the social issue, with merely 5% of difference.

5. The category of recreation and celebrities neither has anything to do with my studies nor has any significant influence on the quality of my daily life.

準關係代名詞讓寫作迎向頂標

as、than 不是 wh-words，但是搭配一些語詞時充當關係代名詞，稱為準關係代名詞。準關係代名詞是頂標寫作常用的語詞，引導的形容詞子句增添句子的訊息，同時巧妙呈現句子的從的部分。由於使用時機明確，容易入手。

as

1. 連接詞性質的 as 有如同的意思，充當準關係代名詞時，先行詞搭配 as、such、the same 等語詞。

   1) I have studied as many books as my homeroom teacher recommended.

   說明

   1. as many books 是先行詞，搭配副詞 as，修飾形容詞 many，「像……這麼多」的意思。
   2. as my homeroom teacher recommended 是形容詞子句，準關係代名詞 as 移自 recommended 的受詞位置。

   2) It is preferable to use any such material as can be easily cleaned.

   說明 as can be easily cleaned 是形容詞子句，as 是主詞，any such material 是先行詞，搭配限定詞 such。

3) My cousin went to the same school as I did.

我表妹跟我上同一所學校。

4) This is the same bag as I lost last week.

這個袋子和我上星期弄丟的袋子相似。

說明 the same...as 可表示同一個或相似的一個。

5) The guest sat in the same row that/as we did.

該名賓客與我們坐的是同一排。

說明 the same...that 表示同一個。

2. as 常以主要子句作為先行詞，如……的 的意思，置於句首、句中或是句尾。

1) As is often the case, Tom was late again.

Tom was late again, as is often the case.

Tom was late again, which is often the case.

2) As was expected, the candidate won the election.

The candidate won the election, as was expected.

As expected, the candidate won the election.

說明 as 搭配形容詞或是分詞，be 動詞可以省略。

Tom was late for class today, as is usual with him.

Tom was late for class today, as usual.

這是常有的事，Tom 又遲到了。

說明 as 是 something like a fact that 的意思。

than

準關係代名詞 than 用於比較級的句子，than 可作主詞或是受詞。

1) We raised more money than we had expected.

我們募得超出我們之前所期待的金額。

說明 than 移自形容詞子句受詞位置。

比較 Tom swam faster than expected（for him to swim）.

= Tom swam faster than it was expected for him to swim.

Tom 游得比預期來得快。

說明 than expected 是副詞子句，沒有先行詞。

這是一篇影片觀賞心得報告，請將提示的語詞填入空格中。

A. undoubtedly

B. as a result

C. as we all know

D. to tell the truth

E. at least a semi-vegetarian or flexitarian first

F. when having a great delicacy with friends at a nice restaurant

題目

Ray's video has impressed me and inspired me to think about being a pescatarian.

First, __1__, I think it is never easy for people like Ray to make a decision to become a pescatarian because they need to resist the lure of the delicious and familiar smells from meat, especially __2__. Also, sometimes, they have to repeatedly and patiently explain to their friends the reasons.

Second, __3__, Ray's sharing sounds informative and inspirational to me. __4__, meat consumption will increase carbon emissions because farm animals emit greenhouse gases all the time, which have already caused severe damage to the atmosphere as well as extreme climate change. __5__, human beings are forced to face and even suffer from a variety of existential challenges. It will result in a series of tragic disasters for human civilization. I was deeply touched by Ray's talk and it drove me to give him my sincere response that it was time to join him and become a pescatarian or, __6__. It is high time for me to do my part for the global environment where I am living.

羅東高中 陳圩呈同學

1. D 2. F 3. A 4. C 5. B 6. E

技巧 15

進入故事山，故事架構穩如泰山

記敘文描述事件，若是搭配圖片，便是看圖寫作，寫作的目的都是要讓讀者身歷其境，感同身受，事件的開始、發展、結束都要完整而清晰。

記敘文必須遵循故事的情節架構，呈現故事的元素，展現故事的脈絡，就是「故事山」。寫作時，若能在「故事山」中寫出故事的元素、架構，刻畫重要橋段，必能完成一篇佳作。

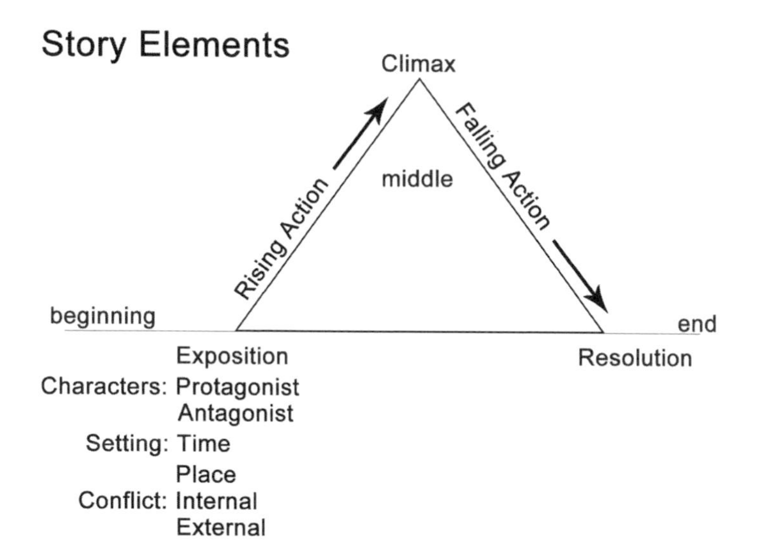

我們就以「Three Little Pigs」為例，進入故事山，找尋故事的元素與脈絡。

1. 説明 exposition

1) 角色 characters

最重要的故事元素，能夠思考的人、能夠感覺或談話的動物、產生動作的生物等都是故事的角色。依照故事情節，角色可分為主角及製造主角問題的反派角色，例如三隻小豬是主角，大野狼是製造問題的反派角色。

2) 場景 setting

包括故事的地點 where（little pigs' house）及時間 when（during the day）。

3) 衝突 conflict

- 內部衝突，導致外部衝突的主角負面特質，例如第一及第二隻小豬不願工作。
- 外部衝突，反派角色製造的衝突，就是大野狼想吃到三隻小豬。

2. 故事中最刺激或最有趣的橋段 Climax。

主角面對且解決衝突的當下，就是大野狼無法擊倒第三隻小豬的房子時。

3. 動作 action

1) Climax 之前的上升動作，就是導致最精彩部分的一連串衝突。

2) Climax 之後朝向結束的下降動作。

4. 解決問題 resolution

故事的結束，衝突解決了，就是大野狼跑掉了。

我們現在就以 Jack 的一段生活經驗為例來說明「故事山」的架構。

15

Jack had not realized the meaning of the saying, "out of extreme joy comes extreme sorrow," until last Saturday when he played sports with his friends. That day, Jack and two of his friends, Hank and Jimmy, played baseball in the park. Hank threw a baseball to Jack, and he hit it. Seeing that Jack hit the ball, Jimmy ran and tried to catch it. On the other side of the park, there was a dog napping on the grass. It was peacefully sound asleep.

The baseball accidentally hit the sleeping dog on its right eye. The poor dog was really hurt and it howled loudly. It became furious! So, with a black and blue mark on its face, the dog got up, barked loudly at the boys and ran after them. All these boys were too scared to cry out while they hurriedly ran away.

The boys experienced a horrible and unforgettable day, but they felt lucky to escape from the attacking dog.

註解

第一段	HOOK 故事的場景 順敘說明衝突前的動作
第二段	衝突 解決方式
第三段	對事件的感想

1. HOOK：以一段諺語預告事件的結果：Jack had not realized the saying “out of extreme joy comes extreme sorrow.” until last Saturday when he played sports with his friends.
2. 第一段介紹故事的場景，包括 Jack、Hank、Jimmy 等角色，時間是 Last Saturday，地點是 in the park，這些場景說明是第一段的重點：On that day, Jack and two of his friends, Hank and Jimmy, played baseball in the park.
3. 第二段是故事的主體，順敘說明衝突、最緊張的橋段與解決等三部分。

   衝突 The ball accidentally hit the sleeping dog on its right eye.

   最緊張的橋段 the dog got up, barked loudly at the boys and ran after them

   解決 ran away
4. 第三段是結論，可以提及事件的結果、感想或學到的功課，這篇故事是以感想作為結論：Lucky enough to escape from the dog’s bite, they experienced a horrible and unforgettable day.

故事山寫作順序：

1. 先寫角色、時間、地點等情景。

2. 陳述角色遇到的衝突。

3. 描述故事最精彩的部分。

4. 說明衝突的解決。

5. 故事的結束。

寫作技巧：衝突、最精彩的部分、解決等是故事的重要橋段，應以句子表示。

Jack 直到上周六與朋友一起運動時才了解諺語「樂極生悲」的意義。

那一天，Jack 與他的二位朋友 Hank 及 Jimmy 在公園打棒球，Hank 丟棒球給 Jack，他隨即擊球。看到 Jack 擊出球，Jimmy 跑步，努力要接住球。在公園的另一邊，有一隻狗正在草地上休憩，安靜地酣睡著。

那顆球意外擊中正睡覺的狗的右眼，可憐的狗痛得大叫，勃然大怒。因此，帶著臉上黑青的印痕，這隻狗起身，向著男孩大叫，隨後追過去。這些男孩趕緊跑走時全都嚇得叫不出來。

男孩們經歷恐怖而難忘的一天，但是覺得很幸運能夠逃離要攻擊他們的狗。

1. 那顆球意外擊中正睡覺的狗的右眼。
2. 臉上帶著黑青的印痕，這隻狗起身，向著男孩大吠，隨後追他們。
3. 男孩們經歷恐怖而難忘的一天，但是覺得很幸運能夠逃離要攻擊他們的狗。
4. 可憐的狗痛得大聲嚎叫。
5. 這些男孩趕緊跑走時全都嚇得叫不出來。

✐ 參考答案

1. The baseball accidentally hit the sleeping dog on its right eye.
2. With a black and blue mark on its face, the dog got up, barked loudly at the boys and ran after them.
3. The boys experienced a horrible and unforgettable day, but they felt lucky to escape from the attacking dog.
4. The poor dog was really hurt and it howled loudly.
5. All these boys were too scared to cry out while they hurriedly ran away.

寫作時應該知曉的語詞面向

形意搭配是英文語詞的特性，語詞形式承載語意，語意藉由語詞傳達，二者相互為用，達成溝通目的。

英文語詞結構分為單詞、片語、句子，對應不同份量的訊息，這是結構上的形意搭配。

寫作導向的語詞視角包括結構、詞性、功用三面向，而功用包含文法及寫作二方面。

（出處：英文文法原來如此增訂版，蘇秦老師）

功用 / 結構	必要成分			修飾				
	主詞	受詞	補語	名詞	動詞	形容詞	副詞	句子
名詞片語								
形容詞片語								
副詞片語								
不定詞								
動名詞								
分詞								

介係詞片語								
名詞子句								
形容詞子句								
副詞子句								

例如以下這一段生活隨筆，描述一份食物引發的感官及情緒反應，流露作者的生活與美食之間的強烈對比。

Today, my mom made me a cup of avocado milk as a summer treat. It smelled so wonderful and totally aroused my appetite. I couldn't wait to drink it, but I preferred to drink it leisurely and enjoyed all of its appealing flavors to add comfort to my life of boredom and fatigue. My encounter with this nice snack brought me a day of pleasure and refreshment.

寫作導向的語詞分析

1. Today, my mom made me a cup of avocado milk as a summer treat.
   "as a summer treat" 是介係詞片語，形容詞詞性，修飾名詞片語 "a cup of avocado milk"，説明作説者對於該物的認定。

2. I couldn't wait to drink it, but I preferred to drink it leisurely and enjoyed all of its appealing flavors to add comfort to my life of boredom and fatigue.
   "to add comfort to my life of boredom and fatigue" 是不定詞結構，副詞詞性，修飾 "enjoyed all of its appealing flavors"，表達品嚐美好食物的結果。

3. My encounter with this nice snack brought me a day of pleasure and refreshment.
“of pleasure and refreshment” 是介係詞片語，形容詞詞性，修飾名詞片語 “a day”，傳達一杯酪梨牛奶對生活的影響。

請試著說出粗體語詞的結構、詞性、功用。

It was one o'clock in the morning, but Jack was lying in bed **awake and anxious** because of the noises of a mahjong game **coming from upstairs**, which sounded **like hundreds of machine guns were shooting at him**. "It must be Mrs. Lin, **who is playing mahjong with her friends**. What a lousy neighbor!" he thought.

Not willing to tolerate it any longer, Jack got up, went upstairs and knocked on the neighbor's door. "How come you are still playing mahjong and making noises **so late** at night? It is high time **to sleep**." **Scolded by Jack**, Mrs. Lin was so embarrassed **that she apologized to him by saying sorry over and over again**.

Mrs. Lin and her friends stopped **playing mahjong** and turned off the lights. The night became silent. Jack finally fell asleep **at two o'clock**, one hour **after he asked Mrs. Lin to stop disturbing him**. For him, it took a long time **to get a good night's sleep**.

✎ 參考答案

1. awake and anxious

 形容詞片語，主詞補語，說明 Jack 躺在床上的情緒，後續事件發展的伏筆。

2. coming from upstairs

 分詞片語，形容詞詞性，說明 the noises of a mahjong game 的來源。

3. like hundreds of machine guns were shooting at him

 介係詞片語，描述 the noises of a mahjong game，誇飾的明喻手法。

4. who is playing mahjong with her friends

 形容詞子句，說明 Mrs. Lin 進行的活動。

5. Not willing to tolerate it any longer

 形容詞片語，主詞補語，說明 Jack 採取行動的情緒因素。主詞已知，主詞補語是新訊息，置於句首，直接感受主詞的狀況，節奏較為緊湊、鮮明。

6. so late

 副詞片語，說明 making noises 的時機。

7. to sleep

 不定詞片語，形容詞詞性，修飾 high time。

8. Scolded by Jack

 分詞構句，主詞補語置於句首，凸顯 Mrs. Lin 感到尷尬的原因。分詞構句在文法教學或測驗中是著重其結構，但寫作中是凸顯其語意功用。

9. that she apologized to him by saying sorry over and over again

 副詞子句，表示程度 so 的結果，over and over again 透露不斷道歉的意味，較單詞 again 到位。

10. playing mahjong

 動名詞片語，stopped 的受詞。

11. at two o’clock

介係詞片語，副詞詞性，fell asleep 的時間。

12. after he asked Mrs. Lin to stop disturbing him

與 one hour 共同形成副詞片語。

13. to get a good night’s sleep

不定詞片語，名詞詞性，填補主詞 it 的後行詞。

技巧 16

主題必須一致，語意必須連貫

英文作文評分要項包括內容、組織、句構、拼字，正好顯示一篇文章的四大要素：文字（拼字）、文法（句構）、文理（組織）、義理（內容），知曉文章要素，便是掌握作文評分要項。

一篇文章只談一個主題，細節針對主題提出說明、證明、舉例，結論句呼應主題，這便符合「一致」的寫作要求。

除了一致，文章的主題與細節、細節與細節之間必須脈絡清晰而合乎邏輯，這是連貫，也就是流暢性。

例如以下生活隨筆，從班上二名確診同學起首，接著是一連串的結果：同學必須在家，遵守防疫規定，每天線上上課，返回學校時就有一場重要考試，細節與主題一致。

範文參考

範文1

16-1

There are two confirmed COVID-19 cases in our class. We must stay at home and follow the epidemic prevention measures until next Thursday. We will have online classes as scheduled every day. We will have a big test on the day that we go back to school. Mr. Lin wants to ensure we will study as usual, even when classes are closed.

↘ 若是加入連接語詞，訊息關聯將更為明確，段落讀起來更為流暢。

There are two confirmed COVID-19 cases in our class, **and therefore**, we must stay at home and follow the epidemic prevention measures until next Thursday. **However**, we will have online classes as scheduled every day. **What's more**, we will have a big test on the day that we go back to school **because** Mr. Lin wants to ensure we will study as usual, even when classes are closed.

政治大學附屬高中 陳鼎鈞同學

↘ 再看以下段落，細節與主題，細節與細節之間都不見連貫，這不是寫作應該呈現的文字。

There are two confirmed COVID-19 cases in our class. A long line of people is waiting to buy COVID-19 rapid test kits at the drug store. The new coronavirus outbreak is continuing to grow. Some residents in this affected area are asked to self-quarantine at home. According to authorities concerned, nearly three million pandemic insurance policies have been sold so far this year.

段落達到連貫的技巧有重複主題關鍵字、使用同義字或反義字、上層字、代詞、轉折語詞等。例如這篇介紹河豚的文章，主題關鍵字是 pufferfish，先是一個 HOOK，再來是主題句，介紹河豚的物種、分布及特質，支持句說明河豚經過專業烹調仍是老饕美食，結論句呼應主題，合乎連貫與一致的段落要求。

範文 2

16-2

What kind of fish is this? Is it really edible?

The pufferfish is a type of fish that is usually found in warm or tropical seas, and it can make itself larger by filling its stomach with water or air.

Most species of pufferfish are toxic and may cause serious injury to other living things, so it is really dangerous to consume this creature as a food. However, it is famous in Japan, Korea and China, because numerous people regard pufferfish as a delicacy, and it is prepared only by specially-trained chefs who are aware of which part is safe to eat and in what quantity.

The pufferfish is really a unique species on the Earth, especially prized by specific consumers in some countries. Unfortunately, even though it is poisonous, there is a demand to consume this fish, putting this unique creature in danger of disappearing from our oceans.

語意連貫的語詞：

- 主題關鍵字：pufferfish
- pufferfish 的上層字：living things, species, creature, fish
- 轉折語詞：so, because, however
- 指涉語詞：food, delicacy

範文 1

我們班上有二名新冠確診同學，因此我們必須在家，並且遵守防疫規定直到下周四。然而，我們必須每天按課表上網課，還有，我們回學校那天有一場重要考試，因為林老師要確定即使停課我們仍照常讀書。

範文 2

這是哪種魚？真的可以吃嗎？

河豚是一種經常在溫暖或熱帶海域發現的魚類，牠會藉著以空氣或水將肚子充滿而使自己體型變得較大。

大多數種類的河豚有毒，對其他生物可能造成嚴重傷害，因此，食用這種生物當作食物非常危險。然而，在日本、韓國及中國卻是享有名氣，因為許多人將河豚視為一道美食，只由受過專門訓練、知道哪一部位吃起來安全及吃多少量的主廚料理來料理。

河豚是地球上非常獨特的物種，尤其受到一些國家的特定饕客的珍視。可惜的是，儘管具有毒性，這種魚的消費需求仍存在，這會將這種獨特生物置於消失於我們海洋的危險中。

1. 我們必須在家，並且遵守防疫規定直到下周四。
2. 河豚會藉著以空氣或水將肚子充滿而使自己體型變得較大。
3. 大多數種類的河豚有毒，對其他生物可能造成嚴重傷害。
4. 河豚只由受過專業訓練，知道哪一部位吃起來安全及吃多少量的主廚來料理。
5. 儘管具有毒性，這種魚的消費需求仍存在，這會將這種獨特生物置於消失於我們海洋的危險中。

參考答案

1. We must stay at home and follow the epidemic prevention measures until next Thursday.
2. The pufferfish can make itself larger by filling its stomach with water or air.
3. Most species of pufferfishare toxic and may cause serious injury to other living things.
4. The pufferfish is prepared only by specially-trained chefs who are aware of which part is safe to eat and in what quantity.
5. Even though it is poisonous, there is a demand to consume this fish, putting this unique creature in danger of disappearing from our oceans.

修飾動詞就是呈現事件樣貌

情態副詞呈現動作的樣貌，彼此緊密搭配，許多詞彙題即是測驗動詞或句子與情態副詞的搭配。

以下是政大附中特招詞彙題：

1. We don't have much time today. Let's _____ talk about the schedule first and discuss the details next time.

   (A) briefly (B) carelessly (C) legally (D) politely

2. Many people think Mary looks great in that black dress. _____, I think pink is a much better color for her.

   (A) Carefully **(B) Honestly** (C) Namely (D) Thankfully

3. I _____ forgot that it's Marilyn's birthday today. It was embarrassing that I didn't buy her any birthday gift.

   (A) completely (B) immediately (C) deliberately (D) regularly

4. Unfamiliar with the local dialect, Bob _____ knew what other people were talking about when he first got to the town.

   (A) fairly **(B) barely** (C) certainly (D) possibly

以下是統測詞彙題：

1. The shy little boy spoke so _____ that I had a hard time hearing what he said.

   (A) bravely (B) clearly (C) openly **(D) softly**

2. Jack invited me _____ on two occasions last week to visit his family.

(A) barely (B) monthly (C) hardly **(D) repeatedly**

3. Even though Nancy is busy at work, she still goes fishing <u>from time to time</u> on weekends.

(A) always (B) generally **(C) sometimes** (D) usually

4. I'm sorry I didn't reply yesterday, for I was _____ busy and could not find any time at all to return your phone call.

(A) casually **(B) extremely** (C) loosely (D) scarcely

情態副詞的位置表達不同的語意，這是詞序上的形意搭配。

1. 通常置於動詞或受詞的右側，尤其是 badly, fast, hard, well 等。

1) We will have to act fast.
我們必須快速行動。

2) It has been raining hard most of the morning.
幾乎整個早上都在下大雨。

3) My niece plays the piano well enough.
我姪女鋼琴彈得很好。

2. 置於時態動詞左側，強調動作。

1) The boy quietly slipped out of the back door.
男孩悄悄從後門溜出去。

2) The janitor carefully folded the note and put it in his pocket.
管理員小心地摺好字條，然後放入口袋。

3) The buyer has quickly agreed to sign the contract.
買家很快就同意簽約。

3. 句子包含數個動詞時，置於所修飾的動詞右側。

1) The buyer has agreed to sign the contract quickly.
買家同意快速簽約。

2) The janitor folded the note carefully and put it in his pocket.

管理員小心地摺好字條，然後放入口袋。

3) The janitor folded the note and put it in his pocket carefully.

管理員摺好字條，然後小心地放入口袋。

4. 情態副詞置於句首，表達對於句子所述事件的評論。

1) Quickly, the buyer has agreed to sign the contract.

很快地，買家同意簽約。

2) Quietly, the boy slipped out of the back door.

悄悄地，男孩從後門溜出去。

5. 情態副詞代換為介係詞片語，受詞是情態副詞的名詞形式，介係詞片語運用較為靈活，句子結構較為平衡。

1) The athlete won the 400-meter race **with ease**.

該名運動員輕鬆贏得 400 公尺賽跑。

2) They always looked at each other **with hostility**.

他們一向相互敵視。

3) I love most classical music, **in particular** Bach and Vivaldi.

我最喜愛古典樂，尤其是巴哈和韋瓦第。

請將以下 A, B, C, D, E 等五個句子依照事件發展排列成一段落：

A. No matter where she is, she always carries a small bottle of alcohol with her and is ready to spread it onto almost everyting she is about to touch.

B. Due to the COVID-19 pandemic, a huge number of people tend to use alcohol for the purpose of disinfection.

C. What's more, she spreads alcohol onto hands of each of her students around her.

D. My homeroom teacher, a little nervous and sensitive, is among them.

E. She never forgets to remind them to keep clean and prevent themselves from getting infected.

✐ 參考答案

Due to the COVID-19 pandemic, a huge number of people tend to use alcohol for the purpose of disinfection. My homeroom teacher, a little nervous and sensitive, is among them. No matter where she is, she always carries a small bottle of alcohol with her and is ready to spread it onto almost everyting she is about to touch. What's more, she spreads alcohol onto hands of each of her students around her. She never forgets to remind them to keep clean and prevent themselves from getting infected.

新店高中 郭品使同學

技巧 17

除了連貫，還要銜接，敘述才能順暢

連貫是指主題連貫，銜接是指語詞或句子有意義地連結，若是缺乏連貫，文章將難以理解；若是缺乏銜接，想法將難以連結。連貫與銜接兼具才能使文章流暢、清晰、容易閱讀。

When my pet dog gets hungry, it brings its bowl to me in its mouth, with its tail wagging, and demands immediate attention. **However**, when it is satisfied, it looks at me and barks, asking me to play with it.

↗ However 使前後訊息產生連結，語意連貫。

When my pet dog gets hungry, it brings its bowl to me in its mouth, with its tail wagging, and demands immediate attention. When it is satisfied, it looks at me and barks, asking me to play with it.

↗ 略去 however，前後訊息未銜接，語意不連貫。

說明文多以時間作為發展的脈絡，例如以下文章以 first, then, finally 等轉折語詞標示活動順序而達到銜接。

17-1

範文 1

Nicole, a backpacker from Africa, visited an elementary school in Nantou during her trip to Taiwan. She had a lot of fun while playing music with children there.

First, Nicole invited some of the children to play a musical game with her. They wanted to play a piece of tribal music and the children would clap their hands, and cup their mouths while shouting loudly. They were to act like a group of hunters ready to go hunting.

Then, Nicole sang a Zulu song while three boys beat African drums. She sounded like a great singer. **Finally**, Nicole sang an old African song to the children who were sitting in a semicircle. She said the song had been sung in Africa for more than five hundred years and she loved to sing it very much.

All of the children had fun and Nicole loved her visit to Taiwan.

範文 2

這篇描述鯰魚獵食鴿子的說明文，連貫與銜接能使文章容易理解，流暢閱讀。

17-2

Unbelievable! Is it real?

In the park, there is a big pond where there is a school of catfish, which is actually a fierce and omnivorous living thing. To enjoy pigeons as a special snack, it swims around the side of the pond and catches them when they fly down for a drink of water. In addition, the unusual animal is always patient enough to wait for the best time for an attack. At the moment that any pigeon gets close, the catfish opens its mouth wide, bites the poor bird tightly and drags it into the water, leaving some broken feathers on the surface of the water. It is really cruel. However, it happens there from time to time. It has become a sort of morbid attraction for visitors to the park.

這篇文章包括以下具有銜接功能的語詞：

1. 連接語詞 where, which, when, however, and
2. 介係詞片語 in addition, at the moment
3. 代詞 it, they, them, there
4. 定冠詞 the
5. 上層字 animal, living thing
6. 代換字 snack, bird
7. 句子結構 leaving some broken feathers on the surface of the water

範文 1

Nicole，一位來自非洲的背包客，前往台灣的旅遊期間造訪位於南投的一所小學，她與當地孩童演奏音樂時非常開心。

首先，Nicole 邀請一些孩童與她一起玩一種音樂遊戲，他們要演奏一首部落音樂，孩童拍手，大聲喊叫時手貼著嘴巴成杯子狀，表演得像一群獵人預備出發打獵。

然後，Nicole 在三名男孩拍打非洲鼓時唱了一首祖魯歌曲，她聽起來像是一名優秀歌手。最後，Nicole 為坐成半圓形的孩童唱一首古老非洲歌曲，她說這首歌在非洲已傳唱五百多年，她非常喜愛這首歌。

所有孩童都玩得很開心，Nicole 也喜愛她的這趟臺灣參訪。

範文 2

難以置信的！這是真的嗎？

公園裡有一大池塘，裡面有一群鯰魚，那是一種兇猛的雜食生物。為了享用鴿子作為特別的點心，鯰魚在池塘邊游著，就在鴿子飛下來喝水時捕獵牠們。此外，這種獨特的動物總是耐心等候一擊的最佳時機，任何鴿子一接近，鯰魚就大大張口，緊緊咬住可憐的小鳥，然後拖入水中，留下一些殘破羽毛在水面上，真是殘酷。然而，這在那裏時常發生，而且已成為遊客前往這座公園的一種著迷吸引力。

1. 有一裡面有一群鯰魚的大池塘，那是一種兇猛而雜食的生物。
2. 此外，這種獨特的動物總是夠耐心地等候一擊的最佳時機。
3. 鯰魚大大張口，緊緊咬住可憐的小鳥，然後拖入水中，留下一些殘破羽毛在水面上。
4. Nicole 向坐成半圓形的孩童唱一首古老非洲歌曲。
5. 它已成為遊客前往這座公園的一種著迷吸引力。

參考答案

1. There is a big pond where there is a school of catfish, which is actually a fierce and omnivorous living thing.
2. In addition, the unusual animal is always patient enough to wait for the best time for an attack.
3. The catfish opens its mouth wide, bites the poor bird tightly and drags it into the water, leaving some broken feathers on the surface of the water.

4. Nicole sang an old African song to the children who were sitting in a semicircle.
5. It has become a sort of morbid attraction for visitors to the park.

文法不起眼，寫作超重要的代詞 -- 連貫訊息的鉚釘

代詞代替前面的單詞、片語、子句或句子，避免訊息重複的語詞，虛詞性質。

代詞不僅代替名詞，還可代替動詞、形容詞、副詞，結構上包括片語或句子。

“指涉明確，易於辨識”是最重要的代詞使用原則。

名詞的代詞

名詞與代詞在人稱、數目、性別、指涉性質上必須一致。

1) *Tom found his wife talked to himself in her sleep last night.

→ Tom found his wife talked to herself in her sleep last night.

湯姆發現他太太昨夜睡覺時自言自語。

2) *The name of the people comes from the name of its land.

→ The name of the people comes from the name of their land.

該民族的名稱來自他們土地的名稱。

說明 land 的所有者是該民族的人們。

3) * In the hospital, a doctor should do one's morning and evening rounds.

→ In the hospital, doctors should do their morning and evening rounds.

在醫院，醫師應該晨間及夜間巡房。

說明 泛指通常搭配複數主詞及所有格，one 是泛指，不搭配 a doctor 當先行詞。

4) *My cousin is an AI engineer, and it is what I choose to major in in college.

→ My cousin specializes in AI engineering, and it is what I choose to major in in college.

我表弟專精 AI 工程，那是我決定在大學主修的領域。

說明 it 的指涉對象是 AI engineering。

助動詞的代詞功用

1) Your smartphone is dead. So **is** mine.

說明 is 代替 is dead。

2) My wife got vaccinated three times, and I **did**, too.

說明 did 代替 got vaccinated three times。

3) Tom has been to the Arctic, and I **have**, too.

說明 have 代替 have been to the Arctic。

so, the same 常代替形容詞，充當形容詞的代詞。

1) A. I'm allergic to shrimp.

B: So is my sister.

說明 so 代替 allergic to shrimp。

2) A: New York is very hot and humid in the summer.

B: It is so in my hometown.

說明 so 代替 very hot and humid。

3) A: This fried pork chop smells terrible.

B: This steak smells the same.

說明 the same 代替 terrible。

4) A: I feel pitiful that the school team lost the game.

B: I feel the same.

說明 the same 代替 pitiful。

代詞功用的副詞

so

1) Sloths move very slowly, and so do koalas.

說明 so 代替 very slowly。

there

1) I got my Master's degree in Edinburgh, and I met my wife there.

說明 there 代替 in Edinburgh。

2) Tomas Georgeson, famous as a painter, knew the Milton Keynes Museum very well because he had worked there before.

106 台南特招

說明 there 代替 in the Milton Keynes Museum。

then

1) The earthquake hit around midnight, and I was sleeping then.

說明 then 代替 around midnight。

代詞與動詞存在固定搭配

1. believe 搭配 it，hope, think 搭配 so。

1) George and Mary say they will get married next week, but I don't believe it.

說明 it 代替 George and Mary will get married next week。

2) A: Will she be here soon?

B: I hope so.

A: Do you think it will rain?

B: I hope not!

說明 so 代替 she will be here soon，not 代替 it will not rain。

3) The pandemic will impact our lives far into the future, and I really think so.

說明 so 代替 The pandemic will impact our lives far into the future，英美人士認為清楚的講法：The pandemic will impact our lives far into the future, and this is something I truly believe.

A. 這是一篇讀書心得報告，請圈出具有銜接功能的連接語詞。

Many people think that there are four oceans in the world, including the Atlantic Ocean, the Indian Ocean, the Pacific Ocean and the Arctic oceans. However, a search on the Internet shows that there is one more ocean, the "Southern Ocean," around the South Pole and Antarctica. Also, the National Geographic Society has now officially accepted that this body of water around Antarctica is a real ocean. In addition, Geography teachers are now teaching their students that there are five oceans in the world. In fact, the Southern Ocean will lead students to a better understanding about climate change. Not everyone knows that the Southern Ocean has its own unique marine ecosystems that are home to wonderful marine life, such as whales, penguins and other sea creatures. From my perspective, this news is very surprising, and I look forward to learning more about it!

越南胡志明市 台灣學校 陳璐雅同學

參考答案

Many people think **that** there are four oceans in the world, including the Atlantic Ocean, the Indian Ocean, the Pacific Ocean and the Arctic oceans. **However**, a search on the Internet shows **that** there is one more ocean, the "Southern Ocean," around the South Pole and Antarctica. **Also**, the National Geographic Society has now officially accepted **that this** body of water around Antarctica is a real ocean. **In addition,** Geography teachers are now teaching their students **that** there are five oceans in the world. **In fact**, the Southern Ocean will lead students to a better understanding about climate change. Not everyone knows that **the** Southern Ocean has **its** own unique marine ecosystems **that** are home to wonderful marine life, such as whales, penguins and other sea creatures. From my perspective, **this** news is very surprising, and I look forward to learning more about **it**!

B. 這是一篇影片觀看心得報告，請將選項語詞填入適當空格以使文章完整。

A.Before I signed up for it, to tell the truth

B. which will certainly not only enable me to enhance my confidence

C. Although I was not among the winners

D. after watching this informative video

E. because feelings of frustration and depression always bring me down for a while

F. but it seems to be difficult for me to overcome my own obstacle

G. especially when I am assigned to make a presentation or speech in public

The lecturer's humorous but inspiring speech has created a deep and touching impression. In my mind, I am not confident enough in many ways, __1__. Sometimes, I tend to avoid or refuse to do it __2__. I know it is never positive and constructive, __3__.

Luckily, the situation has changed recently. Several days ago, I was involved in a self-study report in Yilan, my hometown. __4__, I was not so willing to face the challenge and compete with a number of peers.

Nevertheless, __5__, I changed my mind and gathered my courage to accept the challenge and join in it. During the activity, I spared no effort to develop my potential and perform well. __6__, I was sure I obtained valuable experiences and I would perform better next time. I am convinced that I have benefitted a lot from my eager participation in the keen competition, __7__ but also empower me to face further challenges with full confidence.

羅東高商　陳玗呈

✎ 參考答案

The lecturer's humorous but inspiring speech has created a deep and touching impression. In my mind, I am not confident enough in many ways, **especially when I am assigned to make a presentation or speech in public**. Sometimes, I tend to avoid or refuse to do it **because feelings of frustration and depression always bring me down for a while**. I know it is never positive and constructive, **but it seems to be difficult for me to overcome my own obstacle**.

Luckily, the situation has changed recently. Several days ago, I was involved in a self-study report in Yilan, my hometown. **Before I signed up for it, to tell the truth**, I was not so willing to face the challenge and compete with a number of peers.

Nevertheless, **after watching this informative video**, I changed my mind and gathered my courage to accept the challenge and join in it. During the activity, I spared no effort to develop my potential and perform well. **Although I was not among the winners**, I was sure I obtained valuable experiences and I would perform better next time. I am convinced that I have benefitted a lot from my eager participation in the keen competition, **which will certainly not only enable me to enhance my confidence** but also empower me to face further challenges with full confidence.

技巧 18

寫作邏輯明確，適切表情達意

無論是描述圖片、敘述事件、論述觀點，很重要的是主題一致、語意連貫，脈絡清晰，內容合乎情理，才能無所挑剔，引發共鳴，這就是寫作邏輯。

例如不要貿然以 you 當主詞，寫作不是向著聽話者陳述，不可穿越時空出現 you，而應以 one 泛指不特定的閱聽者。

*You cannot predict when the disease will strike again.

→ No one can predict when the disease will strike again.

→ The disease cannot be predicted when to strike again.

說明 主事者泛指不特定的對象，不須提及，搭配被動語態。

以下句子的問題是，目前人人可上大學，上大學不是祈求上天的 wish，而是能夠心想事成的 hope。

*I am working hard, and I wish that I could go to college.

→ I am working hard, and I hope that I will go to college.

全球暖化是肇因於人類的行為，若說是人類造成的就不合邏輯，畢竟古代就有人類，但沒有全球暖化。

*Global warming is caused by humans.

→ Global warming is caused by human behavior.

再看以下事件，寫作邏輯明確，便能適切表情達意。

18

Watch out! Better safe than sorry.

Last Sunday, Judy went to the shopping mall to buy a vase for her cousin's wedding. She picked one up from a shelf that had three layers of vases on display. She held it in her hands and looked at it carefully. A salesperson came up to Judy, telling her about the vase and its price.

Unfortunately, the vase in her hands suddenly dropped onto the floor, and broke into small pieces with a crashing sound. Judy and the salesperson were both astonished by the accident and stood frozen, looking at the vase pieces with no idea about what to do next.

After the shock and silence, the salesperson told Judy that she had to pay for the broken vase. She had no choice but to do as she was told, in spite of her unwillingness. Two thousand dollars was paid for her carelessness. It was really the worst shopping experience Judy has ever had.

以下是一些不合邏輯的寫法

Last Sunday, Judy went to the shopping mall to buy a vase for her cousin's wedding. She picked one up from a shelf that had three layers of vases on display. She held it in her hands and looked at it carefully. A salesperson **ran** to Judy, telling her about the vase and its **history**.

Surprisingly, the vase in her hands dropped onto the **ground**, and broke into small pieces with a crashing sound. Judy and the salesperson were both astonished by the accident and stood frozen, looking at the vase pieces with no idea about what to do next.

After the shock and silence, the salesperson told Judy that she had to **buy** the broken vase. She had no choice but to do as she was told, in spite of her unwillingness. Two thousand dollars was paid for her carelessness.

註解

① 花瓶專櫃區空間不大，不會也不該跑步到顧客身邊。

② 賣場的花瓶是大量製造，而且只賠償 2000 元的商品不是骨董，應無歷史可言。

③ 花瓶是從手上掉落至地面不是令人驚訝的事。

④ 賣場專櫃不是室外，不該用 ground。

⑤ 造成商品破損而付出金錢是賠償，不是購買，除非 Judy 帶走花瓶碎片。

小心！安全勝於後悔。

上周日，Judy 為了她表妹的婚禮去大賣場買一支花瓶。她從一個展示花瓶的三層櫃子上拿起一支花瓶，然後握在手上仔細端詳。一名銷售員到 Judy 那裏，告訴她這支花瓶及價格。

不幸地，她手中的花瓶突然掉落到地上，然後隨著撞擊的聲音破裂成小碎片。Judy 及銷售員都被這起意外嚇到站著不動，看著花瓶碎片不知道接下來要怎麼辦。

驚嚇及寂靜過後，銷售員告訴 Judy 她必須賠償這支摔碎的花瓶。她別無選擇只好照著要求賠償，儘管不願意，為了她的粗心而付出二千元，這真是 Judy 未曾有的最糟購物經驗。

1. 她從一個展示花瓶的三層櫃子上拿起一支花瓶。
2. 她手中的花瓶突然掉落到地上，然後隨著撞擊的聲音破裂成小碎片。
3. 她別無選擇只好照著要求賠償，儘管不願意。
4. Judy 和銷售員看著花瓶碎片，不知道接下來要怎麼辦。
5. 他們二人都被這起意外嚇到站著不動。

參考答案

1. She picked one up from a shelf that had three layers of vases on display.
2. The vase in her hands suddenly dropped onto the floor, and broke into small pieces with a crashing sound.
3. She had no choice but to do as she was told, in spite of her unwillingness.
4. Judy and the salesperson looked at the vase pieces with no idea about what to do next.
5. They were both astonished by the accident and stood frozen.

錯用 it, one, they，事情原委兜不攏

it

1. 指涉前面的單數名詞，且是同一物。
   1) My husband bought me a necklace for my birthday but I don't like **it**.
      我丈夫買給我一副項鍊當作生日禮物，但我不喜歡。
   2) The company was losing money, and **it** had to downsize.
      公司一直虧錢，它得縮編。

2. 指涉片語或子句。
   1) The foreigner likes **it** in Taiwan.
      那名外國人喜歡待在臺灣。
      說明 後行詞是 in Taiwan。

2) Teenagers who stay away from school do it for different reasons.

輟學的青少年都有這樣做的不同理由。

說明 先行詞是 stay away from school。

3) It is necessary for all of us to be present at the meeting this morning.

我們今天早上出席會議是必要的。

說明 it 是填補主詞，後行詞是 for all of us to be present at the meeting this morning。

4) It's unlikely that we will arrive on time.

我們準時抵達是不可能的。

說明 it 是填補主詞，後行詞是名詞子句 that we will arrive on time。

5) I find it convenient to be able to do my banking online.

我發現能夠線上處理銀行事宜是方便的。

說明 it 是填補受詞，後行詞是 to be able to do my banking online。

6) I thought that it was convenient that we didn't have to check in or check out by ourselves.

我發現我們不須自行報到及退房很方便。

說明 it 是填補主詞，後行詞是名詞子句 that we didn't have to check in or check out by ourselves。

one

one 代替前述單數名詞，指涉同類但不是同一物，或同類中的任一個，等於 "a / an + 單數名詞 "。ones 是 one 的複數形，代替前述複數名詞中的一些，搭配 the 表示特指。

1) I need a USB, and I'll have to buy one.

我需要一支隨身碟，所以得買一支。

說明 one 代替 a USB，但不是前述同一個。

2) I have a few recipes on Italian vegetarian cuisine pasta. You can borrow one if you want.
我有一些義式菜蔬義大利麵食譜，你若要可以借一本。
說明 one 代替 a recipe ，指涉前述 recipes 中的任一個。

3) Please make a copy for everybody in the office and a few extra ones for the visitors.
麻煩辦公室每人印一份，然後多印幾份給訪客。
說明 ones 指涉已知資料中的一些。

4) Which pie would you like? 你要哪一個派？
The one on the left. 左邊那個。
說明 The one = The pie，on the left 限定哪一個 pie。

5) I have three smartphones. One is an iPhone, another is a Galaxy S5, and the other is MIUI.
我有三支手機，一支是 iPhone，另一支是 Galaxy S5，其它一支是 MIUI。
說明 首先提及的一個用 one。

that

代替並特指前述單數名詞，表示對比，等於 "the + 單數名詞 "。that 的複數形是 those，代替並特指前述複數名詞，同樣表示對比，等於 "the + 複數名詞 "。

1) The weather in Kaohsiung is much warmer than that in Keelung.
高雄的天氣較基隆的天氣暖和多了
說明 that = the weather，若是 it，則指 the weather in Kaohsiung。

2) Today's copy machines are more functional than those of the past.
今天的影印機較過去的影印機功能好多了。

後行詞

1. *He is in his late thirties, but John behaves like a teenager.

   說明 對等子句中的代名詞 he 不可後指 John，John 不是 he 的後行詞。

   比較 John behaves like a teenager though he is in his late thirties.

   雖然就要 40 歲了，約翰表現得像個青少年。

2. If you want some, there's coffee in the pot.

   你若要一些，鍋子裡有咖啡。

   比較 If you want coffee, there's some in the pot.

   你若要咖啡，鍋子裡有一些。

3. When the client called him, Mr. Lin was in a meeting.

   客戶打給他時，林先生正在會議中。

   比較

   1. When the client called Mr. Lin, he was in a meeting.

      客戶打給林先生時，他正在會議中。

      說明 Mr. Lin 是 he 的先行詞。

   2. He was in a meeting when the client called Mr. Lin.

      他正在會議中，就在客戶打給林先生時。

      說明 Mr. Lin 不是 he 的後行詞，he 是另指他人。

   3. This is my recommendation: you tell the truth.

      這是我的建議，就是你講實話。

   4. Looking at herself in the mirror this morning, Cindy found a pimple on her nose.

      說明 Cindy 是 herself 的後行詞，也是 her 的先行詞。

名詞片語的結構

中心詞是名詞的片語稱為名詞片語，包含中心詞、補語、加接詞、指示詞等四個成分，以 “a new English teacher” 為例，說明如下：

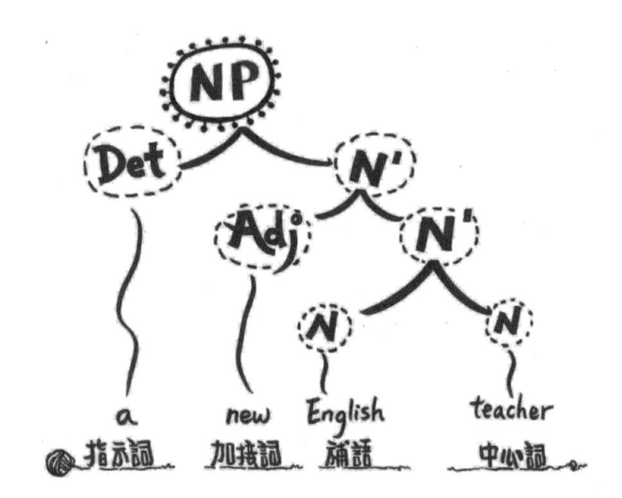

中心詞

teacher，名詞片語的必要成分，決定動詞的單複數。

補語

English，補語表示名詞的身分、原料等，與名詞關係密切，詞序相鄰。名詞片語只有一個補語，但可缺項。

加接詞

new，加接詞修飾名詞，包括單詞形容詞、形容詞片語或形容詞子句，前位修飾的形容詞至多三個，依照與名詞的關聯程度排列，逐漸呈現名詞的樣貌，但也可缺項。

指示詞

a，指示詞標示中心詞的數量與指涉，限定詞的功用即是充當名詞片語的指示詞。

說明

1. it 代替中心詞為單數名詞的名詞片語，they 代替中心詞為複數名詞的名詞片語。
2. one 只代替名詞片語中的中心詞，其他成分皆保留。

請依粗體語詞提示修改，以使句子敘述合乎邏輯。

1. In order to prevent infection from dangerous diseases, it's important that pet owners **vaccinate their pets**.

2. Mary was not hired at the veterinary clinic because she was not experienced enough to interact with **the patients**.

3. Students in Taiwan always **sit tight** during class because they are asked to listen to their teachers carefully.
   In America, students are not asked to **sit tight** because it is not necessary or helpful for learning. They are encouraged to participate in discussion and be active in learning during class.

4. **At** noon, I bought a chicken salad and a cup of ice cream black tea for lunch at the convenience store in my neighborhood. **The chicken salad tasted delicious, though a little expensive**. Feeling relaxed and comfortable, **I had my light lunch in my room with the air conditioner on**. Anyway, I will choose it as my lunch again.

✐ 參考答案

1. In order to prevent infection from dangerous diseases, it's important that pet owners **get their pets vaccinated**.
2. Mary was not hired at the veterinary clinic because she was not experi enced enough to interact with **the pet owners**.
3. sit tight 表示 don't move， sit quietly 表示 don't talk，上課時應該是要求 don't talk!
4. **Around** noon, I bought a chicken salad and a cup of ice cream black tea for lunch at the convenience store in my neighborhood. **Feeling relaxed and comfortable, I had my light lunch in my room with the air conditioner on. The chicken salad tasted delicious, though a little expensive.** Anyway, I will choose it as my lunch again.

   1) 不會正好 12：00，around noon，大約正中午較合理。

   2) 吃完食物之後才會提到食物嚐起來美味的評論。

技巧 19

句型有備無患，但與內容要相符

句型用於陳述或強調觀點，延伸前一話題或是提出結論，善用句型，下筆就輕鬆明快。

強調觀點

1. I am greatly convinced / assured that

   我深信，強調自己的立場

   1) I am greatly convinced / assured that practice makes perfect.

2. It goes without saying that

   不消說，強調陳述內容的真實性。

   1) It goes without saying that smartphones have played an incredibly important role in our lives.

   說明 It goes without saying that 可代換為

   It is needless to say that

   It is obvious that

Needless to say

Obviously

3. There is no way of

無法、不可能，常搭配 knowing。

1) There is no way of knowing when we can travel abroad again.

說明 There is no way of 可代換為：

There is no

There is no possibility of

It is impossible to

It is out of question to

We cannot

No one can

4. Among various kinds of

在各種之中，搭配比較級、最高級或表示程度的副詞。

1) Among various kinds of sports, I like tennis in particular.

= Of all the sports, I like tennis in particular.

簡潔的寫法

Among all the sports, I like tennis in particular.

延伸前一話題

1. We have reasons to believe that

我們有理由相信，陳述具有共識的話題，說明結果或影響。

1) We have reasons to believe that wearing masks will continue to be strongly recommended.

2. If we can really put these points into practice

如果我們能夠落實這些要點。

1) If we can really put these points into practice, tourism will develop in

harmony with the environment.

3. By doing these small things

   藉由做到這些小事。

   1) By doing these small things, we certainly can conserve energy without too much trouble.

句型運用的注意事項

1. 內容遠比句型重要，漂亮的句型搭配合適的內容才是速配，光有句型是加不了分的。

   1) It goes without saying that we have to keep early hours.

      → We had better keep early hours.

      早睡早起只是個人生活作息，不須強調或妄下定論，否則反而會自曝其短。

   2) It's obvious that a high school student's top priority is to get good grades.

      → It's obvious that a high school student should try to achieve their full potential.

      「中學生優先要做的是得到好成績」不是大家都贊同的觀點，若搭配「不用說」，就是在強調武斷的內容，也是自曝其短。

2. 句型與內容在風格上必須相符，例如不要以論證的句型表達情感，否則語意邏輯會出狀況。

   1) I am greatly convinced that prevention is better than cure.

      句型與內容相符

   2) I am greatly convinced that I am so grateful for all that my parents have done for me.

      → I am so grateful for all that my parents have done for me.

      直接表示對父母的感激就好，不須我深信。

3. 寫作力求簡潔、清晰，應該避免無助於語意的語詞，例如一般認為 "that is to say" 用於提供進一步或更為正確的訊息，但不須用於寫作上。

I will meet you in the city tomorrow, that is to say, if the trains are running.

→I will meet you in the city tomorrow, if the trains are running.

以下文章因加入一些不合適的句型而導致邏輯或流暢的問題。

19

Due to food safety concerns, **it goes with saying that** more people choose to prepare meals at home as often as possible. However, some people have no choice but to eat out for different reasons.

Here are three reasons why I eat out more often.

First of all, I tend to savor the experience of tasting exotic cuisines from different cultures and I enjoy trying different dishes. Only specific restaurants are able to offer these choices. Therefore, I usually eat out with my family on different occasions.

Second, due to my parents' tight schedules, **I am greatly convinced that** it is difficult for them to prepare meals at home. What's more, they also need to drive me to and from school during rush hours, so **there is no way that** they have time to prepare food at home. Thus, eating out will reduce their hardship and, on the other hand, it will provide rewards for their hard work.

Finally, I enjoy the precious occasion of family happiness when we eat in a restaurant. It is a time when we have close talks, sharing with each other what happens in our lives. Sometimes, **I have reasons to believe that** I benefit a lot from their words.

In spite of the habit of eating out, I have my own ideas about a balanced diet.

Most importantly, we should prioritize avoiding too much oil, salt and sugar to have a balanced diet because they are not healthy for our bodies. Second, consuming various natural foods, including fruit, vegetables and meats, will offer us a nutritious, balanced diet, and give us a healthy and productive life.

Even though we need to eat out frequently for different reasons, **by doing these small things**, we can balance our diet as much as possible for our health.

若是略去不需要的句型，文章的可讀性將大幅提升。

Due to food safety concerns, more people choose to prepare meals at home as often as possible. However, some people have no choice but to eat out for different reasons.

Here are three reasons why I eat out more often.

First of all, I tend to savor the experience of tasting exotic cuisines from different cultures and I enjoy trying different dishes. Only specific restaurants are able to offer these choices. Therefore, I usually eat out with my family on different occasions.

Second, due to my parents' tight schedules, it is difficult for them to prepare meals at home. What's more, they also need to drive me to and from school during rush hours, so they really don't have time to prepare food at home. Thus, eating out will reduce their hardship and, on the other hand, it will provide rewards for their hard work.

Finally, I enjoy the precious occasion of family happiness when we eat in a restaurant. It is a time when we have close talks, sharing with each other what happens in our lives. Sometimes, I feel that I benefit a lot from their words.

In spite of the habit of eating out, I have my own ideas about a balanced diet.

Most importantly, we should prioritize avoiding too much oil, salt and sugar to have a balanced diet because they are not healthy for our bodies.

Second, consuming various natural foods, including fruit, vegetables and meats, will offer us a nutritious, balanced diet, and give us a healthy and productive life.

Even though we need to eat out frequently for different reasons, we still have to balance our diet as much as possible for our health.

政治大學附屬高中 陳鼎鈞同學

由於食品安全的關注，越來越多人選擇儘量常在家裡烹煮，然而，一些人因著不同原因而只好外食。

這些是我較常外食的三個原因。

首先，我喜好品嚐不同文化的異國料理的體驗及嘗試不同菜餚，但只有特色餐廳能夠提供這些選擇，因此，我經常在不同時機與家人上館子。

其次，由於我父母行程緊湊，要在家預備飯食不容易。還有，他們還得交通尖峰時刻開車載我往返學校，實在沒有時間在家下廚。因此，外食將減輕他們的辛勞，另一方面，也是犒賞他們的辛苦工作。

最後，我喜愛全家人在餐廳用餐的珍貴天倫之樂的場合，那是我們親密談話，彼此分享生活經歷的一段時間。有時候，我覺得從他們的話語中獲益良多。

儘管外食習慣，我對於飲食均衡有自己的想法。

最重要的是，應該優先避開過多的油、鹽、糖以擁有均衡飲食，因為它們對我們的身體不健康。

其次，攝取包括蔬果及肉類等各種天然食物將提供我們營養且均衡的飲食，帶給我們一個健康而豐富的生活。

儘管因不同理由而須外食，為了健康，我們仍須儘量均衡我們的飲食。

1. 我喜好品嚐不同文化的異國料理的體驗及嘗試不同菜餚。
2. 由於我父母行程緊湊，要在家預備飯食不容易。
3. 外食將減輕他們的辛勞，另一方面，也是犒賞他們的辛苦工作。
4. 儘管外食習慣，我對於飲食均衡有自己的想法。
5. 攝取包括蔬果及肉類等各種天然食物將提供我們營養且均衡的飲食。

✎ 參考答案

1. I tend to savor the experience of tasting exotic cuisines from different cultures and I enjoy trying different dishes.
2. Due to my parents' tight schedules, it is difficult for them to prepare meals at home.
3. Eating out will reduce their hardship and, on the other hand, it will provide rewards for their hard work.
4. In spite of the habit of eating out, I have my own ideas about a balanced diet.
5. Consuming various natural foods, including fruit, vegetables and meats, will offer us a nutritious, balanced diet.

遵守會話四大公理，寫作就四平八穩

會話是合作原則，包括**量**、**相關**、**方式**、**質**等四大公理，寫作也應知曉、遵循這些溝通原則，文字才能簡潔、明確。

一篇可讀性高的閱讀文本，必然遵守會話四大公理，這是讀者能夠輕易察覺、體驗的。題組經過嚴謹考量與精確設計，編寫過程同樣符合會話四大公理。因此，知曉會話四大公理，於寫作、閱讀、測驗皆有莫大助益。

量：訊息不多於或少於陳述主題所需的量。

相關：細節與主題相關，描述與圖片相關。

方式：陳述簡潔、清晰，訊息先後有序，避免閱聽者誤解。

質：準確陳述主題或圖片。

選字、詞綴、詞序、句構都與語意息息相關，這是「形意搭配」的原則。藉由句式結構集結、統整相關訊息，達到主題鮮明、陳述完整、訊息簡潔的效果，這是「形意搭配」的應用，也是會話四大公理的表現，更是重要的筆頭功夫，應當熟習。

寫作的訊息產出有三步驟：

1. 想寫什麼？自己主觀的發想。
2. 讀者看得懂嗎？從讀者的角度批判自己的發想。
3. 怎麼表達？選擇最佳的句式結構，並以四大公理丈量自己的文字。

這是一篇關於校園演講的說明文，文中有違反四大公理的量、相關、方式、質等原則各一處，請試著找找看。

If my school is going to hold a lecture next Saturday, it would be a precious occasion to interact with such a famous figure online. The reasons are as follows. First, high school students choose to exercise to release their stress and make friends on the court. Second, some famous players attract a huge number of fans and even become their idols. James' performance is great that there are so many people crazy about him. Last but not the least, the rise of superstar Michael Jordan helped the NBA achieve its global position. He must make a lot of effort to obtain his achievements and become what he is now. Thus, I will look forward to the rare occasion that will inspire and encourage me to become a new person, stronger in mind, more focused on my goal and braver to work for it.

If he gave a speech to us, he would share why he chose to become a professional athlete and what frustration he underwent in the past so that he could become a big star. At the beginning, he may tell us about his passion for basketball from childhood. Then, he might share his training process and the turning point in his career. With his determination, he eventually became more and more distinguished and outstanding on the court. Finally, his conclusion would be "no pain no gain." If I desire to pursue success, I should work hard for it willingly. The question I would like to ask him would be, "How did you overcome the frustrations that you encountered?" To conclude, I think I would benefit a lot from his speech.

✎ 參考答案

質：online

相關：Last but not the least, the rise of superstar Michael Jordan helped the NBA achieve its global position

方式：At the beginning, he might share his training process and the turning point in his career. With his determination, he eventually became more and more distinguished and outstanding on the court. Then, he may tell us about his passion for basketball from childhood.

建議寫法：At the beginning, he may tell us about his passion for basketball from childhood. Then, he might share his training process and the turning point in his career. With his determination, he eventually became more and more distinguished and outstanding on the court.

量：If my school is going to hold a lecture next Saturday, it would be a precious oc casion to interact with such a famous figure face to face.

建議寫法：If my school is going to hold a lecture next Saturday, I hope they can invite Lebron James, a big star in NBA, and the topic should be about basketball and becoming successful. It would be a precious occasion to interact with such a famous figure.

技巧 20

片語起首，句首結構更多樣

句子結構富變化是高分寫作的要項，而增添修飾功用的片語能使句子枝葉繁茂，生氣盎然，若是置於句首，語意及句式上都是錦上添花。另外，片語結構份量較小，片語在前，句子在後，形成由小到大的平衡排列，句子結構的評分項目必然加分。

片語常增添事件的訊息而使語意更為完整，例如：

情緒

1) **Much to our relief**, the boy was found safe and sound by the police last night.
我們鬆了一大口氣

態度

1) **To be honest with you**, I don't think it will be possible.
誠實對你說

評論

1) **Needless to say**, the clerk will be off work for a while.

不用說

2) **Generally speaking**, men are stronger than women.

一般而言

目的

1) **To earn more money**, he took a part time job in a local hotel as a busboy.

為了多賺點錢

結果

1) The man rushed his sick child to the hospital, **only to see a long line of people waiting in front of the entrance**.

不料只看見大排長龍的人在入口等候

背景

1) **Faced with the pandemic**, we're all washing our hands more frequently.

→When we are faced with a pandemic, we're all washing our hands more frequently.

面對大流行

原因

1) **With less time spent at school**, their chances of getting well-paid jobs are small, and they often have no voice in important matters, like who to marry.

因為較少時間花在學校

國中會考

after、on、upon 等介係詞搭配動名詞形成動名詞構句，提供時間訊息，由於指涉明確，動名詞與主要子句的主詞可以不一致。

1) After cleaning his Tesla, Tom drove his son to the resort.

2) On arriving at the station, my uncle was there to greet us.

3) Upon arriving at the campsite, masks are not required, however, we recommend social distancing.

4) Upon arrival, please report to the reception desk.

中文也會在句子前面加上一些情緒、態度、時間、條件等語詞，例如以上句子的中文翻譯，這是中文與英文相通之處，更是學習寫作的好方法。

另外，尤其是說明文，為了使內容條理分明、讀者容易閱讀，句首常搭配表示順序或重要性的轉折語詞，這時句首的片語便具有指引文章脈絡的功能，例如說明個人的防疫作法時，first of all, more importantly, just as importantly, finally 等片語依序說明重要性：

Faced with challenges from the coronavirus pandemic, we can take some steps to protect ourselves and others, and reduce the risk.
First of all, get vaccinated and stay up to date on your COVID-19 vaccines.
More importantly, wear a well-fitting mask indoors in public.
Just as importantly, wash your hands frequently.
Finally, test yourself to prevent spread to others.

110 學測英文作文試題說明是遊客到訪某場所的新聞畫面。你認為圖中呈現的是什麼景象？你對這個景象有什麼感想？請根據此圖片，寫一篇英文作文。文分兩段，第一段描述圖片的內容，包括其中人、事、物以及發生的事情；第二段則以遊客或場所主人的立場，表達你對這件事情的看法。

20

In the picture, a number of visitors went to look at flowers in the flower garden. There was a sign that said, "You are welcome to look and photograph but don't trample the flowers." Unfortunately, some people ignored it and entered the garden, trampling flowers while taking pictures. Some even picked flowers and made a mess.

If I were the owner of this garden, I would get angry at the sight of it. From sowing, watering to fertilizing, the owner spent a lot of time taking care of the garden. Finally, the garden became beautiful with a lot of beautiful flowers. But it was all devastated. I think that some people might have noticed the sign, but when seeing what others did in the garden, they just followed along, making the situation worse.

In case such a mess happens again, the owner should ask the people for a sum of money as a fine for compensation. If this is in vain, the owner should choose to close the garden.

照片中，許多訪客去觀賞花園裡的花，那裡有一個招牌寫著「歡迎觀賞拍照，但勿踐踏花朵。」可惜的是，一些人忽略這個招牌而進入花園，拍照時踐踏花朵，一些人甚至摘下花朵，搞得一團亂。

如果我是花園主人，一看到這景象我就會火大。從播種、澆水到施肥，園主花費大量時間照料花園，終於，因著許多美麗花卉而使花園看起來美麗。但是，現在全毀了。我想一些人可能注意到招牌，但是看到其他人在花園裡所做的舉動時，他們跟進而使狀況更糟。這樣的亂象萬一重演，園主應向這些人要求一筆錢做為賠償的罰金，如果沒有效果，園主應該選擇關閉花園。

1. 一些人忽略這個招牌而進入花園，拍照時踐踏花朵，一些人甚至摘下花朵，搞得一團亂。
2. 如果我是花園主人，一看到這景象我就會火大。
3. 園主應向這些人要求一筆錢做為賠償的罰金。
4. 從播種、澆水到施肥，園主花費大量時間照料花園。
5. 看到其他人在花園裡所做的舉動時，他們跟進而使狀況越糟。

✎ 參考答案

1. Some people ignored the sign and entered the garden, trampling flowers while taking pictures.
2. If I were the owner of this garden, I would get angry at the sight of it.
3. In case such a mess happens again, the owner should ask the people for a sum of money as a fine for compensation.
4. From sowing, watering to fertilizing, the owner spent a lot of time taking care of the garden.
5. When seeing what others did in the garden, they just followed along, making the situation worse.

寫作導向的文法講座

片語修飾語是寫作升級的階梯

片語結構的名詞修飾語添增名詞訊息，擴大句子結構，是應當熟習的寫作技巧。

1. 形容詞片語
   1) He just kept crying, **sad and speechless**.
   2) I was lying looking at the amazing sky **full of bright stars**.

2. 名詞片語，同位語功用
   2.1 非限定同位語，省略而不影響指涉辨識，常搭配 namely, that is, in other words 等。
      1) Three members were mentioned, **namely, Tom, Cindy and Helen**.
      三名會員被提到，也就是湯姆、莘蒂及海倫。

2) Mount Jade, **the highest mountain in Taiwan**, is almost 4,000 meters above sea level.

玉山，台灣最高峰，海拔將近 4000 公尺。

2.2 限定同位語，辨識名詞的必要訊息，與名詞不隔逗號且不可略去。

1) The entrepreneur **Terry** gave the after-dinner speech.

企業家泰瑞發表晚宴後演說。

2) The movie "Fast and Furious" is all about cars, speed and action.

電影「玩命關頭」都是與汽車、速度及動作有關。

3. 分詞片語

3.1 現在分詞，主動、持續狀態。

1) On the other side of the park, there was a dog **napping on the grass**.

3.2 過去分詞，被動、完成狀態。

1) The librarian sat at his desk, **surrounded** by books and magazines.

圖書館員坐在桌前，周圍都是書和雜誌。

2) The car **being repaired** is an automatic.

正在維修的車子是自排車。

說明 being 標記進行、持續的被動狀態，清楚寫法：The car **that is being repaired** has an automatic transmission.

4. 不定詞

1) There is a bench **for patients to sit on**.

有一長凳子讓病患坐。

2) We have many things **to deal with** during this pandemic.

疫情期間我們有許多事要應付。

說明 不定詞後位修飾名詞，名詞若是不定詞的受詞則省略。

5. 介係詞片語

1) Tina saw a little boy crying by the roadside, **with a toy car in his arms**.

2) **With a black and blue mark on its face**, the dog got up, barked loudly at the boys, and ran after them.

這篇是 Tony Coolidge 針對英文寫作 30 技巧課程的推薦文，請找出置於句首、句中、句尾的修飾語詞。

This online course, "30 Writing Techniques," equips learners with everything that is needed to "polish" their writing and make it "shine." All the techniques are understandable and useful for students of different levels.

The course lessons are based on current standard writing theories and principles, including the patterns of the GSAT written test, as well as several English proficiency tests, i.e. TOEFL, IELTS.

These 30 techniques are designed to help you perform well on the four major grading criteria in writing tests, including content, organization, sentence structures, and word use. I believe that if high school students exercise these techniques, their writing skills will become stronger, and they will be able to overcome the challenges of getting a high score on their written parts of their exams.

In addition to the writing instructions, this online course also features methods to help students improve their written grammar. Improved grammar skills, of course, create improved writing. From this, students will gain a clearer understanding of the logical and semantical connection between writing and grammar. This uniquely crafted design, created by Mr. Su, specializes in interpreting grammar logically.

With the enhancements of quality audio files and illustrations, this online course will act as the most beneficial writing material available for high school students and instructors.

Thanks to all the harmonic efforts from the project team, "30 Writing Techniques" will reveal an innovative vision of writing instruction in Taiwan, and guide all the readers to the "promised land" of writing proficiency.

參考答案

This online course, "30 Writing Techniques," equips learners with everything that is needed to "polish" their writing and make it "shine." All the techniques are understandable and useful for students of different levels.

The course lessons are based on current standard writing theories and principles, **including the patterns of the GSAT written test, as well as several English proficiency tests, i.e. TOEFL, IELTS**.

These 30 techniques are designed to help you perform well on the four major grading criteria in writing tests, **including content, organization, sentence structures, and word use**. I believe that if high school students exercise these techniques, their writing skills will become stronger, and they will be able to overcome the challenges of getting a high score on their written parts of their exams.

In addition to the writing instructions, this online course also features methods to help students improve their written grammar. Improved grammar skills, **of course**, create improved writing. **From this**, students will gain a clearer understanding of the logical and semantical connection between writing and grammar. This uniquely crafted design, **created by Mr. Su**, specializes in interpreting grammar logically.

With the enhancements of quality audio files and illustrations, this online course will act as the most beneficial writing material available for high school students and instructors.

Thanks to all the harmonic efforts from the project team, "30 Writing Techniques" will reveal an innovative vision of writing instruction in Taiwan, and guide all the readers to the "promised land" of writing proficiency.

技巧 21

長句短句搭配運用，營造跌宕起伏的氣勢

句式多樣化，簡單句、從屬連接的複句、對等連接的合句、從屬與對等連接兼具的複合句等相互搭配，便足以營造跌宕起伏的氣勢。

簡單句可視為短句，簡潔有力，適合用於主題句或表明觀點、主張。

複句、合句、複合句等可視為長句，結構複雜，訊息繁多，適合用於闡述論點或說明細節。

🎧 21

↘ 主題句是簡單句

Nowadays, on high school campuses, choices for lunch have become diverse.

↘ 複句說明學生午餐的多樣選擇

Some students choose their meals offered from the cafeteria, while some prefer to order food from delivery platforms.

↘ 合句說明不同午餐選擇的特色

The former may be nutritious and economical, and the latter offers teenagers a variety of food choices from restaurants.

↘ 簡單句表明自己最喜愛的午餐形式

What is my preferred source of lunch? Homemade lunch boxes have been my favorite since my childhood.

↘ 二個長句說明自己最喜愛的午餐形式的原因

In addition to delicious food, my mom usually places a small note in my lunch bag when she makes my lunch. The notes show some encouraging words, such as "Fighting," or "Keep going," which touch and motivate me.

↘ 短句揭開另一主題。

In my opinion, homemade lunches have several advantages.

↘ 長句說明喜愛家裡的便當的原因

For me, my lunches are made by my dear mom and they are always delicious, healthy, and full of affection, since she ranks hygiene as her top concern while making my lunch.

✎ 長句結構較為複雜，以下是一些長句的書寫技巧：

1. 句子必須包含一不含連接詞的主要子句。

 * If you go this way, **and** you will soon see the gallery.

 → If you go this way, you will soon see the gallery.

 → Go this way, and you will soon see the gallery.

2. 連寫句（run-on sentence）是數個獨立子句相鄰而無連接詞或逗號，普遍認為是錯誤的，應該避免。

 * There are many ways we prevent the pandemic from triggering another lockdown.

 → There are many ways **for us** to prevent the pandemic from triggering an other lockdown.

→There are many ways **through which** we can prevent the pandemic from triggering another lockdown.

3. 句子主詞必須對應非限定動詞的主事者。

1) *To get good grades, studying hard is essential.

→ To get good grades, **students** should study hard.

2) *Badly hurt, **an ambulance** rushed the injured man to the nearby hospital.

→ Badly hurt, **the injured man** was rushed to the nearby hospital by an ambulance.

4. 片語結構不可當作句子。

1) *There are many ways to prevent ourselves from getting infected. For example, washing hands, wearing masks, distancing and getting vaccinated.

→ There are many ways to prevent ourselves from getting infected, for example, washing hands, wearing masks, distancing and getting vaccinated.

現今，中學校園裡，中餐的選擇變得多樣化，一些學生選擇自助餐廳提供的飯菜，而一些同學偏好平台外送的食物。前者可能營養又省錢，後者提供青少年來自餐廳各式各樣的食物。

我喜歡的午餐來源是什麼？從小時候起，家裡做的便當就一直是我的最愛。除了美味的食物，母親做我的午餐時經常在便當盒袋放一張小紙條，這些紙條寫著一些如「加油」或「繼續前進」這樣的鼓勵話語，讓我感動又得著激勵。我認為家裡做的午餐有好幾的優點。

對我來說，我的中餐都是我親愛的母親做的，一向都是美味、健康、充滿愛，因為她預備我的中餐時將衛生擺在優先考慮。

1. If you go this way, you will soon see the gallery.
   如果往這邊去，你很快會看到美術館。
2. There are many ways through which the pandemic from triggering another lockdown.
   有許多我們能夠憑藉而防止疫情引起另一次封城的方法。
3. There are many ways for us to prevent the pandemic from triggering another lockdown.
   有許多我們防止疫情引起另一次封城的方法。
4. To get good grades, students should study hard.
   為了得到好成績，學生應該用功讀書。
5. Badly hurt, the injured man was rushed to the nearby hospital by an ambulance.
   因為傷勢嚴重，該名受傷男子被救護車緊急送到附近醫院。

6. There are many ways to prevent ourselves from getting infected, for example, washing hands, wearing masks, distancing and getting vaccinated.
有許多預防感染的方法，例如洗手、戴口罩、保持社交距離及接種疫苗。

1. 現今，中學校園裡，中餐的選擇變得多樣化。
2. 一些學生選擇自助餐廳提供的飯菜，而一些同學偏好平台外送的食物。
3. 有許多我們防止疫情引起另一次封城的方法。
4. 除了美味的食物，母親做我的午餐時經常在便當盒袋放一張小紙條。
5. 我媽媽預備我的中餐時將衛生擺在優先考慮。

參考答案

1. Nowadays, on high school campuses, choices for lunch have become diverse.
2. Some students choose their meals offered from the cafeteria, while some prefer to order food from delivery platforms.
3. There are many ways for us to prevent the pandemic from triggering another lockdown.
4. In addition to delicious food, my mom usually places a small note in my lunch bag when she makes my lunch.
5. My mother ranks hygiene as her top concern while making my lunch.

掌握語詞的語意特徵，洞悉字裡乾坤

語詞的定義要項就是該語詞的語意特徵，我們常以 + / - 符號標示是否具有某一語意特徵，例如 happy、sad 的語意特徵標示如下：

happy	sad
+ emotional state	+ emotional state
+ positive	- positive

又如 father, mother, boy, girl 的語意特徵包括：

father： + human + male + adult，通常包含 + married

mother：+ human + female + adult，通常包含 + married

boy： + human + male + young

girl： + human + female + young

1. 只有一語意特徵相異的語詞可視為相反詞，father 與 mother 互為相反詞，boy 與 girl 互為相反詞。

2. 除非必要，語意特徵若伴隨出現，語意特徵的字詞即是贅字，應該略去。

   1) The girl is **young** and pretty.

      那位女孩年輕又漂亮。

      略去 young：The girl is pretty.

      那位女孩漂亮。

   2) My father is a married, handsome man.

我父親是一位已婚、英俊的男士。

略去 married：My father is a handsome man.

我父親是一位英俊的男士。

說明

1. 凸顯具有 handsome 特性的 man，強調類別中具有某特性的個別或群體。
2. 略去 man：My father is handsome.
   純粹描述 father 的外觀。

3. 以下句子中的 new, actual, building, imaginary 都是贅字，應該略去。

   1) We must encourage **new** innovation if the company is to remain competitive.
   公司若要維持競爭力，我們就必須鼓勵創新。

   2) The book is full of **actual** facts about COVID-19 vaccines.
   這本書充滿新冠肺炎疫苗的真相。

   3) My uncle is the **building** architect of this gallery.
   我叔叔是這棟美術館的建築師。

   4) In my **imaginary** dream I flew to a forest of enormous trees.
   說明 imaginary 是 dream 的本質，贅字。dream 可搭配 frightening, unpleasant, bad, strange, weird, vivid 等。

4. 比較以下句子：

   1) My brother is a student, who is studying at school.
   說明 修飾語與 student 的語意特徵重複，可以略去。

   2) My brother is a student, who is studying at a private high school in town.
   我弟弟是一名學生，目前就讀市區的一所私立中學。
   說明 修飾語包含 student 語意特徵以外的訊息，語意與結構份量相稱。

5. 若是考量語詞結構與訊息量，可運用不同面向的語詞或是譬喻來修飾名詞。

1) The marble table is round in shape.

這張大理石桌子形狀是圓的。

說明

1. shape 是 round 的語意特徵，也是上層字，贅字，可改寫如下：

This is an amazing round marble table.

這是一張很棒的圓形大理石桌。

This is a round marble table, **which looks like an elegant mirror**.

這是個圓形大理石桌子，看起來像一面高雅的鏡子。

2. 考量結構對稱，語意特徵或上層字可以保留。

The island is round **in shape** and is approximately 18 km **in diameter**.

這位島嶼形狀圓形，直徑大約 18 公里。

3. 以下介係詞片語表示特定訊息，不是贅字，不應略去。

A gingerbread man is a cookie **in the shape of a stylish man**.

薑餅人是一種以時尚男子作為形狀的餅乾。

名詞搭配的形容詞就是該名詞可能的語意特徵或性質，例如 a delicious meal，meal 搭配 delicious，meal 可能具有 delicious 的性質。

A. 請將提示單字填入正確空格以形成搭配：

basic deep furious constant natural regular

1. The guest was fed up with the __________ noise of traffic.
2. In Taiwan, we are having a __________ debate about the death penalty.
3. Eating __________ meals helped me lose weight.
4. This is the most __________ model.
5. I slept a __________ sleep last night.
6. The monk died a __________ death the night before.

B. 以下句子若有形容詞的錯誤，請訂正，若無，請打 O：

___ 1. The new comedy show is quite fun.

___ 2. The egg sandwich tasted a little funny.

___ 3. I think playing dodge ball with my friends is funny.

___ 4. The operator spoke in a tired voice.

___ 5. It's a very friendly restaurant with a nice relaxed atmosphere.

___ 6. My parents are relaxed about me staying out late.

___ 7. He's quite an interested guy.

___ 8. I'd be interesting to hear more about your work.

___ 9. My cousin was unable to join the army because of ill health.

___ 10. The patient was kept living on a life-support machine.

參考答案

A.

1. constant 2. furious 3. regular 4. basic 5. deep 6. natural

B.

1. funny 2. O 3. fun 4. O 5. O 6. O 7. interesting 8. interested 9. O 10. alive

技巧 22

製造焦點有技巧，強調部分要倒裝

一篇好的文章，除了短句與長句搭配得宜之外，句子結構也須隨著語意而變化，例如分裂句是為製造焦點而將強調的語詞前移至主要子句，倒裝句是將強調語詞移至句首，以特殊的詞序引起注意。分裂句與倒裝句都是寫作常見且重要的修辭技巧。

中華民國第十四屆總統就職演說中的一段話就是藉由分裂句而凸顯強調的焦點。

1) It is not **the leader** who makes a country great; it is **the collective striving of the people** that makes this country great.
   使一個國家偉大的不是領導者，使這個國家偉大的是人民的集體奮鬥。

基本詞序的句型不具強調的功能，無法製造焦點訊息：

2) The leader does not make a country great; the collective striving of the people makes this country great.

倒裝句將強調語詞移至句首，凸顯訊息焦點，並使句首結構多樣化，例如：

3) Not until I completed all my homework did I go to bed.
強調我是什麼時候去睡覺的

4) Only when we follow the epidemic prevention measures can we prevent viruses from spreading.
強調預防病毒傳播的條件

另一倒裝句型是表示位置的主詞補語前移至句首，主詞置於句子的右側。

5) Next to the lake is a small village.

主詞置於句子的右側，若是加接修飾語，不僅擴增訊息，句子結構也富變化，這是英文寫作的好招。

6) Next to the lake is a small village, **named after a great hero from Greek mythology**.

7) Next to the lake is a small village, **which is famous for its locally produced goat's cheese.**

8) Next to the lake is a small village, **where there are boat hire businesses and snack bars**.

22

This afternoon, there was a temple procession passing through my neighborhood. Two huge marching effigies of gods looked magnificent but serious, like ancient moving artifacts. Each of their ghostly costumes felt as heavy as thick carpets hanging on a moving rack. **Near the two gods were Techno Princes**, another type of puppet god, performing fun and active dances to noisy pop music, which sounded like a live concert.

Along both sides of the parade route were long lines of vendors selling local snacks, like bubble tea, stinky tofu, wheel pies, fried chicken and Taiwanese sausage with sticky rice, which smelled absolutely delicious. The smells in the air made everyone's mouth water in anticipation. However, not everything tasted delicious to everyone. To some people, some food, like stinky tofu, tasted like kitchen waste.

Obviously, a temple procession seems to be a combination of religion and sensual stimulation, which can fully satisfy believers' spiritual and physical desires.

今天下午，一個廟宇遶境隊伍經過我家附近，二尊行進的巨大神像看起來壯觀而嚴肅，像移動的古代工藝品，而每一件鬼裝扮的服裝感覺跟吊在移動架上的厚地毯一樣沉重。二尊神祇旁邊是電音三太子，那是另一種傀儡神，和著聽起來像現場音樂會的喧鬧熱門音樂表演逗趣而活潑的舞蹈。

沿著繞境路徑二邊都是一長串賣著地方小吃的攤販，泡沫茶飲、臭豆腐、車輪餅、炸雞和大腸包小腸等聞起來非常美味，空氣中的香味讓每個人垂涎三尺。然而，不是每樣小吃都讓每個人嚐起來美味的，對一些人來說，像臭豆腐的一些食物嚐起來像餿水一樣。

明顯地，一趟廟宇繞境隊伍似乎是宗教及感官刺激的結合，能夠完全滿足信眾的心靈及食慾。

1. 今天下午，有一個廟宇遶境隊伍經過我家附近。
2. 二尊行進中的巨大神像看起來壯觀而嚴肅，就像移動的古代工藝品。
3. 每一件鬼裝扮的服裝感覺跟吊在移動架上的厚地毯一樣沉重。
4. 一趟廟宇繞境隊伍似乎是宗教及感官刺激的結合。
5. 空氣中的香味讓每個人垂涎三尺。

參考答案

1. This afternoon, there was a temple procession passing through my neighborhood.
2. Two huge marching effigies of gods looked magnificent but serious, like ancient moving artifacts.
3. Each of their ghostly costumes felt as heavy as thick carpets hanging on a moving rack.
4. A temple procession seems to be a combination of religion and sensual stimulation.
5. The smells in the air made everyone's mouth water in anticipation.

寫作導向的文法講座

結構與語意之間的形意搭配－倒裝

寫作上的形意搭配有三種方式一形式、搭配、詞序。

1. 形式

1) I **must** get some sleep.

說明 must 傳達作說者的意見或感覺。

2) The customer **has to** pay the bill on schedule.

說明 have to 表示客觀的事實。

3) If I **had had** enough money, I **would have gone** to London.

說明 had 加接過去分詞，would 加接 have pp，表示過去事實相反。

2. 搭配

Have you finished **reading** that magazine?

說明 ing 有存在的意涵，搭配表示完成的 finish。

3. 詞序

倒裝是指一個結構的正常詞序改變，目的是形成疑問、強調語氣或尾重原則。疑問句是最常見的倒裝形式，屬於必要的變形，藉由主詞與動詞詞序改變而形成要求聽者回答的疑問語氣。

否定詞倒裝

正式用法中，否定語意的副詞移至句首以表示強調，助動詞移至主詞前面配合演出，標示否定副詞移位的詞序變化，屬於非必要的變形。

1) Never have I been so furious!

→ I have never been so furious!

2) Never again will I offer to help Tom!

→ I will never offer to help Tom again!

3) Not a single book did Tom read last week.

→ Tom didn't read a single book last week.

4) Not until did I begin to work that I realized how much time I had wasted.

→ I didn't realize how much time I had wasted until I began to work.

說明 not until 的意思是 **not before a particular time or event**，表示 "I realized how much time I had wasted" 不是在 "I began to work" 之前發生的，而是直到 "I began to work" 才發生，達到變形後語意保留的效果。

搭配 only 的語詞

具有限定意涵，強調訊息移至句首。

1) Only by constant practice can you master a foreign language.

2) Only when Tom apologizes sincerely will I forgive him.

3) Only his father will Tom obey.

→ Tom will obey only his father.

so、such

正式用法中，強調首次提及的單數可數名詞的程度時，包含程度副詞的形容詞片語前移至 "a/an 名詞 " 前面。

1) Tom is **too polite** a person to refuse.

2) I couldn't afford **that expensive** a car.

3) Tokyo is not **as expensive** a city to visit as you think it is.

4) **How great** a basketball player Tom is!

5) It was **so cold** a day that we decided to stay indoors.

說明 程度副詞 so 不可加接 a/an 引導的名詞片語，以下句子錯誤：

*It was **so a day** that we decided to stay indoors.

such 作為限定詞，「如此、這麼」，置於名詞片語首表示強調，名詞片語即使不含形容詞，同樣表示程度很高。

1. 不含形容詞的單數名詞片語

1) I'm glad your presentation was **such a success**.

2. 含形容詞的單數名詞片語

1) Tom is **such a hard-working colleague**.

*Tom is so a hard-working colleague.

說明 so 是程度副詞，強調形容詞或副詞。

3. 複數名詞

1) I really admire those who can work in **such difficult conditions**.

* I really admire those who can work in so difficult conditions.

說明 so 只搭配單數可數名詞。

4. 不可數名詞

1) It was **such good juice** that we couldn't stop drinking it.

* It was so good juice that we couldn't stop drinking it.

5. many, much, few, little 等數量詞搭配副詞 so，不搭配限定詞 such。

1) She has only **so much time** to do her housework.

2) There are **so many mistakes** in this book.

3) Tom has **so few books**.

4) We have **so little information**.

注意 He is such a little boy. 中的 little 是小的意思，搭配 such。

6. so, such 強調形容詞的程度，that 引導的副詞子句表示結果。

1) Tom was so tired that he could do nothing but yawn.

2) The professor is such a good lecturer that all his courses are full.

7. 搭配表示結果的 that 子句，形容詞片語是主要子句的**訊息焦點**，常移至句首以示強調，be 動詞倒裝至主詞前配合演出。

So sleepy was Tom that he fell asleep during the meeting.

→ Tom was so sleepy that he fell asleep during the meeting.

8. 搭配 such 的組成成分是名詞片語，強調 such 時，名詞片語前移至句首，be 動詞同樣倒裝配合演出。

Such a serious condition was it that there was nothing that could be done.

→ It was such a serious condition that there was nothing that could be done.

說明

1. 代名詞性質的 such 表示「這樣的人或事物」，指涉名詞，賦予強調的意涵。

   Such were his words.

2. 正式用法中，代名詞 such 移至句首以示強調，be 動詞倒裝配合演出。

   Such is the elegance of this typeface that it is still a favorite of designers.

   — Oxford Dictionary

   → The elegance of this typeface is such that it is still a favorite of designers.

關於 so、such 倒裝句型，仍是從**詞性**著手—so 是副詞，such 是限定詞，再來根據詞性所構成的組成成分—so 構成**形容詞片語**，such 構成**名詞片語**。搭配表示結果的 that 子句時，so, such 是訊息焦點，其組成成分可移至**句首**以標記強調，be 動詞移至主詞前面配合演出，完成倒裝套路。知曉詞性、組成成分、強調詞序，掌握句型構成的脈絡，便能輕鬆學習 so, such 的倒裝句型。

讓步

讓步是指**狀況不影響結果**，搭配雖然、儘管等語意的連接詞－ as though。非常正式的美式英語中，as 子句中的名詞、形容詞、副詞，甚至動詞移至句首以強調與結果對比的狀況。同樣是美式英語，as 子句的主詞前常搭配 as，形成 as…as 的結構，表示達到某種程度。

名詞

though 引導的讓步子句的名詞前移是 outdated，寫作時不應使用。

前移的名詞片語省略限定詞。

1) Child as he was, he did quite well.

2) Japanese as he was, he supported the Chinese team.

形容詞

1) Strange as it may seem, I like housework.

*Strange although it may seem, I like housework.

說明 although 不置於句中。

2) As cold as it was, we went out.

3) Even as the man is rich and famous, he is living a simple life.

說明 as 可搭配副詞 even。

副詞

1) Bravely as they fought, they had no chance of winning.

2) As much as I respect your point of view, I can't agree.

動詞

Try as he might, Tom couldn't get the door open.

說明 搭配情態助動詞的動詞才能移至 as 前面。

as 引導的子句表示原因，同樣可以形成強調詞序。

1) As Tom was exhausted, he went to bed as soon as he came back.

→ Exhausted as Tom was, he went to bed as soon as he came back.

→ Because Tom was exhausted, he went to bed as soon as he came back.

比較 Exhausted as Tom was, he stayed up late.

儘管 Tom 非常疲憊。他仍熬夜，as 表示讓步。

A. 請寫出以下句子未倒裝的形式

1. Seldom did she raise her voice.
2. No longer will they stay with us.
3. Not a word would the man say.
4. Stupid as I was, I believed whatever he said.
5. Late as it was getting, Tom decided to check into a hotel.
6. Such a good lecturer is the professor that all his courses are full.

B. 請將以下句子翻譯成英文。

1. 那名男子儘管富有又有名，他過著純樸的生活。
2. 儘管生氣，Tom 不禁笑了。
3. 我們的決定就是這樣。
4. 他們其中只有二位有任何臨時照顧孩童的經驗。
5. 這樣的殘酷真是超越我的理解。

參考答案

A.

1. She seldom raised her voice.
2. They will no longer stay with us.
3. The man would not say a word.
4. As I was stupid, I believed whatever he said.
5. As it was getting late, Tom decided to check into a hotel.

= Because it was getting late, Tom decided to check into a hotel.

6. The professor is such a good lecturer that all his courses are full.

B.

1. Even as rich and famous as the man is, he is living a simple life.
2. Angry as he was, Tom couldn't help smiling.
3. Such is our decision.
4. Only two of them had any experience at babysitting kids.
5. Such cruelty really is beyond my comprehension.

技巧 23

文字呈現感官知覺，描述更加生動鮮活

描述物品或場景，色彩、聲響、味蕾、觸感等感官元素能將文字呈現在眼目前、舌尖上、耳際間，既是寫實，又是創意，二者堆疊，描述更顯鮮活。

呈現感官知覺的方式，除了直接描述，明喻是普遍而重要的技巧。

1) This sauce tastes strange.

   tastes strange 直接描述 this sauce。

2) The man stood completely still, not making a sound.

   I could feel the sweat trickling down my back.

   分詞片語描述場景的聲音或感官知覺，語意與句子結構都加分。

3) The street performer stood motionless like a statue of bronze.

   表達譬喻的介係詞片語傳達街頭藝人的視覺效果。

4) The boy's face went pale and he looked as if he might faint.

   描述搭配譬喻，訊息連貫而完整。

5) We could tell from the lady's voice that she wasn't pleased.

   藉由評論讓人聯想到聲音傳達的情緒。

以下這篇逛士林夜市的信函充分藉由食物呈現感官知覺，生動的描述足以引人身歷其境。

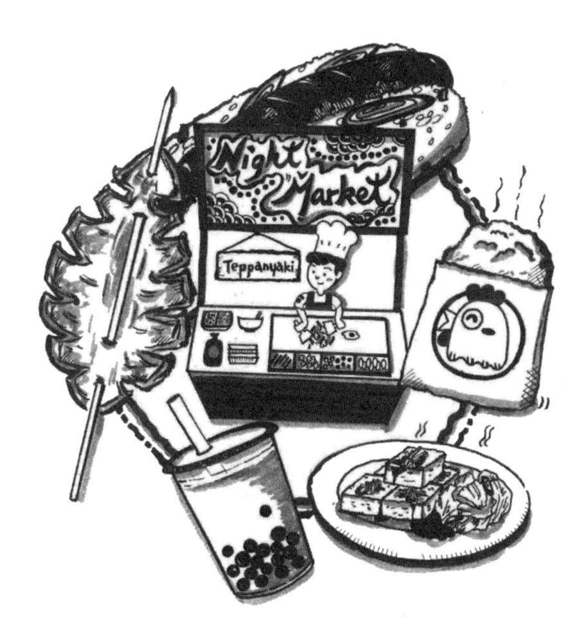

23

Dear mother and father,

I finally finished my quarantine, and I am safe.
Now, I have some time to explore this big city of Taipei before I start my new job.

My first day of exploring Taipei was incredible. The city is a feast for the senses. **Visually**, the city **looks as huge and diverse as New York City or Hong Kong**. There is so much to experience. A friend of mine brought me to the Shilin Night Market. Taiwan has many night markets, but this is one of the most famous ones.

Before we even reached the food area, I was assaulted by **a variety of smells**. I could **smell the pungent odor of stinky tofu**, which **smelled as foul as a dead animal**. But you know what? My friend forced me to try stinky tofu and it actually **tastes pretty good**. **The smell of grilled squid bathed in sesame oil and soy sauce** beckoned me, and I loved eating that, too.

When I walked past an outdoor teppanyaki stand, I was stopped in my tracks by **a chorus of smells and sounds**. The teppanyaki grill master was like **a composer**, using his spatula to **direct a symphony of food**.

The scraping of the grill, the cracking of the eggs, and the stirring of the vegetables and chopped meat were sounds that followed **the rhythm of the chef**. And **the smells of each item** he placed on the grill wafted to my nose as if they were luring me to sit down and take a taste. I ordered the most unusual item on the menu, which was grilled ostrich. I was taken by surprise, as the ostrich meat melted in my mouth **like the most tender steak I have ever eaten**.

I can't wait to go back and explore more of the night market.

Don't worry. I will really enjoy living here.

Stacy

親愛的爸爸媽媽，

終於完成隔離，安全了。

現在，開始新的工作之前，我有一些時間探索台北這個大城市。

探索台北的第一天棒極了，這城市簡直是一感官饗宴。視覺上，這城市看起來如同紐約市或香港一樣廣闊、多采多姿，有好多可以去體驗。我的一位朋友帶我去士林夜市，臺灣有許多夜市，而這是最有名的夜市之一。

我們抵達食品區之前，我受到各種氣味的侵襲。我聞到臭豆腐強烈的臭味，聞起來如同一隻死亡的動物一樣臭。但是您們知道嗎？我朋友強要我試一下臭豆腐，嚐起來真的很棒。浸在芝麻油及醬油的烤魷魚香氣誘惑我了，我也超愛吃這味的。

走過一攤戶外鐵板燒時，一陣氣味夾雜吆喝聲把我的步伐止住了。鐵板燒烤物師傅就像一名作曲家，用他的煎鏟指揮一首食物交響樂，烤架刮來刮去、雞蛋裂開，攪拌蔬菜及切肉全是跟隨主廚節奏的聲音。他放在烤架上每一食材的氣味都飄到我的鼻子，宛如誘惑我要坐下來嚐一口。我點了菜單上最獨特的一項，烤鴕鳥。我驚呆了，鴕鳥肉融化在口中，就像吃過的最鮮嫩牛排一樣。

我迫不及待要回去更多探索這夜市。

請勿擔心，我會很喜愛住在這裡的。

Stacy

1. 視覺上，這城市看起來如同紐約市或香港一樣廣闊、多采多姿。
2. 我們抵達食品區之前，我受到各種氣味的侵襲。
3. 我聞得到臭豆腐強烈的臭味，聞起來如同一隻死亡的動物一樣臭。
4. 他放在烤架上每一食材的氣味都飄到我的鼻子，宛如誘惑我要坐下來嚐一口。
5. 我驚呆了，章魚肉融化在口中，就像吃過的最鮮嫩牛排一樣。

參考答案

1. Visually, the city looks as huge and diverse as New York City or Hong Kong.
2. Before we even reached the food area, I was assaulted by a variety of smells.
3. I could smell the pungent odor of stinky tofu, which smelled as foul as a dead animal.
4. The smells of each item he placed on the grill wafted to my nose as if they were luring me to sit down and take a taste.
5. I was taken by surprise, as the ostrich meat melted in my mouth like the most tender steak I have ever eaten.

寫作導向的文法講座

扉頁上的感官知覺

形容詞常搭配程度副詞而構成形容詞片語，加添形容詞的意涵。最常見的程度副詞是 very，搭配 very 的形容詞通常是較為常用的簡單字，以字源而言，大多是英語的本族語。以選字及結構而言，若以單詞代換則較為簡潔；以測驗與評量而言，單詞難度較高，屬於中級以上詞彙測驗的命題範疇。

very good → excellent

very nice → kind

very bad → awful

very rich → wealthy

very warm → hot

very simple → basic

1. 有些「very 形容詞」可代換為黏接字尾 less 的單詞。

   very clean → spotless

   very perfect → flawless

   very easy → effortless

2. 有些近義的「very 形容詞」可代換為同一單詞。

   very light/very bright → luminous

   very smart/very clever → intelligent

3. 有些單詞可搭配 very 而以另一單詞代換，三者呈現程度上的升冪排列。

   very boring → dull，very dull → tedious

   very pretty → beautiful，very beautiful → gorgeous

   very fast → quick，very quick → rapid

very willing → eager, very eager → keen/very sharp → keen

4. 其他代換例示：

very sorry → apologetic	very worried → distressed
very angry → furious	very accurate → exact
very big → massive	very evil → wicked
very noisy → deafening	very calm → serene
very dear → cherished	very lively → animated
very deep → profound	very cheap → stingy
very excited → thrilled	very difficult → arduous
very fancy → lavish	very scared → petrified
very fat → obese	very scary → chilly
very open → transparent	very serious → grave
very stupid → idiotic	very shiny → gleamy
very happy → ecstatic	very shy → timid
very weak → frail	very wet → socked
very strong → forceful	very sad → sorrowful
very long → extensive	very colorful → vibrant
very soft → downy	very confused → perplexed
very wide → expansive	very mean → cruel
very wise → sage	

A. 請將句中「very 形容詞」代換為合適的提示單字。

a. adorable b. amiable c. cautious d. costly e. exceptional f. fearful
g. freezing h. huge i. terrific j. starving

__________ 1. My colorful caterpillar is **very hungry**.

__________ 2. Mr. Lee and his staff are **very friendly** and professional.

__________ 3. Our Christmas meal was **very special**.

__________ 4. The plan sounds **very great** to me.

__________ 5. This kind of design looks **very expensive**.

__________ 6. It is a **very cute** puppy.

__________ 7. I'm not **very afraid** of the dark.

__________ 8. A mountain climber must be **very careful**.

__________ 9. Icebergs are **very large** chunks of ice that float in waters in **very cold** areas of the world.

B. 請寫出提示字對應的 "very 形容詞 "。

1. certain ________________

2. pouring ________________

3. delicious ________________

4. obvious ________________

5. ancient ______________

6. innovative ______________

7. brief ______________

8. gifted ______________

9. exhausted ______________

10. ecstatic ______________

参考答案

A

1. j 2. b 3. e 4. i 5. d 6. a 7. f 8. c 9. h g

B

1. very sure 2. very rainy 3. very tasty 4. very clear 5. very old

6. very creative 7. very short 8. very talented 9. very tired 10. very happy

技巧 24

平行修辭技巧，平添寫作文采

文法使一段文字正確，邏輯使一段文字真實，修辭使一段文字優美，文法、邏輯、修辭三者兼備的文章才得以登上頂標。

文法錯誤與修正

1) *Tom has **gone** to London twice.

→ Tom has **been** to London twice.

2) *I want to travel because I enjoy **to meet** people and see new places.

→ I want to travel because I enjoy **meeting** people and **seeing** new places.

文法正確，但邏輯有誤

1) *My sister is the only **child** in my family.

→ My sister is the only **daughter** in my family.

2) * I saw **an ostrich** flying in the sky.

→ I saw **a hawk** flying in the sky.

語氣不夠委婉而需要修辭

1) *My grandfather **died** last month.

→ My grandfather **passed away** last month.

2) *Who **made gas**?

→ Who **did a fart**?

修辭藉由選字或結構而使文字臻於優美，修辭技巧可以透過學習而自然流露。

我們先介紹與文法關連密切的修辭技巧—平行。

1. 平行是數個相同結構的語詞形成的對等連接。

名詞片語

1) I have an online class and several important phone calls to make.

不定詞

1) Today, I need to clean my bedroom, do the laundry, go grocery shopping and get my smartphone fixed.

動名詞

1) In the resort, we enjoyed walking along the beach, making sand sculptures and watching stars in the sky.

介係詞片語

1) Students in this school go to school by MRT, by car or on foot.

2) Your car key was placed either on the end table or in the cupboard.

John F. Kennedy 就職演説中開頭一句話就以平行結構闡述對於自由的堅定信念。

*"We shall **pay the price, bear any burden, meet any hardship, support any friends** or **oppose any foe** to ensure the survival and the success of liberty,"*

說明 以下句子對等連接的語詞結構不一致，不形成平行結構。

1) *He is a **delivery** person **but joyful** all the time.

→ He is a delivery person but he is joyful all the time.

2) *The receptionist is **tall**, beautiful, **and with elegance**.

→ The receptionist is **tall**, beautiful, and **elegant**.

3) *I don't know what the device is, where it is and how to fix it.

→ I don't know what the device is, where it is and how I can fix it.

2. 平行講求對等連接的語詞結構一致，內容對稱。

1) *I had a quick breakfast, rushed to school and had dinner with my family at home.

→ I had a quick breakfast, rushed to school and attended the first class.

說明 rushed to school 連接的是在學校的活動。

2) *Many sanitarians predict that the COVID-19 pandemic will end soon but that many others have predicted otherwise.

→ Many sanitarians predict that the COVID-19 pandemic will end soon but many others have predicted otherwise.

許多公衛專家預測新冠肺炎大流行很快會結束，但是許多其他公衛專家預測並非如此。

說明 "that many others have predicted otherwise" 不是 Many sanitarians 預測的內容。

3. 為避免結構混淆，限定動詞組結構太大時，應改為獨立子句。

1) I tend to savor the experience of tasting exotic cuisines from different cultures and enjoy trying different dishes.

→ I tend to savor the experience of tasting exotic cuisines from different cultures and I enjoy trying different dishes.

2) Eating out will reduce their hardship and, on the other hand, will provide rewards for their hard work.

→ Eating out will reduce their hardship and, on the other hand, it will provide rewards for their hard work.

接下來我們介紹遞增修辭技巧。

平行是數個結構一致的語詞形成的對等連接，語詞的排列未講究語意關聯，若是按照語意特徵，份量由輕而重，逐漸呈現高峰而形成遞增的層次，這是遞增修辭技巧。

印度詩人泰戈爾的詩集《飛鳥集》中的一段文字展現遞增的修辭美學：

I love three things in this world.

Sun, moon and you

Sun for morning, moon for night, and you forever.

浮世三千，吾愛有三：日、月與卿。日為朝，月為暮，卿為朝朝暮暮。

美國總統 Abraham Lincoln 在一段演説辭中藉著遞增修辭技巧強調誠實的重要。

"You can fool all the people some of the time and some of the people all the time, but you cannot fool all the people all the time."

你可以欺騙所有人一段時間，欺騙一些人所有時間，但是無法所有時間欺騙所有人。

16 世紀英國 Francis Bacon 在短文《論學習》中的一段文字以遞增簡潔而雋永地描述書的層次。

"Some books are to be tasted, others to be swallowed, and some few to be chewed and digested."

有些書是用來品嚐的，有些書是可以一口吞下的，少數的一些書是讓人咀嚼、消化的。

遞增可以出自名人名言，也可以出自我們的日常寫作，只要有梗，稍作安排，便能營造文章的亮點。

1) Tom started a fast break; he shot the ball; he scored another three-pointer; again, the school team won the game.
   籃球動作串成遞增，緊湊的節奏躍然紙上，但是一些英美人士較少用分號而寫成以下句子：
   Tom started a fast break, and he shot the ball. He scored another three-pointer and again, the school team won the game.
2) Before, I really disliked English, hated English and almost quit English, but now, I like it, enjoy it, and have a good command of it.
   遞增修辭技巧陳述對英文的愛恨情結，生動而令人動容。

範文參考

這篇故事包括一連串的動作及伴隨的情緒，由於平行結構，情節發展顯得連貫而緊湊，讀起來流暢而脈絡分明。

🎧 24

Last Saturday afternoon, Brian went to the park with his dog, Lucky. Brian sat on a bench **and** read his favorite novel. Lucky was quietly sitting by Brian's side. Suddenly, a squirrel appeared in front of Lucky, **and** out of curiosity, it followed the squirrel wherever it moved, **but** Brian was totally unaware of Lucky's encounter.

All of a sudden, Brian noticed Lucky was not around. He put down his book, stood up, **and** looked around, **but** he did not see his beloved dog. Then, he looked for Lucky everywhere around the park, calling "Lucky" **over and over again**. At last, he quit **and** left the park, tired **and** depressed.

To Brian's surprise, the moment he got home, he saw Lucky sitting by the door. The dog was looking at Brian, its tail wagging with excitement as usual. It filled him with a sense of relief **and** delight, **and** he felt **not only** thankful **but** lucky.

上周日，Brian 帶著他的狗狗，Lucky，去一處公園。Brian 坐在長凳讀他最喜愛的小說，Lucky 安靜地坐在他旁邊。突然，一隻松鼠出現在 Lucky 前面，出於好奇，它就隨著松鼠到處移動，但是 Brian 完全沒有察覺 Lucky 遇到了什麼。

突然，Brian 注意到 Lucky 不在附近，便放下書，站起來，四周張望，但就是看不到心愛的狗狗。他在公園四周到處尋找 Lucky，一次又一次喊著「Lucky」，最後放棄了，離開公園，疲累又沮喪。

令 Brian 驚奇的是，他一到家就看見 Lucky 坐在門邊，望著 Brian，一如往常興奮地搖著尾巴，這一幕讓他充滿了寬心及喜樂，感到欣慰又幸運。

1. Lucky 隨著松鼠到處移動，但是 Brian 完全沒有察覺到它遇到了什麼。
2. 他放下書，站起來，四周張望，但就是看不到心愛的狗狗。
3. 最後他放棄了，離開公園，疲累又沮喪。
4. 那隻小狗望著 Brian，一如往常興奮地搖著尾巴。
5. 這一幕讓他充滿了寬心及喜樂，感到欣慰又幸運。

參考答案

1. Lucky followed the squirrel wherever it moved, but Brian was totally unaware of its encounter.
2. He put down his book, stood up, and looked around, but he did not see his beloved dog.
3. At last, he quit and left the park, tired and depressed.
4. The dog was looking at Brian, its tail wagging with excitement as usual.
5. It filled him with a sense of relief and delight, and he felt not only thankful but lucky.

超越文法，平行結構是修辭起手式

平行結構是指「語法結構相同、語意內涵相關的語詞或句子對等排列」，對等連接詞 and, but, or, nor 對等連接，例如：

1) They kissed and hugged each other.

2) Every morning, we make our bed, eat breakfast and feed our dog.

說明 時態動詞平行結構，and 右側動詞常縮減為現在分詞構句。

The manager came into the office and gave his assistant a name list.

→ The manager came into the office, **giving his assistant a name list**.

3) She likes to dance and sing songs.

4) Ashley likes to ski, swim and climb mountains.

5) We enjoy relaxing and sitting out in the sun.

6) They practiced dribbling and passing.

7) In your bedroom, you will find the following: a bed, a desk, **and** a closet.

說明 平行結構的名詞不須搭配限定詞

1. We walked **arm in arm** along the river bank.
2. My father earned very little and there were four kids, so we lived **from hand to mouth**.
3. Prosperity goes **hand in hand** with investment.

Cambridge Dictionary

4. The whole party was a disaster **from start to finish**.

Cambridge Dictionary

8) The stray dog was wet and tired.

說明 一些形容詞平行結構可視為複合形容詞。

rich and famous

rich and poor

wise and foolish

strong and weak

both young and old

not only good but also cheap

9) Mary wanted to make sure that she made her presentation creatively, effectively and persuasively.

說明 以下 and 副詞平行結構表示反覆。

to and fro

backward and forward

up and down

in and out

10) Tim was considered to be a good employee because he was always on time, he was very motivated **and** he was a good leader.

11) As for giraffes, **both** males **and** females have horns.

12) An amphibian can live **both** in water **and** on land.

13) Either you leave now **or** I call the police.

Cambridge Dictionary

14) Many subspecies of the tiger are **either** endangered **or** extinct already.

15) The editor is **either** proud, overconfident **or** inexperienced.

16) Strangely, **neither** Carlo **nor** Juan saw what happened.

17) We can **neither** change **nor** improve it.

18) Some beggars are **neither** poverty-stricken **nor** homeless.

說明 neither 強調 nor，連接語詞數量不限，都是否定意，不搭配其他否定詞。另外，neither...nor 不連接子句。

19) If this project fails, it will affect **not only** our department, **but also** the whole organization.

20) **Not only** did she turn up late, she also forgot her handout.

21) Some people in China **not only** eat tortoise jelly **but** they kill tortoises for food.

→ **Not only** do some people in China eat tortoise jelly **but** they kill tortoises for food.

22) I think you'd call it a lecture **rather than** a talk.

23) She uses lemon **rather than** vinegar in her salad dressings.

24) I'd like to stay at home this evening **rather than** go out.

25) We merely suggested or advised **rather than** gave orders.

26) My nephew enjoys dancing **rather than** singing.

27) The smartphone is functional **rather than** expensive.

28) Mandy had dinner with her roommate **rather than** with her instructor.

29) My uncle is allergic to seafood **rather than** the fish is not fresh enough.

30) Jennifer failed because the test was too difficult **rather than** because she was not well-prepared for it.

說明

1.rather than 表示 but not 時，對等連接詞性質，形成平行結構，例如以上 (22) - (30)。

2. rather than 加接動詞時，動詞原形或動名詞都可以，但儘量形成平行結構，若是加接動名詞，rather than 是介係詞性質，例如：

Tom takes the MRT rather than drive his car to work.

Tom takes the MRT rather than driving his car to work.

但是，寫作時最好是搭配 instead of：

Tom takes the MRT instead of driving his car to work.

請依照各句的提示語詞填入空格以形成適當的平行結構：

例如：

Let a spirit of thanksgiving guide and bless your _____. day / night

答案：

Let a spirit of thanksgiving guide and bless your days and nights.

1. Don't __________. drink / drive
2. The clerk __________.
   ran out of the store / shouted at the drunkard at the door.
3. My parents worked __________, seven days a week. dawn / dusk
4. When we stand __________, my chin comes to your shoulders.
   side / side
5. I wonder what sort of a conversation we'd have… if we came
   __________. face / face
6. __________.
   you tell the truth now / I will report you to the police
7. __________. I will not sing a song / I will not dance.
8. I __________. not know / not care what happened to him
9. My uncle didn't go to university. / My aunt didn't go to university.
10. I saw swallows flying __________ low in the air and heard them
    chirping. to / fro

参考答案

1. Don’t drink and drive.
2. The clerk ran out of the store and shouted at the drunkard at the door.
   → The clerk ran out of the store, shouting at the drunkard at the door.
3. My parents worked from dawn to dusk, seven days a week.
4. When we stand side by side, my chin comes to your shoulders.
5. I wonder what sort of a conversation we’d have... if we came face to face.
6. Either you tell the truth now or I will report you to the police.
7. I will not sing a song, nor will I dance.
8. I neither know nor care what happened to him.
9. Neither my uncle nor my aunt went to university.
10. I saw swallows flying to and fro low in the air and heard them chirping.

技巧 25

被動語態該用則用，左右開弓大勝利

網球比賽中，右手拍的選手隨時會用到反手拍來處理左側來球，左右開弓才能火力全開。同樣，寫作時，主動語態縱使寫起來得心應手，但是，被動語態是該用則用，不能迴避。

被動語態的使用時機

1. 主事者不確定

主事者是指蓄意產生動作的人或物，主事者不確定，難以扮演主詞角色，因此以受事者充當主詞而形成被動語態。

1) It is believed that the castle was built in 1850.

2) It is expected that COVID-19 will continue to impact us.

2. 受事者作為闡述或説明的主題

受事者是指受動作影響者，受事者作為主題，當然要將受事者置於主詞位置而搭配被動語態。

1) The drug has been widely used for decades.

2) Joe Biden was elected as the 46th president of the United States.

3) The bench was painted in rainbow colors to show support for the gay community.

3. **強調受事者或動作**

1) All the cakes have been eaten.

2) The old town was destroyed by an earthquake.

3) Several people were killed in the car accident this morning.

4. **與格動詞**

同樣因為不提及主事者，有些動詞以主動語態表示受事者的狀態，這類動詞稱為與格動詞，用法非常普遍。

比較以下句子：

1) A boy broke the vase.

說明 主事者當主詞，著重動作產生影響。

2) The vase broke.

說明 受事者當主詞，著重受事者的狀態，主事者不重要或不知道。

3) The vase was broken by a boy.

說明 主事者置於動詞右側的介係詞片語中，強調主事者。

再看一些與格動詞的例句：

1) The book is **selling** well.

2) The door will **open** automatically.

3) Water **boils** at 100° Celsius.

4) The meat was **roasting** in the hot oven.

5) Make sure the beef has fully **defrosted** before **cooking**.

說明 烹飪動作搭配主動語態，著重食物的狀態。

6) The motorcycle **crashed** into a tree.

7) The car **stopped** at the traffic lights.

8) The plane has been **flying** for 10 hours.

說明 一些交通工具的動作也有與格動詞的用法。

9) The cost of the projecthas **increased** dramatically since it **began**.

10) Our share of the market has **decreased** sharply this year.

11) The economic situation has **changed** significantly since the breakout of the pandemic.

說明 與格動詞用法是商用書信常見的風格。

被動語態的句子合併運用

主要子句尾的名詞成為形容詞子句的受事者主詞時，主從分明中呈現連貫的流暢風格，而轉折功用的關係代名詞更凸顯語意銜接的鋪陳，這樣的文字操弄，比起對等連接要精湛多了。

1) Tom bought his wife a coat, and it was made in Italy.

→ Tom bought his wife **a coat**, **which** was made in Italy.

2) Professor Lin recommended this book, and it has been translated into multiple languages.

→ Professor Lin recommended **this book**, **which** has been translated into multiple languages.

由於正確而妥當運用被動語態，以下這篇生活隨筆顯得自然而節奏緊湊。

This morning, I went by bus to **get vaccinated** at school and, due to my carelessness, something was wrong. Not until I was ready to get off the bus did I find that my vax card was missing. It made me upset and worried. Therefore, upon arrival at school, I hurried to ask everyone for help. Luckily, one of my classmates told me that the vax card could actually **be reissued**. Then, I rushed to the activity center, where **I got vaccinated. As expected**, I obtained my reissued vax card and **got vaccinated** successfully. Feeling relieved and delighted, I sincerely appreciated what the medical staff did for me today.

內壢高中 曹祐誠同學

今天早上，我搭公車到學校打疫苗，但由於我的粗心，一件事不對勁。我一直到準備下車時才發現我的小黃卡不見了，這令我不安又擔心。因此，一抵達學校，我就趕緊去向每個人求助。幸運地，我的一位同學告訴我小黃卡事實上可以補發。隨後我就衝去活動中心，接種疫苗的地方。就如預期，我拿到補發的小黃卡又順利打到疫苗，覺得鬆了一口氣又愉悅，衷心感謝醫護人員今天為我的付出。

1. 我一直到準備下車時才發現我的小黃卡不見了。
2. 一抵達學校，我就趕緊去向每個人求助。
3. 幸運地，我的一位同學告訴我小黃卡事實上可以補發。
4. 就如預期，我拿到補發的小黃卡又順利打到疫苗。
5. 覺得鬆了一口氣又愉悅，衷心感謝醫護人員今天為我的付出。

參考答案

1. Not until I was ready to get off the bus did I find that my vax card was missing.
2. Upon arrival at school, I hurried to ask everyone for help.
3. Luckily, one of my classmates told me that the vax card could actually be reissued.
4. As expected, I obtained my reissued vax card and got vaccinated successfully.
5. Feeling relieved and delighted, I sincerely appreciated what the medical staff did for me today.

掌握事件中的角色，語意邏輯更到位

名詞在事件中扮演不同的角色，不同的角色具有不同的功用。

主詞角色

1. **主事者**

1) 蓄意產生動作的生命體，典型的主動語態主詞角色。

The attacker kicked him in the stomach.

They live only a few miles from the coast.

說明 不是蓄意進行的動作不可搭配祈使語氣。

Go to bed now. 現在去睡覺。

*Fall asleep now.

Kill the cockroach. 弄死那隻蟑螂。

*Cockroach, die.

2) 擬人化的非生命體

This morning my car could not start again.

3) 低等生物的本能動作

Omicron viruses contain a minimum of 30 mutations in the Spike protein.

Germs may spread to a bone from infected skin.

2. **受事者主詞**

1) 受動作影響者，典型的被動語態主詞角色。

The package has been tied with strong string.

The driver was rushed to hospital with serious head injuries.

2) 狀態改變者，不及物用法的與格動詞主詞是狀態改變者。

The durians were growing well.

The trees shook in the wind.

3) 授與動詞的目標，直接受詞的接收者

Let me buy **you** a drink.

I will show **you** the earrings we have available.

3. **事件主詞**，名詞子句結構的主詞是事件主詞。

The event took place two months ago.

The match could not have been more exciting.

What happened to me is not your business.

4. **描述主詞**，常搭配連綴動詞。

The lamb stew smelled delicious.

The food tasted better than it looked.

5. **經驗者**，感官或心理狀態是一種經驗，經驗者主詞搭配感官動詞或心理動詞。

1) 感官動詞，感官知覺不是蓄意使然，而是感官經驗。

I saw Tina leave a few minutes ago.

The security guard heard a sudden loud crash.

2) 心理動詞

I admire him for his courage.

My mother hates me staying out late.

6. **造成影響者**

1) 無意志動作的物體

A strong wind blew down the trees and power lines.

2) 對心理狀態產生影響者

My pet dog's reaction surprised me.

7. **所有者**

Mr. Lin has never owned a suit in his life.

Cancer cells have more genetic changes, compared to normal cells.

8. **工具**，工具主詞是擬人化的呈現。

The key opened the door.

受詞角色

1. **受事者**，受動作影響者，典型的及物動詞受詞角色。

A boy kicked **the stray dog**.

2. **被創造者**，受事者是及物動作產生前即存在，被創造者是因著及物動作而產生，動作前並不存在。

My sister fixed **breakfast** this morning.

I made **a cup of coffee** for the visitor.

3. **經驗者受詞**

The manager insulted **the new hire**.

The woman comforted **her daughter**.

4. **同系受詞**，不及物動詞加接**同源名詞**當受詞，同源名詞是同系受詞。

breathe one's last **breath** 呼最後一口氣

die a natural/an unnatural **death** 壽終正寢／死於非命

dream a sweet **dream** 做一場甜蜜的夢

live a simple **life** 過一個簡樸的生活

smile a little **smile** 露出一抹淺淺的微笑

sleep a good **sleep** 睡一眠好覺

A. 請寫出以下句子主詞的語意角色。

1. English has been widely used in almost all international forums.

2. Kids were playing and chasing each other.

3. My smartphone refused to connect to the computer.

4. Heartworms can live for 5 to 7 years in a dog.

5. The ship had to be towed into the harbor.

6. The plane flew at twice the speed of sound.

7. The director finally gave me permission to leave.

8. Being a YouTuber is not right for you.

9. You sound as if you've got a cold.

10. The boy felt a sudden pain in his leg.

11. The screwdriver can lock on tighter to the screw.

12. The flood washed away many cars in the community.

13. The newcomer amazed everyone with his skill.

14. My boss has plenty of money but no style.

B. 請寫出以下句子受詞的語意角色。

1. The warm water melted the snow.

2. Alexander Graham Bell invented the telephone in 1876.

3. It matters to me.

4. The monk died a natural death the night before.

參考答案

A.

1. 受事者主詞 2. 主事者 3. 主事者 4. 主事者 5. 受事者主詞 6. 受事者主詞 7. 受事者主詞 8. 事件主詞 9. 描述主詞 10. 經驗者 11. 工具 12. 造成影響者 13. 造成影響者 14. 所有者

B.

1. 受影響者 2. 被創造者 3. 經驗者 4. 同系受詞

技巧 26

名詞標記數目指涉，正確使用代名詞

名詞標記數目是英文的重要特性，除了單複數，一些搭配語詞也要標記數目，這是寫作時應該注意的細節，例如：

1. 山區以複數形 mountains 表示。

   *After being lost in the **mountain** for two days, all the climbers arrived home safe and sound.

   → After being lost in the **mountains** for two days, all the climbers arrived home safe and sound.

2. vocabulary 的複數形是 vocabulary words。

   *Tom knows more than twenty thousand **vocabularies**.

   →Tom knows more than twenty thousand **vocabulary words**.

3. waters 指國家的領海、海域或湖泊、河流或海洋的水域。

   *The country depends on its clean coastal **water** for its income.

   → The country depends on its clean coastal **waters** for its income.

限定詞標記名詞的數目與指涉，限定詞與名詞在數目上尤其必須一致，例如：

1. 搭配單數名詞的限定詞

   each person

   every person/**every two** days

   another day/**another two** days

2. 搭配不可數名詞的限定詞

   a little money

   a huge amount of paper

   a great deal of effort

3. 搭配複數名詞的限定詞

   a few slices of cake

   a great number of students

4. 搭配可數或不可數名詞的限定詞

   plenty of options

   plenty of rice

   a large quantity of weapons

   a very small quantity of cement

   說明 quantity 較 amount,number 正式。

除了數目，名詞也必須標記指涉的對應，這是達到銜接的方式之一，例如：

1. 無陽性或陰性區分的通性單數名詞所有格用 their，因為單數形的 his 或 her 會產生性別差異，只好搭配陽性與陰性通用的複數形 their。

   *Every child has **his** own room.

   →Every child has **their** own room.

2. each 不用於否定句，應用 none 表示否定，not every 表示不是每一。

   ***Each** of the answers was not correct.

   → **None** of the answers was correct.

3. that 代替前述的不可數名詞。

*The population of Germany is larger than **those** of France.

→ The population of Germany is larger than **that** of France.

範文參考

以下說明文中的名詞在數目、指涉及代名詞等皆正確標記，就是首次提及的單數可數名詞搭配 a/an，再次提及時搭配 the 或代名詞。另外，共同認知的名詞搭配 the，例如 the riverbank。因此，全文細節銜接得宜，情節流暢有致，這是說明文應有的寫作技巧。

26

It was sunny last Sunday. To beat the summer heat, **a boy** went swimming in **the river**. **He** enjoyed **it** and shouted to **a passerby** with **his hands** waving above **his head**, but **the passerby**, with **a vest** and **a pair of slippers**, just walked leisurely along **the riverbank** without noticing **the boy**.

Suddenly, **the water flow** ran so rapidly that **the boy** almost drowned. Scared and frightened, **he** cried out, "Help!" with **his hands** beating **the water** over and over again. Luckily, **the passerby** heard **his cries** for help. **He** stopped, jumped into **the river** and pulled **him** to **the riverbank**.

On the **riverbank**, **the boy** was standing frozen, tired and scared. **The passerby** was unhappy. **He** pointed at the sign that displayed, "no swimming." **The man** asked **him** to look at **it** and told **the boy** that **the river** was actually **a rapid stream** that **no one** was allowed to swim in, because it was too dangerous. Embarrassed and regretful, **the boy** said "sorry" and "thank you" to **the passerby**, **his savior**.

上周日天氣晴朗，為了打敗暑夏熱氣，一名男孩去河裡游泳。他好喜歡，就向一名路過的人喊叫，雙手往頭上揮舞，但是該名路人，穿著背心及一雙拖鞋，就是悠閒地沿著河岸走過去而沒注意到這名男孩。

突然，水流加快，以致男孩幾乎溺水，害怕又驚恐，他大喊「救命！，雙手一再拍打水。幸運地，路人聽見他的求救聲，便停下來、跳入水中，然後將他拉到河岸。

在河岸上，男孩呆站著，疲累又害怕。路人不高興，他指向顯示「禁止遊游泳」的標示。男子要他看這標示，然後告訴男孩這條河事實上是一條急湍溪流，沒有人可以在河裡游泳，太危險了。尷尬又懊悔，男孩向路人，他的救命恩人，道歉又道謝。

1. 男孩喜歡在河裡游泳，向一名路過的人喊叫，雙手往頭上揮舞。
2. 這名路人，穿著背心及一雙拖鞋，就是悠閒地沿著河岸走過去而沒注意到男孩。
3. 路人停下來、跳入水中，然後將男孩拉到河岸。
4. 這條河事實上是一條急湍溪流，沒有人可以在河裡游泳，太危險了。
5. 害怕又驚恐，男孩大喊「救命！」雙手一再地拍打水。

參考答案

1. The boy enjoyed swimming in the river and shouted to a passerby with his hands waving above his head.
2. The passerby, with a vest and a pair of slippers, just walked leisurely along the riverbank without noticing the boy.
3. The passerby stopped, jumped into the river and pulled the boy to the riverbank.
4. The river was actually a rapid stream that no one was allowed to swim in because it was too dangerous.
5. Scared and frightened, the boy cried out, “Help!” with his hands beating the water over and over again.

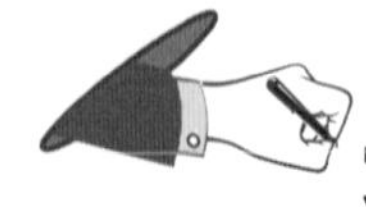

寫作導向的文法講座

名詞有標記，數目、指涉不可少

名詞扮演主詞、受詞、補語等句子的必要成分，是最重要的字詞。寫作上，名詞的重點有**標記**與**修飾**二方面，本講座要談的是名詞的數目。

1. 可以個別化的是可數名詞，單數不須標記，數目複數才須標記。

1) I missed my aerobics class yesterday.

2) We keep your records on file for five years.

3) I have two smartphones: one for work and the other for personal use.

2. 不可個別化的是不可數名詞，不須標記數目。

1) My parents don't eat **meat**.

2) I went outside to get some fresh **air**.

3) I am going to get my **hair** cut this weekend.

3. 不可數名詞搭配計量單位，計量單位標記數目。

3.1 度量衡

1) The island was blanketed in **eight inches of snow**.

2) The recipe needs **three ounces of soft brown sugar**.

3.2 容器

1) **Two glasses of lemonade**, please.

2) Mom just bought **three cartons of milk** today.

3.3 形狀或形象

1) She wrapped **a piece of roast meat** with a fragrant leaf.

2) **A school of fish** has plenty of eyes that can scan for food or threats.

4. 不可數名詞常因語意需求而具可數性質，但仍應明確表達，避免混淆。

1) Tom drank **a black coffee** during the flight.

2) The café restaurant serves **different types of coffee**.

說明 英語人士注重語意清晰，避免使用 two juices、coffees。

3) Peter ordered **a small cola**, **a green salad** and **three pizzas**.

4) My husband had **two gray hairs** at a very young age.

5) For weeks, we had **cloudless blue skies**.

6) We're off to **the sunny skies of Kenting**.

說明 表示某種天氣狀況或地方的天空，sky 是可數性質。

7) There was **a light rain** during the night.

8) **Heavy rains** and **strong winds** hit parts of the U.S.

9) The French are known as **a food-loving people**.

10) We went for a walk in the **woods** after breakfast.

11) The beach covers more than three miles of golden **sands**, which wrap around the island.

12) It's bad **manners** to eat with your mouth open.

5. 不可數名詞表示**種類**，可數性質。

1) The aquarium has **a number of fishes** of various sizes.

2) Our Yemen Mocha Mattari is **an excellent coffee**.

3) Genmaicha is **a special tea** made from the brown rice and green tea.

4) My uncle collected **a wide range of old wines**.

5) Mangos, watermelons and strawberries are **summer fruits**.

6) Everyone, to a certain extent, has a desire for **sweet-tasting foods**.

6. 集合名詞表示人物的群體，視為一個整體時，單數語意；表示成員時，複數語意，不標記複數，但搭配複數動詞，而美式英語著重形，搭配單數動詞，英式英語形意並重，動詞數目不拘。

1) **My family members** are quite well. Thank you.

說明 寫作應避免以 my family 表示我的家人。

2) Mr. Lin gave **the whole class** extra homework for a week.

3) **My class** was/were rather noisy this morning.

4) **Our class members** are having a picnic this weekend.

說明 寫作應避免以 our class 表示我們班上同學。

請依照文章敘述，填寫正確的冠詞、代詞、名詞。

文章出處：108 國中會考

Animals have __1__ special ways to deal with hard times in nature. __2__ superb fairy-wren, __3__ kind of bright-blue bird in Australia, is __4__ example. This year, __5__ ten-year study showed that this small bird has eggs of different sizes in different kinds of weather. When __6__ weather is hot and dry, there is less food for young superb fairy-wrens, and they die easily. So __7__ mother bird will make larger eggs to help __8__ babies grow stronger inside before __9__ break out of __10__ eggs into __11__ "hungry" world.

However, not all mother birds are able to do this trick. Only __12__ with at least one male child can. When __13__ weather is "good," __14__ mother will make smaller eggs, and __15__ sons will bring food back for __16__ baby brothers and sisters from __17__ eggs. With __19__ sons' help, __21__ mother can save more energy to make larger eggs when __20__ weather is bad. Isn't this amazing?

參考答案

1. their 2. The 3. one 4. one 5. a 6. the 7. the 8. her 9. they 10. the 11. the 12. those 13. the 14. the 15. her 16. their 17. the 18. her 19. the 20. the

技巧 27

動詞標記時態及語態，時間及主被動要明確

標記事件的時間是英語的溝通特性，動作是事件的核心，時間標記在動詞，標記時態的動詞稱為時態動詞。

圖片題或是敍述文大多描述已發生的事件，搭配過去簡單式，背景動作搭配過去進行式，過去之前的動作搭配過去完成式。除了標記時間之外，動作還須標記主動或是被動，現在分詞或過去分詞必須正確。

27-1

範文 1

This morning, while **walking** my dog along the pavement, I **witnessed** a taxi **pull** over onto the slow lane, and then the driver **opened** the left door without **noticing** the situation behind. Unfortunately, a scooter **coming** from behind it **hit** the car door. The female rider **fell** off onto the fast lane and **lay** on the ground motionless. A van **hit** the emergency brake with a harsh sound because it almost **hit** the **injured** rider. The **frightening** accident **scared** me and made me **tremble**.

說明一個過去、現在、未來都存在的現象時，搭配表示泛時的現在簡單式。例如這篇國中會考的題組文章。

27-2

範文 2

In Daraya, a city in Syria, there**'s** a library, and it **has** 15,000 books on almost any subject you **can think** of. However, it **is** different from any libraries you **know**: It **is** a secret underground library, and only people in Daraya **know** where it **is**.

Over the years, war **has shaken** Daraya badly. Every day, houses **are bombed** and people **are killed**. Stores **are closed** one after another, and so **are** schools. To help the kids in Daraya with their learning, Anas Ahmad, a 19-year-old student, and his friends **decided** to build a library. They **built** the library under the ground to keep it safe from bombing. But it **is** dangerous to collect books for the library. Often, Ahmad and his friends **look** for books in houses that **were bombed**. They **need** to be careful because they **may be killed** in another bombing.

You **may ask**, "In a place like Daraya, why **would** people **be** interested in books?" "Just like the body **needs** food, the mind **needs** books," **says** one library user. In the library, people **enjoy** their time reading and **forget** about the terrible world above, so their life **doesn't** seem so hard. Through reading, they **are** able to dream of a better life after war.

範文 1

今天早上，我沿著人行道溜我的狗時，目睹一輛計程車路邊停車到慢車道，而司機未注意後面狀況就打開左側車門。不幸地，一部後方過來的輕型機車撞到車門，女騎士摔落到快車道，躺在地上不動。一部廂型車緊急煞車，發出刺耳聲，因為幾乎撞到該名受傷騎士。這起意外讓我驚恐而直顫抖。

範文 2

德拉雅，敘利亞的一座城市，有一座圖書館，擁有 15,000 冊書籍，你想得到的主題幾乎都有。然而，它跟你所知道的任何圖書館不同：它是一間祕密的地下圖書館，只有德拉雅人才知道在哪裡。

幾年來，戰亂使德拉雅嚴重動盪，每天都有房子遭到轟炸，人民遭到殺害，商店一家一家地關閉，學校也是。為了幫助德拉雅孩童學習，Anas Ahmad，一名 19 歲的學生，與他的朋友決定蓋一間圖書館。為了躲避轟炸、保持安全，他們將圖書館蓋在地下。但是，為圖書館收集書籍是危險的，Ahmad 與他的朋友常在遭受轟炸的房屋裡尋找書籍，他們必須小心，因為可能在另一波轟炸中喪命。

你可能會問：「在像德拉雅的地方，人們為什麼會對書籍感興趣？」「就像身體需要食物，心思需要書籍。」一名圖書館使用者說。在圖書館裡，人們享受他們的閱讀時光，忘卻上面可怕的世界，因此他們似乎不是那麼辛苦。藉由閱讀，他們能夠夢想戰後較為美好的生活。

1. 今天早上，我沿著人行道溜我的狗時，目睹一輛計程車路邊停車到慢車道。
2. 一部廂型車緊急煞車，發出刺耳聲，因為幾乎撞到該名受傷騎士。
3. 為了躲避轟炸、保持安全，他們將圖書館蓋在地下。
4. 女騎士摔落到快車道，躺在地上不動。
5. 司機未注意後面狀況就打開左側車門。

參考答案

1. This morning, while walking my dog along the pavement, I witnessed a taxi pull over onto the slow lane.
2. A van hit the emergency brake with a harsh sound because it almost hit the injured rider.
3. They built the library under the ground to keep it safe from bombing.
4. The female rider fell off onto the fast lane and lay on the ground motionless.
5. The driver opened the left door without noticing the situation behind.

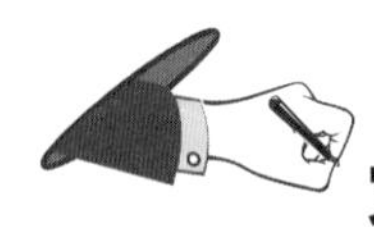

寫作導向的文法講座

寫作才知道語氣這麼簡單

溝通時，一般都是直述事實，就是存在的事件，若是陳述不存在的狀況，就是假設語氣，藉由動詞形式標記非真，這是「形意搭配」的英語句式特性。

英文重視形意搭配，詞綴、選字、詞序、句構都具有標記功能，假設語氣表達異於直述的訊息，中文則無明確而嚴謹的假設語氣句式或用字。

中英差異是英語測驗重點，假設語氣當然是熱門考點，文法學習重點，假設語氣教學各式各樣，但是，不乏令學習者無所適從，英美人士感到無俚頭的公式，不得不慎重！

其實，英美人士的表達首重清楚而不混淆，寧可多一字釐清狀況，也不少一字造成困惑，這就是寫作導向的假設語氣學習要點一清晰、清晰、再清晰！

以下是寫作導向的假設語氣重要學習內容。

1. 必然發生的結果、條件及結果都可搭配現在簡單式。

→ 自然現象

1) If you **heat** ice, it melts.

2) If water **is heated** to 100°C, it turns to steam.

3) If the wind **blows**, trees move.

→ 常理

1) It is easier to relax if you **close** your eyes.

2) Animals get hungry if they **don't** have food.

→ 重複發生的生活經驗

1) If I **drink** coffee after dinner, I can't sleep well enough at night.

2) If you **push** this button, the lights come on.

2. 未來可能發生

1) If I **see** him tomorrow, I will speak to him.

比較 If I **see** him tomorrow, I **may/might** speak to him.

說明

1. 結果不一定成真。

2. 該句不搭配 could，could 表示一種選擇，不是未來的動作。

2) If someone **is annoying** you, block them.

3) If you**'ve finished** work for today, you can go home.

4) Quit smoking if you **have been diagnosed** with hypertension.

3. 情態助動詞 should 表示「萬一」，可能性低的假設。

1) If anyone **should** actually ask for me, I'll be in the briefing room.

2) **Should** you actually need anything, please don't hesitate to contact me.

4. 現在不可能成真

1) If I **were** you, I would accept her apology.

2) I **wish** I **were** rich.

3) I **wish** we **had** a new van.

4) I'm freezing. **If only** it wasn't so cold.

5. 未來不可能

1) If pigs **were to** fly, I would go out on a date with you.

2) If only we **could** stop for a drink.

3) I don't like my work. I wish I **could** get a better job.

4) That's a strange noise. I wish it **would** stop.

6. 過去事實相反，不可能發生

1) 過去假設的條件，過去假設的結果。

1. If I **had seen** Tom yesterday, I **would have talked** to him.

2. If I **had had** some time last weekend, I **would have tidied** up my room.

→ It is **certain** that I **would have tidied** it up my room.

比較 If I had had some time last weekend, I **could/might** have tidied up my room.

→ It is **possible** that I would have tidied up my room last weekend.

2) 過去假設的條件，現在假設的結果。

If I **had studied** medicine, I **would be** a doctor now.

→ I didn't study medicine, so I am not a doctor now.

3) 過去假設的條件，現在可能的結果。

If Tom had not quit school last year, he might still be working part-time with me.

4) 但願，表示對過去懊悔。

John **didn't study** hard at school. Now he **wishes** he **had studied** harder then.

這是一篇抒發確診心情的生活隨筆，請依照空格右側粗體字填寫正確的動詞形式。

I __1__convince that the odds of contracting viruses were minuscule. However, when getting infected with Covid-19, I __2__experience extreme illness. I __3__overcome with coughing, body aches, pains and a nasty fever, one after another. What's worse, even taking a breath became difficult. Though in serious panic, I still resisted __4__ see a doctor. The lesson from my suffering was that I should __5__bemore cautious to protect myself from getting infected. Unfortunately, as long as COVID remains, it __6__ be a life lesson that I will never forget. I initially believed that I was strong enough to fight against any viruses, but now, not only did I suffer from the consequences, but I __7__ expose those around me to high risk of infection. In retrospect, I realize that I have been reckless and selfish. __8__ face with matters of life and death, overreacting may be more advantageous than underreacting, because we should never gamble with our lives.

板橋高中 劉杰宥同學

參考答案

I **had been convinced** that the odds of contracting viruses were minuscule. However, when getting infected with Covid-19, I **experienced** extreme illness. I **was overcome** with coughing, body aches, pains and a nasty fever, one after another. What's worse, even taking a breath became difficult. Though in serious panic, I still resisted **seeing** a doctor. The lesson from my suffering was that I should **have been** more cautious to protect myself from getting infected. Unfortunately, as long as COVID remains, it **will be** a life lesson that I will never forget. I initially believed that I was strong enough to fight against any viruses, but now, not only did I suffer from the consequences, but I **exposed** those around me to high risk of infection. In retrospect, I realize that I have been reckless and selfish. **Faced** with matters of life and death, overreacting may be more advantageous than underreacting, because we should never gamble with our lives.

技巧 28

修飾語如影隨形，語意擴增更精采

名詞與動詞是最重要的語詞，名詞扮演主題的角色，搭配修飾語，主題顯得具體而生動；動作是事件的核心，情態副詞呈現動作的樣貌，不定詞交代目的或結果。名詞與動詞都要修飾語如影隨形，這是文章必然展現的鋪陳，也是佳作必備的高分工法。

98 年學測英文作文題目便適合發揮「修飾語如影隨形，語意擴增更精采」的寫作技巧，題目說明如下：

「請根據下方圖片的場景，描述整個事件發生的前因後果。文章請分兩段，第一段說明之前發生了什麼事情，並根據圖片內容描述現在的狀況；第二段請合理說明接下來可能會發生什麼事，或者未來該做些什麼。」

這篇文章的寫作清單如下：

主題句	HOOK 主題句
第一段	之前發生了什麼事情 現在的狀況
第二段	接下來可能會發生什麼事 未來該做些什麼
結論句	呼應主題

↘ HOOK

What happened to the house?

↘ 之前發生了什麼事情？

The night before, an earthquake happened around the east part of the island, where earthquakes occur **frequently**.Therefore,almost all the **local** buildings have been strengthened **under government subsidy** to become **earthquake-resistant**. Such a 4.2 magnitude earthquake neither made residents scared nor caused **serious** losses in that area.

↘ 現在的狀況

Unfortunately, this **deserted old** house, located on an **empty** plain, was **severely** damaged, with the walls and roof **on the southern side** falling, beam-columns collapsing and bricks scattering. Now, it is **totally** a ruin. After the earthquake, the owner of the house, a **senior** villager, was informed by the rescue relief unit that his property had been **seriously** damaged for the sake of the earthquake, so he set out on foot **alone** to the house. It seemed to be **difficult** to get close to it because the ground was covered with **scattered** debris. He just looked toward the **empty** house, **with a deep long sigh**, **but without any idea about what to do with it**.

↘ 未來該做些什麼

I think the house owner will go to see the Village Chief and ask for assistance, telling him what happened to his **old** house though it had been deserted for a **long** while. The Village Chief can perhaps do two things for him. First, according to the **current** law, if the house was recognized as an **earthquake-damaged** building, the house owner would be **eligible** to apply for the government grants regarding **natural** disasters. So, the Village Chief will help him conduct the **necessary** procedures. Second, under the house owner's permission, the **damaged** building has to be **completely** demolished **as soon as possible**, considering **public** safety and the **scenic** view. Therefore, the Village Chief will contact a **reliable** construction contractor to do it. However, the house owner has to pay the demolition expenses by himself because it is his own **private** property.

➘ 我們對照缺乏修飾語的寫法，除了訊息不完整而導致事實無法充分陳述，場景描述也會不清楚，無法讓人感受到事件的真實樣貌。

What happened to the house?

The night before, an earthquake happened around the east part of the island, where earthquakes occur. Therefore, almost all the buildings have been strengthened to become earthquake-resistant. Such a 4.2 magnitude earthquake neither made residents scared nor caused losses in that area.

This house was damaged. Now, it is a ruin. After the earthquake, the owner of the house, was informed by the rescue relief unit that his property had been damaged for the sake of the earthquake, so he set out on foot to the house. It seemed to be difficult to get close to it because the ground was covered with debris. He just looked toward the house.

I think the house owner will go to see the Village Chief and ask for assistance, telling him what happened to his house though it had been deserted for a while. The Village Chief can perhaps do two things for him. First, according to the law, if the house was recognized as a building, the house owner would apply for the government grants regarding disasters. So, the Village Chief will help him conduct the procedures. Second, the building has to be demolished. Therefore, the Village Chief will contact a construction contractor to do it. However, the house owner has to pay the demolition expenses by himself.

這房子怎麼了？

前天夜晚，島嶼東邊附近發生一起地震，那個地區地震頻繁發生，因此，幾乎所有當地建築物都受到政府補助而強化以達到耐震。這樣的 4.2 級地震既不會引起居民驚嚇，也不會在那地區造成嚴重損失。

不幸的是，這棟位於空曠平原的廢棄老舊房屋受到嚴重損壞，南邊牆壁及屋頂掉落、樑柱倒塌、磚塊散落一地，現在就是一片廢墟。地震過後，屋主，一位年長村民，接到救援單位的通知說他的房屋由於地震而遭受到嚴重損壞。因此他獨自步行前往這棟房子。因為地面佈滿散落的破瓦殘礫，要靠近似乎不容易，就是望著空房子，深深地長嘆一口氣，對於怎麼處置是一無所知。

我認為屋主會去見村長並向他求助，告訴他自己的老房子怎麼了，儘管已長時間廢棄。村長可能會為他做二件事。首先，根據當前法律，房屋若被認定為地震損壞建築物，屋主將合乎資格申請天然災害補助。因此，村長將協助他執行必要的程序。第二，在屋主的許可之下，考量公共安全及景觀，受損建築物必須儘快完全拆除。因此，村長將聯絡一家可靠的營造商執行，但是，屋主必須自行支付拆除費用，因為它是他自己的私人財產。

1. 幾乎所有當地建築物都受到政府補助而強化以達到耐震。
2. 這樣的 4.2 級地震既不會引起居民驚嚇，也不會在那地區造成嚴重損失。
3. 南邊牆壁及屋頂掉落、梁柱倒塌、磚塊散落一地，現在完全是一片廢墟。
4. 房屋若被認定為地震損壞建築物，屋主將合乎資格申請天然災害補助。
5. 在屋主的許可之下，考量公共安全及景觀，受損建築物必須儘快完全拆除。

參考答案

1. Almost all the local buildings have been strengthened under government subsidy to become earthquake-resistant.
2. Such a 4.2 magnitude earthquake neither made residents scared nor caused serious losses in that area.
3. The walls and roof on the southern side fell, beam-columns collapsed and bricks scattered. Now, it is totally a ruin.
4. If the house was recognized as an earthquake-damaged building, the house owner would be eligible to apply for the government grants regarding natural disasters.
5. Under the house owner’s permission, the damaged building has to be completely demolished as soon as possible, considering public safety and the scenic view.

練就語意擴增術，成就寫作飆高分

描述分為客觀描述與主觀描述，客觀描述是寫實的，明確記錄事實，主觀描述是帶著情感、意念，傳達一種氛圍。客觀描述與主觀描述相輔相成，事實中散發氛圍，氛圍中看見事實。

訊息的擴增使說明清晰而完整，從閱聽者的視角，這是作說者考量閱聽者對於事件的認知、理解、感受而進行的必要處理，這些考量宛如一把量尺，測度訊息的質與量。

訊息的擴增主要目的有四：

1. 提供作說者對於事件的評論、意念。
2. 提供事件的時空背景、方式、情緒、動機、目的、樣貌等訊息。
3. 增進閱聽者對於訊息的認知、理解，避免造成隔閡或不明確。
4. 作說者為加深閱聽者對於事件的感受或印象而增添的文字。

1. 提供作說者的評論或意念，增進閱聽者對事件的了解。

寫作導向而言，語詞學習除了構詞、發音、字義之外，還要擴及所蘊含的訊息功用，這是**語詞學習**的第四面向。

1) So, what **actually** happened?
2) **Hopefully**, we'll be able to rearrange the dates of our annual holiday.
3) **Undoubtedly**, having got vaccinated does not make an individual 100% immune against the viral variants.
4) **To tell the truth**, I couldn't hear a word the woman said.
5) **To sum up**, fighting COVID-19 is a team effort.

6) **Briefly speaking**, the omicron COVID-19 variant will inevitably hit the United States.

7) **In a word**, the man is lying.

2. 提供事件相關訊息。

時空背景

1) We're going to Ilan for the weekend **next Friday**.

2) **Today on the way home**, I saw a guy driving an electric car.

3) I found these coins **while I was cleaning out my cupboards**.

方式

1) Hank came to the gymnasium **by scooter**.

情緒或原因

1) **Feeling scared**, the girl managed to find a group of people.

2) **Depressed and frustrated**, he turned to computer games as distraction.

動機、目的

1) **To attend the morning meeting**, my roommate left the dormitory earlier than usual.

原因

1) **Having** completed the **course**, we'll get an email asking for feedback on the course.

2) **Looking at her son who died of hunger**, the poor mother could just cry.

結果

1) I was so tired **that I fell** asleep in this **chair**!

2) This soup is too hot to eat.

條件

1) Staff members may use paid sick leave **if required to** leave work **under these circumstances**.

附帶狀況

1) The assistant left the office, **with a parcel** to mail.

2) Cut the avocado in half lengthwise, **leaving the** seed intact.

3) Brian stared at the fashion model, **amazed by her** elegant **looks**.

3. 增進閱聽者對於訊息的認知、理解

以測驗與評量而言，題組文本若出現特別的語詞，上下文常伴隨相關的敍述以消弭考生的認知隔閡，或將此特別的語詞設計為猜字的臆測題。

1. 109 國中會考題組

1) Now I'm going to show you how to work with chocolate. I'll do it in a "**bainmarie**," or, well, some people call it "**water bath**."

2) During lunch time, on 53rd Street, you'll see a long line of people in front of a Taiwanese food truck for their "**bian-dang**," **a Taiwanese word for "lunch box."**

2. 106 政大附中特招猜字題

53-56

After the first phase of Rat Park, Alexander took this test further. He reran the early experiments, where the rats were left alone in the cage for 57 days and became heavily addicted to the drug. Then he took the rats out of isolation and placed them in Rat Park. What happened is again striking! The rats did show some signs of dependence, but they soon stopped their heavy use and went back to having a normal life. Whether the results of these experiments can be applied to human beings remains to be proved. Yet, Alexander's theory offers us a different way to examine what really causes addiction.

What does the word isolation mean in the last paragraph?

(A) **The condition of being alone by oneself.**

(B) The condition of being free of drugs.

(C) The condition of being in a group.

(D) The condition of being addicted.

57-60

Ancient Egyptians first mummified their dead by burying them in hot sand. Over centuries they developed the process where bodies were wrapped in cloth and dehydrated to remove all moisture. The inner organs including the brain were taken out, because the bacteria inside might start to decay the body. A mask was placed over the face of the mummy, and then it was sealed inside a large wooden or stone coffin. By this time, Egyptians started burying their dead in special tombs underground. The organs were also buried in the tomb, contained in jars next to the coffin. Sometimes wealthy Egyptians had pets mummified and buried with their owner so that they could be accompanied by their pets even after death.

Which of the following best replaces dehydrated in the third paragraph?

(A) **Dried up**. (B) Swept off. (C) Torn down. (D) Crossed out.

增進閱聽者對於訊息、認知、理解的方式：

1. 同位語

1) In the storybook, Woollie was taken to see Ms. Stella Clark, **the leader of our city then**.

（110 國中會考試題）

說明 同位語提供名詞的身分，必要訊息。

2) Well, if you're a Matisse fan, you'll know this is, in fact, another painting by him, **Woman on a High Stool**.

（110 國中會考試題）

說明 "Woman on a High Stool" 說明 "another painting" 的指涉對象，必要訊息。

2. 同位語子句

1) In his resignation speech, he blamed his failings on the fact **that he was blood type B**.

（105 學測）

2) The police came to the conclusion **that at least four men were involved in the kidnapping**.

3. 形容詞子句

1) However, it was on August 27, the day **when Confucius's birthday was celebrated**.

說明 形容詞子句限定 "the day" 而賦予特定意涵。

2) In the desert, **where there are no trees**, grass is the only thing **with which people build their house**.

說明 "where there are no trees" 提供 "desert" 訊息，避免閱聽者因先備知識不足而產生語意上的隔閡；"with which people build their house" 提供 "the only thing" 的必要訊息。

4. 舉例

舉例藉由細節、共同認知、熟悉的經驗幫助閱聽者了解所述內容，雖然不是引經據典，但總有觸類旁通、撥雲見日的效果。

1) Okawa once said she had lived for so long because she liked to eat good food and rest. **For example**, she ate a lot of vegetables and slept eight hours a day.

（104 政大附中特招）

2) Many names of food or drinks have colors in them, but they don't look that way. **For example**, eggplants are a purple vegetable without the white and yel low color of eggs.

（喬登 CEPT A）

3) A big company **such as** yours should make sure that all products are safe and reliable.

（105 政大附中特招）

4) Costs **such as** travel and accommodation for you to travel to workshops will not be covered by the program.

5. 引用

引用就是引經據典、借力使力，運用普遍認同的格言或諺語強化自己的主張，擴大文字的張力，爭取閱聽者的認同。

1) There is an old proverb that says, "Give a man a fish, and you feed him for a day; teach a man to fish, and you feed him for life. "

6. 明喻：作說者為加深閱聽者的感受、印象而增添或運用的文字。

明喻以 like, as, as if 等字詞引介並對照另一人物而形成的比喻，人物及比喻二者明確而得名。

1. 原級比較中的連接詞 as 引導的是對照的人物。

   1) Mom is usually **as busy as a bee**.

   2) This App runs **as slowly as a turtle**.

2. as if，宛如

   1) The section director took over the meeting **as if he were the boss**.

3. like，與對照的人物構成介係詞片語。

   1) Well, they hope one day there will be a block with Taiwanese food in the city, just like there is a Chinatown, a Korea Town, and a Little Italy.

   （109 國中會考）

   2) You may ask, "In a place like Daraya, would people be interested in books?" "Just like the body needs food, the mind needs books," says one library user.

   （109 國中會考）

請依照語意及結構將提示語詞填入正確空格以完成訊息的擴增：

A.

As a matter of fact	Due to quarantine
Just out of curiosity	Needless to say
Theoretically	upon entering the UK
while crossing the road	

1. ____________, viruses can be identified by a PCR test.
2. ____________, vaccination is the most important aspect of the disease prevention.
3. ____________, I've only lived here for the last three months.
4. Where can I find information on quarantine ____________?
5. Two children injured after being hit by a vehicle ____________.
6. ____________, I decided to give it a try.
7. ____________, I am feeling lonely and disconnected with other people.

B.

As the proverb says　　as if he were the boss　　For example

not knowing what to do

only to find the train had departed ten minutes before

the great Chinese teacher from 2,500 years ago

where there are no trees

8. We hurried to the station, ____________.

9. The boy was helpless, ____________.

10. We also celebrate this day to remember Confucius, ____________.

11. In the desert, ____________, grass is the only thing with which people build their house.

12. ____________, Café Tortoni, a popular and historical coffee shop built in 1858, is a place on everybody's to-do list.

13. ____________, "Where there's a will, there's a way."

14. The section director took over the meeting ____________.

参考答案

1. Theoretically 2. Needless to say 3. As a matter of fact 4. upon entering the UK 5. while crossing the road 6. Just out of curiosity 7. Due to quarantine 8. only to find the train had departed ten minutes before 9. not knowing what to do 10. the great Chinese teacher from 2,500 years ago 11. where there are no trees 12. For example 13. As the proverb says 14. as if he were the boss

技巧 29

遣詞用字，字字珠璣

文字表達語意，遣詞用字關乎寫作品質，必須字字珠璣，而選用精準語詞是達到字字珠璣的必要功夫，例如依照 Longman Dictionary 的定義，devour（狼吞虎嚥）與 swallow（吞下）的區分如下：

devour:to eat something quickly because you are very hungry

swallow:to make food or drink go down your throat and towards your stomach

所以同樣 Longman Dictionary 的句子，“Most snakes **swallow** their prey whole.” 若是用 devour 就不對，用 eat 也不到位。

另外，提及小時候居住的地方，寫法如下：

This is the neighborhood where I grew up.

* This is the neighborhood where I lived in my childhood.

以下是幾個展現遣詞用字的起手式：

動詞轉喻

轉喻是運用其他範疇的語詞陳述一個情境，藉由認知的轉移，巧妙地強化、渲染，藉此引發共鳴。轉喻是遣詞用字不可或缺的筆頭功夫，閱讀時觀察、蒐集、運用，寫作時即可自然展現，呈現文字魅力。

1) I've been **caged** in depression and loneliness for a long while.

2) The real estate agent **poured** himself into his work.

3) I **emptied** my mind to concentrate on my speech.

4) A long commute not only **eats up** your time but also hurts your health.

詞性轉化

語源功能轉換是指單字衍生語意，改變詞性，這是零衍生的造字方式。語源功能轉換輕鬆增添主動詞彙，拓化寫作選字範疇，非常值得熟習。名詞與動詞都承載重要訊息，兩者之間的語源功能轉換最為頻繁。詞性轉換是同義字的運用，常使單字轉換為片語，具有緩和語氣、豐潤語意的文字效果。

1. 動詞轉換為名詞

名詞形式表示動作，名詞片語增添修飾語詞，活化結構鋪陳。

1) It's at least an hour's **commute** to work.

   比較 It takes at least an hour to commute to work.

2) He bought a drink at Starbucks for **his ten-minute walk** to the train station.

3) Before you sign the contract, you should **take a careful look** at it.

4) The taxi driver was asked to **make a brief stop** at the post office before taking the passenger to the airport.

5) The mother **cast a loving glance** at her newborn baby.

6) Just when I was passing the man, he raised his head and **gave me the strangest smile** ever.

7) I **had a brief sleep**, **took a quick shower** and then set off.

8) The policeman stopped the thief, but suddenly, he **made a quick move** toward the door of the jewelry store.

2. 情態副詞轉換為名詞

情態副詞常轉換為名詞而以介係詞片語修飾動詞，名詞前面若是搭配形容詞，語意又更豐富了。

1) Fans cheered as the national team entered the field of the stadium **with full confidence**. (confidently)

2) Linda always seems so self-confident, but **in actuality**, she's extremely shy. (actually)

3. 形容詞轉換為名詞

形容詞也常轉換為名詞而以介係詞片語後位修飾名詞，片語置於單字後面，合乎結構平衡的風格。

1) Alaskan Malamutes are **of great importance to** the Inuit people.

形容詞 important 轉變為名詞 importance

2) The loan was **of timely help** to the partners in their promotion of new products.

形容詞 helpful 轉變為名詞 help

3) Trees are also **of great use** to human beings, as they provide us with food, materials and medicines.

形容詞 useful 轉變為名詞 use

108 學測英文作文題目要求描述臺灣最讓你引以為榮的二個面向或事物及原因，同時說明你認為可以用什麼方式來介紹或行銷這些臺灣特色，讓世人更了解臺灣，這樣的題目若要高分頂標，必須言之有物，選用精準語詞具體陳述，並且搭配修飾語詞，展現磅礡的文字氣勢。

這篇文章的寫作清單如下：

<table>
<tr><td>主題句</td><td>HOOK
身為臺灣的一份子感到驕傲</td></tr>
<tr><td>第一段</td><td>引以為榮的面向一及原因
引以為榮的面向二及原因</td></tr>
<tr><td>第二段</td><td>介紹或行銷方式一
介紹或行銷方式二</td></tr>
<tr><td colspan="2">結論句</td></tr>
</table>

29

↘ HOOK

Home, sweet home! There's no place like home, oh, there's no place like home!

↘ 身為臺灣的一份子感到驕傲

Yes, as a Taiwanese person, I am truly and fiercely proud of my **homeland**, Taiwan, which has been praised with the name, **Formosa**, which means beautiful **island**.

↘ 引介引以為傲的二面向

With many distinct features, Taiwan has long been one of the most popular tourist **destinations** in the world. Among these features, local **cuisine** and **ecological resources** give me the most pride.

↘ 面向一

Thanks to **cultural diversity**, a wide variety of traditional and delectable **cuisines** are spread across different **regions** and represent their specific **customs** and **living environment**. These include **bamboo rice**, **Hakka flat noodles** and **milkfish congee**. Each local **dish** not only offers **vitality** but also provides **cultural abundance**.

↘ 面向二

Located in the **subtropical zone**, Taiwan, an island in **the Pacific Ocean**, is rich in distinctive **ecological resources**. Splendid mountains, vast **plains** and long **coastlines** offer **islanders** a wonderful living environment and **breed** a wide variety of **living creatures**. Some are even considered **national treasures** like the **Formosan orchid**, **Formosan landlocked salmon** and **Formosan black bears**. These precious and marvelous **ecological resources** make Taiwan a **wonderland** where tourists can enjoy their impressive, educational and unforgettable trip.

↘ 介紹或行銷方式一

When it comes to **international promotion**, in my opinion, the easiest method is taking advantage of social networking websites, like **Twitter**, **Facebook**, or **Instagram**.We can share **cuisine-related** pictures, information, stories, or even recipes, in order to introduce Taiwan to every part of the world.

↘ 介紹或行銷方式二

In addition, to attract more visitors to Taiwan, the government agencies or **non-governmental organizations** can host various **international events** in different parts of Taiwan during different seasons. This allows those **involved** to **gain fascinating insights into** Taiwan and then spread their personal experience to others around the world.

↘ 結論句

Taiwan is my dear homeland, and I am proud of it. I am pleased to introduce its **beauty** and **majesty** to everyone in the world.

家！甜美家！沒有像家一樣的地方，噢，沒有像家一樣的地方！

是的，身為一名臺灣人，我以我的家鄉臺灣為榮，真實而深刻，它曾經以意思是「美麗島嶼」的「福爾摩沙」之名受到讚揚。

擁有許多顯著特色，臺灣一直是世界上最熱門的觀光去處之一。這些特色之中，地方料理及生態資源給我最大的驕傲。

由於文化多樣，種類繁多的傳統美味料理遍佈不同的區域，代表它們的特有風俗及生活環境，包括竹筒飯、客家粄條及虱目魚粥，每一道地方料理不僅供應活力，也提供文化豐富性。

位於亞熱帶太平洋上的一座島嶼，臺灣擁有豐富的特殊生態資源。壯麗的山脈、廣闊的平原、綿長的海岸提供島民一個美好的生活環境並孕育種類繁多的生物，其中一些甚至被視為國寶，像蘭花、櫻花鉤吻鮭、臺灣黑熊。這些珍貴而令人驚嘆的資源使臺灣成為一個非常好的地方，到這裡觀光客可以享受他們印象深刻、具教育意義、難忘的旅行。

一提到國際推廣，我認為最簡單的方式是善用像推特、臉書或 IG 等社群網站，介紹臺灣到世界每一地方，我們可以分享料理有關的圖片、訊息、故事，甚至食譜。

此外，為了吸引更多觀光客前來臺灣，政府機構或者非政府組織可以在不同的季節、臺灣不同的地方舉辦各種國際活動，這樣可以讓參與的人見識到臺灣美好的面向，然後將個人經驗傳播到全世界其他的人。

臺灣是我親愛的家鄉，我為它感到驕傲。我很榮幸將它的美好及壯麗介紹給世界上每一個人。

1. 擁有許多顯著特色，臺灣一直是世界上最熱門的觀光去處之一。
2. 這些特色之中，地方料理及生態資源給我最大的驕傲。
3. 一提到國際推廣，我認為最簡單的方式是善用像推特、臉書或 IG 等社群網站。
4. 位於亞熱帶太平洋上的一座島嶼，臺灣擁有豐富的特殊生態資源。
5. 政府機構或者非政府組織可以在不同的季節、臺灣不同的地方舉辦各種國際活動。

參考答案

1. With many distinct features, Taiwan has long been one of the most popular tourist destinations in the world.
2. Among these features, local cuisine and ecological resources give me the most pride.
3. When it comes to international promotion, in my opinion, the easiest method is taking advantage of social networking websites.
4. Located in the subtropical zone, Taiwan, an island in the Pacific Ocean, is rich in distinctive ecological resources.

5. The government agencies or non-governmental organizations can host various international events in different parts of Taiwan during different seasons.

寫作導向的文法講座

熟習搭配，寫作、閱讀、測驗無往不利

搭配是一個單詞或片語與另一單詞或片語共同出現且普遍接受的組合，中文的種「稻」、碾「米」、煮「飯」、熬「粥」都是動詞與名詞的搭配，rice 對應不同的中文語詞；「彈」鋼琴、「拉」小提琴、「敲」鑼、「打」鼓也是動詞與名詞的搭配，play 同樣對應不同的中文語詞。對於母語人士，搭配可於語言環境中自然習得，對於外語人士，搭配必須經由學習方能熟習運用。

形容詞修飾名詞，其實就是名詞與其特質之間的搭配，不是名詞特質的形容詞不能修飾該名詞，名詞特質的形容詞才能修飾該名詞，例如：

1) My car is in **excellent condition**.

2) At least one out of four **Americans** are considered **obese**.

3) I was late and **Miss Lin** was **furious** with me.

noise 搭配的形容詞都是 noise 可能呈現的特質：

1) What's that **funny noise**? 那個奇怪噪音是什麼？

說明 funny 也有奇怪的 strange 的意思。

2) The rain made a **loud noise** against the roof.

3) I have enjoyed a peaceful stay with no **traffic noise**.

meal 搭配的形容詞都是 meal 呈現的特質：

1) I'm not hungry enough to eat a **full meal**.

2) My landlady had her **main meal** at lunchtime.

3) A **heavy meal** is likely to make you feel sleepy.

4) It was a **delicious meal**.

5) The visitors will get a **good meal** after the meeting.

6) Mrs. Lin makes **healthy**, **balanced meals** for her family every day.

7) Lisa doesn't have a **big meal** at lunchtime, usually just a **light meal** of salad/a **simple meal** of soup and bread.

描述人特質的形容詞修飾人，例如：careful, clever, foolish, kind, nice, polite, impolite, selfish, thoughtful。

描述事情的形容詞不修飾人，例如：dangerous, difficult, convenient, easy, hard, important, likely, natural, necessary, possible, impossible, proper, safe, useful, useless。

形容詞的結構及語意份量都較修飾的語詞來得小，基於尾重原則，陳述事情的語詞移至形容詞的右側，移位痕跡以 it 填補。

1) It is **convenient** that you live near the office building.

2) I find it **convenient** to be able to do my banking online anytime.

3) It is **necessary** for all of you to be present at the meeting tomorrow.

4) I think it **necessary** for all of you to be present at the meeting tomorrow.

搭配能夠豐富語意、增添訊息質量，是寫作不可或缺，必須不斷精進的工法，而一些線上字典提供條目字彙的搭配及例句，是非常便利有效的學習工具。

這是一篇生活隨筆，請說出粗體語詞的技巧名稱。

Today, I **attended** my great grandmother's funeral. She **died a natural death** weeks ago, at the age of 83. My family arrived at the funeral home early this morning and participated in the ceremony right away. I **witnessed** my mom's friends and relatives **sobbing** uncontrollably, and at that moment, a feeling of sorrow **flooded** into my mind and **drew** out all my tears and memories with my dear great grandmother.

At the end of the funeral, my mom silently reminded me not to say goodbye to others but just make a **respectful gesture**. I had no idea why, but I just followed along. It was an unforgettable day full of sadness.

新店高中 郭品倢同學

參考答案

1. attend：正式的語詞。
2. die a natural death：同系受詞。
3. witness：語源功能轉換，名詞轉換為動詞。
4. sob，cry loudly：精準的語詞。
5. flood：動詞轉喻。
6. draw：動詞轉喻。
7. respectful gesture：搭配。

技巧 30 精簡語詞是王道，跳脫考試框架是技巧

清楚、簡潔是寫作的圭臬，精簡、易懂的語詞使文字感到親切而具説服力，但是，這與預備考試的眉角不同，必須跳脫考試的框架。

以下是幾個精簡語詞的寫作技巧：

1. **使用構詞簡單的單字，精簡有力**

firstly → first

secondly → second

thirdly → third

utilize → use

2. **略去贅字**

以下句中粗體字是贅字，應該刪去

1) Welcome **you** to my house.

→ Welcome to my house.

2) Tom's wife is a **married**, elegant and intelligent woman.

→ Tom's wife is an elegant and intelligent woman.

3) **In my mind**, I think we need to work together to solve this problem.

→ I think we need to work together to solve this problem.

→ In my mind, we need to work together to solve this problem.

→ In my opinion, we need to work together to solve this problem.

說明 I think 與 in my mind, in my opinion 互為贅詞，I think 較 in mind, in my opinion 普遍。

4) **Personally**, I believe COVID-19 will never end.

→ I believe COVID-19 will never end.

3. 避免使用 very 等加強詞

中文習慣在形容詞前面加上「很、非常」，例如「你很棒」、「這家餐廳非常溫馨」，但是，very, so, quite, really, a lot 這些是加強功能的語詞，通常搭配弱形容詞，而不搭配強形容詞，儘量加強語詞能使文章的字數加一，寫作應盡量使用強形容詞。

really happy → ecstatic

quite bad → awful

very rich → wealthy

4. 單字取代片語

1) Recently, **a couple of** infected cases have been reported across Japan.

→ Recently, **several** infected cases have been reported across Japan.

2) **A lot of** people would disagree with your ideas.

→ **Many** people would disagree with your ideas.

5. 避免使用片語動詞

片語動詞是普遍的用語，但較不正式，除非是語意明確、用法固定，寫作儘量援用單詞動詞。

1) 語意明確的片語動詞

The janitor forgot to **turn off** the lights.

I **got on** my school bus in front of the post office.

2) 避免使用的片語動詞

We are willing to **give out** free N95 masks.

→ We are willing to **offer** free N95 masks.

The artist **made up** a new idea.

→ The artist **created** a new idea.

6. **避免虛字起首的句型**

虛字沒有語意，會使訊息疏離而削弱句子的量能，寫作應該避免虛主詞起首的句型。

1) there be 句型

there be 是多餘的填塞語詞，略去後句子顯得有力且中肯。

During pandemic, there are many problems we need to solve.

→ During pandemic, we need to solve many problems.

There are two possible solutions for the company to choose from.

→ The company should choose between the two possible solutions.

There are some people who think that native languages should be more emphasized.

→ Some people think that native languages should be more emphasized.

2) it 填補主詞

it 填補主詞的句子中，真正的主詞移至補語右側，違反重點在前的英語溝通原則，應該避免。

It is important to introduce new policy.

→ Introducing new policy is important.

When conducting experiments, it is essential to record the data accurately.

→ When conducting experiments, recording the data accurately is essential.

7. 縮寫不是精簡語詞，不應出現在寫作

don't → do not

haven't → have not

hasn't → has not

can't → cannot

shouldn't → should not

I'm → I am

he's → he is/he has

she's → she is/she has

e.g. → for example

這是 103 年學測英文寫作題目，四框三圖的說明文，參考範文中展現了遣詞用字及精簡語詞的寫作技巧，這是頂標作文的風采。

30

One afternoon, Ted and his sister Amy were walking to their school on the sidewalk. They were distracted by their electronic devices, and the sidewalk was not straight. Amy was **scrolling through** her messages on **Facebook** and her **photographs** on **Instagram**, while her brother was dancing to his favorite Korean pop music. The **siblings** were so absorbed into their devices that they ignored their surroundings.

Just as Amy was **clicking on the Like button** for a **photograph**, she **walked into a tree**. She **fell flat on the ground** with **a huge scratch on**

her forehead.Ted continued walking, **unaware of** what happened to his sister.

A mother walking her small **child gasped in horror** as she watched Ted step onto the street in front of a car that was **honking its horn**. The driver **hit his brakes hard** and **narrowly avoided running over the boy**.

The man got out of his car and stopped Ted, and the boy finally **took off his earphones**. Ted turned around and could not believe his eyes. His sister was crying, and the car was stopped on the side of the road. He finally understood the danger of being distracted by electronics.

一天下午，Ted 和他妹妹 Amy 走在人行道上要去上學。他們因電子裝置的影響而分心。人行道不是筆直的，Amy 一直在滑她臉書上的信息及 IG 上的相片，而她哥哥一直跟著最喜愛的韓國熱門音樂手舞足蹈，這對兄妹太專注在自己的裝置而忽略周遭狀況。

就在 Amy 在為一張照片點「讚」的按鍵時，她走著撞上一棵樹，臉朝下摔倒在地上，前額一大片擦傷。Ted 繼續走著，沒有意識到他妹妹怎麼了。

一名帶著小孩散步的媽媽看到 Ted 走到街道上的一部狂按按喇叭的汽車前面，她驚恐地倒吸一口氣。司機踩煞車，差一點就輾過男孩。

男子從他的車子出來，要 Ted 停下來，這時男孩終於拔下耳機。Ted 轉身，不敢相信他的眼睛，他的妹妹在哭，而車子就停在路邊，他終於了解因電子產品而分心的危險。

1. Amy 一直在滑她臉書上的信息及 IG 上的相片。
2. 這對兄妹太專注在自己的裝置而忽略周遭狀況。
3. 她走著撞上一棵樹，臉朝下摔倒在地上，前額一大片擦傷。
4. 司機踩煞車，差一點就輾過男孩。
5. 男孩終於了解因電子產品而分心的危險。

參考答案

1. Amy was scrolling through her messages on Facebook and her photographs on Instagram.
2. The siblings were so absorbed into their devices that they ignored their surroundings.
3. She fell flat on the ground with a huge scratch on her forehead.
4. The driver hit his brakes hard and narrowly avoided running over the boy.
5. The boy finally understood the danger of being distracted by electronics.

寫作導向的文法講座

寫作用字有眉角，頂標作文要遵守

不同於私人書信或是個人隨筆，寫作測驗應該採用正式用法的語詞。

1. 使用正式用字

名詞

kids → children，a children's hospital 一家兒童醫院

get → obtain/receive

give → provide/present

show → illustrate/demonstrate/reveal

形容詞

避免使用 bad, not good, not so good 等字，因為語意不清楚，應該使用語意清楚的字，例如：basic, poor, awful, disappointing, disastrous, horrible, inferior, unfortunate, negative。

程度副詞

so/very → extremely

2. 不用剪裁字

bike → bicycle

phone → telephone

fridge → refrigerator

gym → gymnasium

math → mathematics

3. 避免使用頭字詞

asap → as soon as possible

NTU → National Taiwan University

4. 不用貶義字

There was a **cop** directing the traffic during the rush hours.

→ There was a **policeman** directing the traffic during the rush hours.

說明 cop，條子，policeman 的貶義字，不適於寫作體例。

5. 不用口語用法

1) too → also

I am cold, and I am hungry and tired, **too**.

→ I am cold, and I am **also** hungry and tired.

2) We were **kind of/sort of** tired after our long hike.

→ We were **somewhat/rather/slightly** tired after our long hike.

→ We were tired after our long hike **to some degree**.

6. 不用俚語，俚語不是正式用語

1) It's a hot potato.

2) Don't beat around the bush. Get to the point!

7. 數字 1 到 10 以單字書寫

About **three** to **four** out of **ten** adults aged between **30** and **60** do not regularly exercise.

請寫出以下句子修正的用字原因，例如不用俚語。

1. ____________

The government needs to **do something** to help these victims.

→ The government needs to **act** to help these victims.

2. ____________

This project is never **a piece of cake**.

→This project is never **easy**.

3. ____________

They are more likely **gonna** take a part-time job.

→ They are more likely **going** to take a part-time job.

4. ____________

Send me the report **ASAP**.

→ Send me the report **as soon as possible**.

5. ____________

You must avoid taking sweet foods, **e.g**. cake, chocolate, and ice cream.

→ You must avoid taking sweet foods, **for example**, cake, chocolate, and ice cream.

6. ____________

My English is **poor**.

→ My English is **basic**.

7. ____________

The man took lots of **photos** of the kids.

→ The man took lots of **photographs** of the kids.

8. ____________

The test must be repeated **again**.

→ The test must be repeated.

參考答案

1. 使用正式用字
2. 不用俚語
3. 不用口語用法
4. 避免使用頭字詞
5. 避免使用頭字詞
6. 使用正式用字
7. 不用剪裁字
8. 略去贅字

語研力 ***E070***

全方位英語大師英文寫作30技巧：
文法與寫作直覺搭配，立馬下筆寫出高分作文

英檢、學測、生活隨筆、流暢寫作皆適用！

作　　者　蘇秦、王茹萱、解琪◎合著
插圖設計　Morphine
範文錄音　Tony Coolidge
顧　　問　曾文旭
出版總監　陳逸祺、耿文國
主　　編　陳蕙芳
執行編輯　翁芯俐
內文排版　李依靜
封面設計　李依靜
法律顧問　北辰著作權事務所

印　　製　世和印製企業有限公司
初　　版　2022 年 08 月
初版二刷　2023 年 06 月
出　　版　凱信企業集團 - 凱信企業管理顧問有限公司
電　　話　（02）2773-6566
傳　　真　（02）2778-1033
地　　址　106 台北市大安區忠孝東路四段 218 之 4 號 12 樓
信　　箱　kaihsinbooks@gmail.com

定　　價　新台幣 420 元 / 港幣 140 元
產品內容　1 書

總 經 銷　采舍國際有限公司
地　　址　235 新北市中和區中山路二段 366 巷 10 號 3 樓
電　　話　（02）8245-8786
傳　　真　（02）8245-8718

國家圖書館出版品預行編目資料

全方位英語大師英文寫作30技巧：文法與寫作直覺搭配，立馬下筆寫出高分作／蘇秦、王茹萱、解琪◎合著. -- 初版. -- 臺北市：凱信企業集團凱信企業管理顧問有限公司, 2022.08
面；　公分
ISBN 978-626-7097-20-5(平裝)

1.CST: 英語 2.CST: 寫作法

805.17　　111009570